MAKE ME FALL

SARA RIDER

Cover Design by Paper & Sage (www.paperandsage.com)

❀ Created with Vellum

Dear Mr. Humperdinck Von Spackledick III,
Please refrain from further violating Shadow Creek Noise bylaw 2011.684.
Signed, your neighbor
CC: the city bylaw officer

Nora Pitts leaned back in her desk chair to read back her hastily typed letter. She'd considered going with Noisy McPuppyHater, but Humperdinck had a nicer ring. She needed to step up her game after her obnoxious neighbor responded to her last letter asking him to keep the noise down with a hand-scrawled note in her mailbox that said *No problem, Princess.*

Nope, that was not a shudder that just rolled down her spine. Sure, her nameless neighbor had the kind of look that could only be described as panty-dropping, but he also had the obnoxiously lazy charm of a man who'd never had to face any real consequences in his life. Not her type. At all.

The roar of an electric saw ripped through the air, as though her walls were made of clouds instead of hardy insulation and vinyl siding, nearly knocking her off her seat. Just lovely. Now she got to listen to that monstrous sound *and* the pounding bass from his stereo.

She moved her cursor to the bottom of the page and added one more line.

P.S. Your taste in music sucks. P.P.S. Put on a shirt.

Maybe it was mean, but considering he'd woken her up a couple nights ago with some weird disco song from the seventies, he deserved it.

God, why was it so much easier to make enemies than friends? She'd been living in Shadow Creek for six months, and her most significant relationship in all that time was with a man who hated her guts and didn't even know her name.

Hopefully that would change tonight. It was her fifth meeting with her new book club. This time, she was determined to finally work up the courage to ask the women in the club to do something social outside of their monthly meeting, which meant tonight had to go perfectly. No awkwardly putting her foot in her mouth. No fretting about whether anyone actually read the book or spilled wine on her Berber rug. No acting like a skittish raccoon whenever anyone doubled-dipped their crudités in the hummus. All she had to do was relax and act like a normal, easy-going human being.

Why did that have to be so hard?

With a stifled groan, she sent her letter to the printer and checked on the lemon-poached baby artichokes cooling on the stovetop. She'd found the recipe on one of those gourmet foodie websites where every dish had a thousand different ingredients, and made three practice batches before she got it right. So far, it looked perfect and smelled even better. *Please stay that way.*

She popped a tray of meticulously crafted caramelized onion tartlets into the oven next, sending a prayer to the book club gods that her guests would appreciate the effort she'd put into matching the French-themed food to the novel's Parisian setting. When the printer finished its job, she stuffed the letter into an envelope and headed next door. Her nerves lit up like fireworks on the Fourth of July as she opened the mail flap and slid the note inside. Sure, it was a coward's way of getting her point across, but confrontations weren't exactly her strong suit.

The music ended abruptly as soon as the mail flap slammed shut.

She turned to scurry off, but the door flew open. "Got something to say, neighbor?"

Nora turned around slowly, ice freezing her spine straight. He was shirtless, like always, probably because his ego couldn't bear to cover up that perfect six-pack, but this was the first time she'd seen said six-pack up close. His black sweatpants hung so low on his hips that his insanely sexy v-shaped cut lines peeked out.

"It's in the letter," she answered with an uncharacteristically rough voice.

He picked the envelope up from the floor and peered quickly at the note. "Ever consider it might be easier to talk about our problems face-to-face?"

Looking at his face was a bad idea right now because his light brown eyes framed by dark lashes, thick lips currently pulled into a wry grin, and messy brown hair left her completely tongue-tied. Instead, she let her gaze fall to the bead of sweat sliding down his chest, winding down his abs like a glacial river slowly chiseling its way through a rock face.

He laughed. Heat flamed her cheeks as she realized he was watching her watching him. "Are you sure you came here to talk about a noise problem?"

Of course he was the arrogant type who assumed every woman wanted in his pants. "There's nothing to talk about. There are rules in this town and you need to respect them. That means no loud noise after seven p.m."

His smile faded. "I'll keep the noise down, but I need to finish the cuts on the new hardwood floors I'm putting in. I have to install them tonight or it'll be another week before I can get into my kitchen."

She might have had a little sympathy for him if he hadn't spent every other Friday evening when she hosted her book club communing with his weed whacker. "No construction after seven."

"No *commercial* construction after seven. That doesn't apply to personal home repairs. I've read the bylaws, too. But maybe if you ask real nice, I'll try to keep the noise to a minimum."

She sucked in a breath and squeezed her eyes shut. "Please, can you keep the noise down just for tonight? I've had a bad day and I'd really like this evening to go well."

She hated begging, but she was at a breaking point. She needed something to go right in her life, even if it was just a stupid book club. In the six months she'd been here, nothing had gone the way it was supposed to. The lab she was promised at Shadow Creek College turned out to be nothing but a bunch of broken-down equipment and a single master's student named Doug who liked to scratch himself in places she'd rather not be looking. She hadn't made any real friends or found where she fit in. The only thing she had was this stupid rental house that she thought would be her dream home until she discovered it came with the world's worst neighbor. But quitting now would be admitting defeat. Admitting her ex was right when he told her she couldn't make it on her own.

She wasn't ready to do that yet.

She opened her eyes, expecting to find him gloating. Instead, he was looking at her with pity. "Yeah, sure. I'll try, okay?"

She exhaled shakily. "Thank you." She spun around and trotted down his front stairs, needing to escape this foolish feeling as soon as she could.

"Anytime, Princess," he called after her, making her stumble on the last step.

Keeping her mind on everything she needed to do—and off her neighbor's hard, sweaty body—wasn't easy, but at least Nora had made a list. Lists were one of her favorite things, second only to a perfectly organized cupboard. They made her feel in control. Organized. Calm. But for some reason the neatly printed purple words on her periodic table-themed stationery were blending together every time she looked at them.

Stupid, sexy neighbor. The only reason she was distracted by thoughts of him was because it had been a long, lonely time since she'd gotten more than her eyeballs on a man's naked chest. But she wasn't looking for a man, especially not an obnoxious one. She wanted to make friends. Girlfriends with whom she could go to the movies and share all the weird things Doug did at the lab, and cry to whenever life got just too freaking hard.

Friends she kept hoping the women from her book club could be, even though that seemed less likely with every meeting. Making friends was easy in grad school, where no one cared about whether she wore the right clothes or liked the right kind of music, or that she was uptight. It was so much harder in her thirties. Everyone seemed to have their lives established already. There was no one holding up signs saying *Friends Wanted*. No Tinder for people who wanted someone to call and kvetch with. She'd thought this town on the northwestern coast of Washington State would be a friendly, welcoming place, but she'd been wrong. Everyone here knew each other already.

Finding a Craigslist ad for a book club looking for new members had seemed like a godsend, but a few months in, she felt like there was still a big huge wall between her and the others. Like they only included her because of her baking skills.

Oh crap. The tartlets.

She ran to the kitchen and pulled the tray out of the oven. A little over-browned, but by some miracle not burned. She pressed her hands against her cheeks. How could she have forgotten to set the timer? She was a chemist, for God's sake. Precision and dependability were supposed to be her best traits. Unfortunately, she didn't inherit them from her father, who'd called her this afternoon asking her how to renew his car insurance that expired two months ago. How a man who was considered a world expert on theoretical macroeconomics couldn't figure out the basic functions of life after his separation from her mom, Nora would never understand.

Dealing with her dad had thrown her schedule completely off, mostly because she'd had to talk him out of driving anymore until this mess was sorted. She hated being disorganized. It made her stomach roil with nausea. She picked up her list again and read each item out loud, forcing herself to concentrate.

"Chill the wine. Prepare the cheese plate and—" The roar of her neighbor's saw made her shoulders tense so hard, she dropped the paper. She gritted her teeth and picked it back up. "Finish the last chapter."

Oh no. She'd forgotten that, too.

She found her library copy of the paperback on her bedside table and flicked through the pages as she walked back into the kitchen to plate the tartlets on a serving tray. The book was a slog, to put it nicely. Just once, she wished her book club would choose a book that didn't involve weird old white guys waxing poetic about their penises.

The doorbell rang just as she skimmed the last page. Annie, Gemma, and Rose stood on the other side. "Hi—"

The power-saw thundered, drowning her words in the strident noise.

"Yikes," Annie said. "I hope that's not going on all night."

Nora forced a smile on her face. It's not like she wanted to host every frigging time, but after the first time these ladies had caught sight of her neighbor's naked torso, they'd insisted on camping out in her screened-in back porch every single month. And he insisted on putting on a show for them. "He promised to keep it down as much as possible tonight."

"Wait," Gemma said, stepping into the living room. "You talked to Neighbor McStudly? You? The woman who stutters whenever he comes outside?"

She hated that stupid nickname. Even if he couldn't hear them inside the house, she was pretty sure his ego magically grew a few inches every time they called him that. "I—"

"I didn't think you were capable of talking to a man without getting all flustered," Rose added with a laugh before tossing her sweater onto the back of the couch. Nora picked it up and brought it to the closet to hang up, then followed her guests as they traipsed into the kitchen to pick away at the food.

"Hi, um, shoes off, please," she said meekly.

Gemma rolled her eyes and opened the bottle of wine she'd brought.

It's fine, you can sweep later. Just relax and stop being so uptight. Still, Nora couldn't stop herself from immediately wiping up the drop of ruby red wine on her white countertop.

"Yum, these smell good," Annie said, popping one of the tarts into her mouth.

"Thanks, I—" The ear-splitting sound of the saw cut her off again. "They're caramelized onion tartlets. I made them as a tribute to the book, but I also have an assortment of French cheeses. Brie, Roquefort, and gruyère."

Rose frowned. "No dessert?"

Nora groaned. She'd forgotten to put the petit gateaux into the oven. "It'll be ready after the appetizers."

"We should get started before we miss Neighbor McStudly," Annie said with a glint in her eye. She picked up the tray of food and carried it to the patio.

"I wonder if he takes commissions," Gemma mused, lounging on the wicker loveseat with her glass of wine like she was a matriarch from *Dynasty*.

"I guess you weren't as persuasive as you thought, Nora, because he doesn't seem to be slowing down," Annie said, pulling her hardcover copy of the book out of her purse.

Nora cast her glance to his yard. "I'm sure he'll be done soon."

"I don't mind, but it would be a lot nicer if he took his shirt off this time," Rose said.

The fact he'd clothed himself felt like a small victory. Like maybe he was going to finish his cuts and then shut up for the rest of the evening. Probably just wishful thinking. She was so desperate for someone to be kind to her that she was willing to fall for his fake charm when he made that promise.

"Sorry, ladies. Just finishing up," he called out with a wave that made his biceps flex. "And the shirt stays on this time. Unless you're willing to share some of that delicious looking food."

Everyone but Nora burst into a fit of giggles.

Nora flipped through her notebook until she landed on the page where she'd prepared some discussion questions. "So, how did everyone feel about Xavier's relationship to painting? I thought the way he became obsessed with recreating Mary's masterpiece once he became impotent was—"

"Ugh, I didn't even get that far," Gemma said. "The book was such a drag."

"But you chose it," Nora said, setting her notebook down on her lap and carefully placing the delicate string bookmark between the pages. Why was she even surprised at this point? Gemma never finished the book. It frustrated Nora that they insisted on reading the densest, most high-brow books straight from the *New York Times* bestseller list, rather than considering some of her suggestions for more entertaining reads. She spent her days reading dry-as-dust academic papers. When she was off the clock, she wanted to read for fun.

"Well, I thought the prose was lovely and stark. Poetic, almost. In fact, the entire thing was a bleak, lyrical broadside against the tyranny of political correctness." Rose was the English major of the group and never let anyone forget it, even though Nora was pretty sure she was full of it half the time.

"Really? I kind of thought it was terrible." Nora flicked to one of the particularly egregious pages she'd bookmarked earlier in the week "The author described his house as a 'windowless box of melancholy and copper plumbing.'"

Rose shook her head and drained her glass. "You just don't understand good literature."

"I guess I don't either," Annie said, sending a small smile Nora's way. "I agree with Nora. Any guy who calls a vagina 'her pink pit of despair' would not be getting in my bed."

"Maybe that's the problem. Nora just needs to finally get laid so she can loosen up and appreciate the book." Rose punctuated the insult with a high-pitched laugh, then rolled her eyes. "I'm kidding."

Nora sat back in her seat, cheeks flushed with embarrassment. It wasn't the comment that stunned her—it was her own reaction that pissed her off the most. Why was she even trying with these women? These weren't the kinds of people she wanted to be friends with. She'd be better off spending the rest of her lonely Friday nights babysitting feral cats or cleaning her toilet with her own toothbrush than trying to fit in with them. If she couldn't find friends who accepted her for who she was—friends like the ones she had back in Toronto—what was the point?

God, she missed her old life. She stood up and set her book on the glass-topped coffee table. "I'm going to check on the dessert."

Eli Hardin had honestly tried to finish putting in the new flooring before his neighbor's book club started, but rushing inevitably meant he'd measured one of the cuts wrong. Usually he didn't care whether he disturbed the monthly event, since the women spent most of the evening catcalling him anyway, but something about the way his neighbor pleaded with those big brown eyes made him wonder if their reciprocal teasing was more one-sided than he realized.

Pretty brown eyes, too.

Pretty enough to distract him from the backbreaking work of installing the new floors. He'd spent the last three days and more money than he'd like to admit replacing the old parquet and linoleum with new expensive hardwood that would make him feel like an actual accomplished human being, only now he was ninety-nine percent of the way done with one big glaring mistake. Kind of like his life.

He took the last plank from the box and brought it to the backyard where he'd set up his saw. Not having a garage in this old place was a pain in the ass, and if the permit got approved, he'd put one up soon so that he didn't have to keep doing all of this outside. But for now, fixing up the inside of the house was his priority.

Actually, it was more of a distraction, if he was being honest. He didn't give a shit about home improvement, but after his buddy Jake moved out to live with his girlfriend a few months ago, Eli had too much time on his hands to think about things he'd rather forget. Too much time to feel like a failure. Ripping up every spare inch of his old bungalow was probably stupid considering he didn't have a lick of renovation experience, but it kept his hands and his head busy.

He marked off twenty-six and three-quarter inches as precisely as he could and lifted the blade of the circular saw.

"Oh my God, I soooo wasn't kidding," one of the women next door said loudly. "Nora really does need to get laid."

His shoulders tensed. This wasn't the first time he'd overheard the women loudly shit-talking his neighbor behind her back. He had no idea why she hung out with them.

"Maybe you should set her up with someone," another woman added.

The other two laughed. "Can you imagine Nora on a date? She's so uptight and frigid. Who would want to date her? No lay is worth that kind of torture. Can't you just picture her busting out her bottle of sanitizer before the poor sap tries to hold her hand?"

His jaw tensed and he felt the last of his patience snap like an icicle in his warm hands. He sliced the saw through the wood, threw his protective glasses onto the ground, and marched over to the waist-high chain link fence. "I'd do it."

All three women turned to look at him like he was a space alien who'd just beamed down to earth. The one who'd been talking the most leaned forward in her seat. "What did you just say?"

"You heard me. I'd go out with her."

"You can't be serious."

The more this woman pushed, the more he wanted to put her in her place. No, Nora was not the kind of woman he would normally ask out—mainly because she was one of the few who didn't seem to fall for his charm. In fact, he was pretty sure she didn't think he had any charm whatsoever, but she was attractive and smart enough to read a book every month. That alone made her more dateable than half the population in this town. "Sure as hell am."

The woman leaned forward, smiling at him like he was freshly caught prey in her snare. "If you're looking for a date, I could show you a much better time."

He shrugged, keeping his fake smile on his face. "No thanks. Back-stabbing and mean isn't my type."

He probably enjoyed the shocked look on the woman's face a little too much, but it was seriously fucking rude to trash-talk the hostess while sitting on her porch and eating her canapés.

The screen door slid open right at that moment. Nora walked out with a plate of decadent-looking mini chocolate cakes that made his mouth water on sight. Her eyes darted from her friends to him and back again. "Um, what's going on?"

He rested his hands against the old chain-link fence. "What's going on is that your so-called friends are talking trash about your love life behind your back and don't seem to think you can get a date. So I volunteered."

"You what?"

"Volunteered. You and me. Tomorrow night at seven. I'll drive."

She slammed the cake tray onto the coffee table and set her hands on her hips. She looked around, like she couldn't decide where to focus her anger. Of course she settled on him. "Who says I'd want to go out with you?"

He raised his eyebrow, liking the way she got flustered around him a little too much. "Got better plans?"

Even at the distance between them, he could see her suck in a breath. Her mouth hardened into a flat line, but she didn't say no.

"Tomorrow. Seven. Dinner. Oh, and consider making new friends who aren't so damn mean. These ladies don't deserve any of those amazing-looking cakes." He grabbed his plank of wood and headed into the house, wondering what the hell he'd just gotten himself into.

2

*N*ora hesitated with her red pen poised over the front page of the last exam in her pile. She'd checked it over five times to see if there were any extra points she could squeeze out of the answers. She'd already added two bonus points for completing the chemical equation even though the answer was completely wrong.

Points for spelling her name right? Nora glanced at the top of the page and sighed. Nope. Couldn't even give that one, considering the student had only written her first name despite being one of four Emmas in the class. Even though it made Nora's stomach hurt, she marked a D on the exam. She hated giving bad grades. Her students weren't dumb, but they weren't particularly motivated to learn about chemistry either. Then again, wasn't it her job to motivate them? What if she was the one who wasn't giving clear lessons? Her slides were simple, black-on-white instructions. Maybe she needed to make them more dynamic? More pictures? Videos? Inquiry-based learning or whatever the newest buzzword was?

She flipped the exam over onto the pile of graded ones. Ooh, maybe she could give an extra half point for that doodle of an atom on the back.

Nope. Never mind. It was a penis.

God, she missed having TAs to do this dirty work for her. Missed having time to do real cutting-edge research, instead of spending ninety-nine percent of her time unlocking the mysteries of how to make her students care as much about covalent bonds as they did about their latest Snapchat post.

It was all her fault. She'd put all her eggs in one basket and failed to notice the big, giant hole at the bottom. Who else could she blame but herself when everything came crashing down? Accepting a spousal appointment for a tenure-track job at a prestigious university in Boston when her ex-husband, Gavin, got hired seemed like a dream come true at the time—a research-heavy position in the same department as her husband and frequent collaborator. She hadn't expected the cold shoulders, or to be treated by her colleagues like she was a second-class citizen. She was more than qualified for the professorship—heck, even more qualified than Gavin—and spousal appointments were fairly common in academia, but it was still a cutthroat industry and she'd had an uphill battle proving her worth.

When she caught Gavin cheating with the head of the geology department, the cold shoulders turned to an icy freeze-out. Nora had no friends of her own in Boston to turn to when she'd packed up her bags and moved out. No support through those black days. She'd been completely devoted to her job and to Gavin.

And now she had nothing.

Teaching chemistry at Shadow Creek College might not be her dream job, but she'd earned the position on her own. It was a chance to stay in academia, something she'd desperately wanted from the time she was a young kid watching her professor parents sitting around every night in their study reading journal articles or debating current affairs. She'd romanticized their relationship and hoped she would have the same kind of life with Gavin.

Nora squeezed her eyes shut and pushed that memory out of her mind. She'd been too young back then to realize that nothing lasted forever. Not her marriage, and not her parents' marriage either. This time around, she wasn't going to make the same mistakes. No more getting involved with a man before she had her own independent financial and emotional support system firmly in place.

She groaned as her brain immediately sounded a warning bell about her upcoming date tonight. She grabbed her tea and took a sip.

Ugh. Ice cold. If only she could make her libido cool down just as quickly as her Earl Grey. What on earth had possessed her to say yes? Yeah, her neighbor was a good-looking man—okay, maybe a lot more than good-looking—but she wasn't swayed by lean muscles and disarming grins. The idea of him and her on a date was beyond absurd. But after sitting at home alone for the twenty-seventh Saturday night in a row since moving here, she was susceptible to the scraps of kindness he'd dished out to her. She needed some kind of shake-up to her routine. A reason to not spend the rest of her Saturday in the office.

Most of all, she wanted to prove Gemma, Rose, and Annie wrong.

At least her anxiety about tonight's date made her hyper-productive this morning. She hadn't just graded exams, she'd also written up the syllabi for all three courses she was teaching next semester. Maybe it was time to reward herself with something fun.

She logged on to the library system and pulled up the newest edition of her favorite materials science journal. Maybe the latest issue would give her some inspiration for her own sad little research program she ran off the side of her desk.

The first article was on nanoparticle polymer coatings, right up her alley. She read the abstract first, recognizing the topic instantly. It was the same idea she'd worked on back in Boston before she'd had to give up the project. The methods, she realized, were similar, too.

No, not just similar, she realized with a sinking feeling. The exact same as what she'd been trying before she'd moved to Shadow Creek. She continued reading, each word looking more and more familiar until she was filled with dread. This was exactly the idea she'd brought to Gavin the week before she'd caught him cheating—the one he'd dismissed, telling her she was reading too much into her preliminary results. With a deep breath, she finally raised her eyes to look at author listing.

Goddamn her ex-husband. He'd stolen her idea.

Rage filled her entire body, prickling her scalp and curling her toes. This was her idea. Her work. And Gavin was taking all the glory.

She pushed her chair back with a growl. How could he do this to her? Why was she even surprised? Gavin was an opportunistic asshole, which is one of the reasons he'd been such a successful academic. But that wasn't the worst part. No, the worst part was that she had to admit to herself he'd only been able to scoop her because she didn't have the resources or equipment to pursue the idea here at Shadow Creek College. On some level, it was only ethical that the science get published, but it felt like a slap in the face. A brutal reminder that the life she'd worked so hard to build was gone forever.

She scrolled down to the acknowledgements section, then shook her head. The bastard didn't even have the decency to include her name there.

That was it. She was done with men. For good.

"What do you think about the floral archway behind the dais?"

Eli filled the last keg of Repentant Red Ale and picked up the broom to sweep up the day's mess. "I don't know. Mom always liked daisies, right?"

Julia ignored his I-don't-want-to-have-this-conversation-right-now tone and pressed on. "Daisies are terrible for an archway because they'll wilt. We need something longer lasting."

"What about fake ones?"

He could sense his sister's tensed shoulders, pursed lips, and overall annoyance with him before he even turned around. "I'm trying to involve you, but you keep acting like this is a joke!"

He didn't bother to stop sweeping. They'd had this conversation so many times since Julia decided she wanted to do a remembrance ceremony for the ten-year anniversary of their mom's death, and nothing he said or tried to contribute was ever right, apparently. Or maybe she still blamed him for what happened.

"This is your area of expertise, sis. I'm trying, but I don't know what kind of flowers look good in an archway. Hell, I don't even know if I could name more than three types of flowers, and you've already rejected all of those. I always bought Mom daisies for her birthday. For all I know, she probably hated them and just pretended they were here favorite to be nice." The last words came out more choked and garbled than he intended.

He hated all of this. Talking about his mom didn't feel any better now than it did ten years ago. And yeah, that probably made him a huge asshole for resenting Julia's plans, so he tried to play nice, but it felt like he was ramming his head against a brick wall. Every time he tried to help, she reacted like he was screwing up on purpose.

"Maybe I can tuck in a few daisies on the morning of the ceremony," she conceded in a small voice. Like he was an afterthought.

Hell, he pretty much was. Julia was the one who'd organized the funeral even though she'd only been nineteen at the time. Jake, his best friend and co-owner of the Holy Grale brewpub, had stepped up to cover the costs. And Eli had done nothing but drink too much and act like an asshole that entire time. He didn't even have the guts to deliver the eulogy he'd prepared. No wonder Julia didn't trust him with anything more than nodding along to the decisions she'd already made.

He didn't like it, but he understood it. "Can we talk about this later? I'm heading out soon."

He could tell from the way his sister's mouth pressed into a hard line that she was mad. "We were supposed to talk about the fall event schedule for the Holy Grale tonight."

Ah crap. "I'm sorry. I forgot."

"You always forget," she mumbled.

He hoisted a keg onto his shoulder. "We can talk tomorrow. I've got plans tonight."

Jake walked into the brew room and unloaded the keg from Eli's shoulder. "Since when do you take Friday *and* Saturday nights off?"

Eli shrugged. "Since I've got this place running so smoothly—aside from the over-demand for our Lord's Work Lager, which I blame entirely on your girlfriend and her remarkably good taste in beer—I figured I'd grace the Wonder Woman Convention with my presence and show all those lovely ladies a little appreciation for their dedication to those little blue shorts and boots."

"My girlfriend's at that convention," Jake said. "And I can't decide whether to be pissed off at you for that comment, or agree with you."

Eli shrugged. "That's part of my charm."

"Men!" Julia grabbed her clipboard, shaking her head as she left the room.

Jake waited until Julia had closed the door behind her before he spoke. And even then he didn't exactly say anything. Just tilted his head to the side and mumbled, "So…"

Eli ignored him and picked up the broom.

"Given that size of those bags under yours eyes, I should be happy you're taking a Saturday night off. Except you haven't taken a Saturday night off in almost two years. So what gives?"

Eli kept sweeping until some of the tension left his shoulders. He and Jake had been inseparable since they were roommates at college. They'd stuck together while Eli got his Master's in chemistry and Jake his MBA, and then Eli moved to Jake's hometown of Shadow Creek to open the Holy Grale—named because of its location inside an old church. Their relationship had lasted longer than most marriages, which meant they'd had more than their share of ups and downs. But their dynamic was different over the last few months in a way Eli wasn't prepared for. For years, Jake had been sullen, overworked, and generally miserable, to the point that Eli often felt he needed to act like a court jester to balance his moods. But Jake was happier than ever now that he was dating Clementine, and Eli no longer understood who or what he was supposed to be.

Of course Jake didn't take the hint to leave. He just stood there with his head tilted and a curious expression on his face.

Eli sighed. "I've got a date. That's all."

"With who? The redhead who threw up in the bathroom last week after telling you that you look like Clark Kent without glasses?"

"Nope. With my neighbor."

"Mr. Budd?"

"Funny, but no. I'm open-minded about my sexuality, but a guy who insists that his own urine is the best fertilizer for his herb garden isn't exactly my type."

Jake didn't laugh, even though they'd both witnessed Budd delivering the golden juice straight from the source on more than one occasion. "The blond you've been tormenting for the last six months? How the hell did you get her to agree to a date? Do you even know her name?"

"Nora." He crossed his arms defensively. "I'm not sure she knows mine, though."

"How the heck is this possible? You've been driving that poor woman crazy from the moment she moved in."

"Hey, most people appreciate when their neighbors pay attention to their curb appeal. When Mrs. Kocilowicz used to live in that house, she never complained when I left my shirt off to mow the lawn. In fact, she used to bring me homemade lemon squares."

"That's because she had a bad case of glaucoma. And because you used to mow her lawn, too. But as far as I can tell, Nora can see just fine and doesn't appreciate your landscaping. Or your manscaping. So why is she going out with you tonight?"

"I didn't mean to ask her out, but I overheard her friends making fun of her behind her back for being too uptight to get a date, so I volunteered."

"You volunteered? Dude, that's not how you get a date."

He shrugged. "I'm an unconventional guy."

When Jake dropped the keg to the ground, Eli knew he was in for a lecture. "Have you actually thought this through? Sleeping with your neighbor is going to cause a hell of a lot of problems, and I don't think you can handle much more right now."

"What am I supposed to do? Tell her I'm cancelling because I don't want her to hate me? She already does. Besides, I'm not planning on sleeping with her."

Jake raised his eyebrows. Yeah, Eli probably earned his friend's doubt. Long-term relationships weren't his thing, but that didn't mean he was a total manwhore. He and Jake had poured their souls into their brewpub to get it off the ground, leaving them almost no time for anything else. But over the last few months, things had turned around at the Holy Grale. Business was good. The staff was more than competent. The machines were working great. All of which meant he had a lot more time on his hands than he was comfortable with.

"I'm not sleeping with her. I didn't like how mean those women were. I was just trying to be nice." It made no sense. He'd been giving Nora a hard time since she moved in, but the way her friends were talking about her unleashed a weird protective streak in him.

Jake shook his head, holding back a laugh. "A pity date. Christ, you're in over your head. You know that, right?"

Eli nodded, smiling in spite of himself. "Aren't I always?"

Nora pulled up to her driveway later than she intended, but at least she'd gotten all her exam grades entered into the computer program. She'd waited until her anger at her conniving ex had gotten out of her system. Her fingers were still sore from jamming into the keyboard as she punched in the scores, but instead of feeling better, she just had a stabbing pain in her middle finger and a bad case of mental, emotional, and physical exhaustion.

Humperdinck's car was in his driveway as well, dashing her hope he'd forgotten about their date. The last thing she wanted to do was go out tonight, but walking over to her neighbor's house to explain she was breaking the date was a pretty close second. She wanted to curl up on her couch with a good book—one of her own choosing— and ignore the world for a little while. Pretend like the fact every bad thing that happened today wasn't the culmination of her own stupid choices.

She was so caught up in her thoughts, she didn't see the note at the foot of her door until she had her key in the lock.

Seven o'clock. No chickening out.

A tiny yellow buttercup was taped to the bottom.

That shouldn't have thawed the edges of her frozen heart, but it did—just enough to crack the surface and get under her skin.

She closed the door behind her, set her shoes on the rack in the closet, and took a quick shower, hoping the hot water would ease the tension in her shoulders and clear her mind. It didn't, so she did the only thing she could.

She pulled up her text messages and typed four simple words. *I have a date.*

The answer came immediately. *With who?*

Humperdinck.

When a long pause followed with no response, she knew exactly what was coming. She answered the call before the first ring even finished.

"A date? Like a date-date? With hot-neighbor Humperdinck?"

Nora fell back on her mattress with her phone tucked at her ear and closed her eyes. "Yes. No. Maybe? I don't know. I'm pretty sure he just asked me out as a joke."

"Then why are you going out with him?" Alice, one of her best friends since childhood, asked.

"Because she thinks he has abs more ripped than the pair of jeans I wore for my eighth grade school photo," Jessie, her other best friend, shouted into the speakerphone.

It was hard to hear them over the sound of their kids playing together in the background. No surprise they were hanging out together on a Saturday night. Growing up, the three of them had been inseparable. It had been ages since Nora lived in Toronto and got to spend time with Alice and Jessie, and their lives had all taken very different turns since they were children, but their friendship hadn't diminished at all.

"I'm not! I need to find a way to cancel without actually…speaking to him."

"Why would you cancel? You haven't dated anyone since your divorce," Jessie said.

Nora groaned before diving into the entire story about Gavin stealing her idea and the embarrassing way she ended up with this damn date in the first place.

"Well, if you don't go out with him, wouldn't you just be giving those women in your book club a reason to keep believing that you're not very adventurous?" Alice asked in her diplomatic way.

"It's completely anticlimactic if you don't go out with him," Jessie added with the second half of their coordinated one-two punch. "Won't it bug you forever to think about what could have happened?"

"I don't want you to be right," Nora mumbled. It *would* bug her. Almost as much as it would bug her to have to tell Gemma, Rose, and Annie that she'd been too much of a wimp to go through with the date. "But what if I am really just an uptight shrew?"

"So what if you're uptight? It means you're always the one who remembers birthdays," Alice said.

"And you make the best cakes," Jessie added.

"And you never, ever get lost when you're navigating somewhere."

Nora sighed. "I miss you guys."

Not for the first time, she wished for a chance to undo her past decisions. She'd given up a tenure-track offer in Toronto to follow Gavin to Boston, and so much else along with it. Her friends. Her family—complicated as they might be. There was no going back either. Not without giving up her academic career.

Lately, though, she couldn't help but wonder if that would be such a bad thing.

"We miss you, too. Movie and Margarita Night isn't the same without you," Alice said.

"Can we just skip to the part where you tell me what I'm supposed to wear for a date I don't really want to go on? And maybe send me some talking points while you're at it." She was thirty-one years old. How hard could it be to dress herself for a social engagement?

Waaaaayyy too hard.

She couldn't remember the last time she'd gone on a date. Come to think of it, she hadn't ever really been on a proper date at all. She'd been with Gavin since undergrad, and back then, it was less dinners and movies and more casually hanging out until they woke up one day as boyfriend and girlfriend. When Gavin got the offer to move to Boston, they'd quickly eloped so he could secure her a job in the same department. Nothing about her love life had been even a little bit traditional. Or even romantic at all.

"Ask what he does for a living, his long-term financial goals, and what his dental hygiene routine is like," Alice, ever the practical one, said. "Oh, and whether he cleans his own toilet. It says a lot about his character if he's never had to use a toilet brush."

"This isn't a real date. I don't need to know all that stuff."

Jessie giggled, a clear sign she was on margarita number two already. "I agree. All you need to know to have a good time is that he's cute, right?"

"No." Cute didn't even come close to describing the man's lean muscles and chocolate brown eyes. "But he is annoying. I just need to find a way to pass the time. I've Googled a couple of first-date conversation starter lists, but they don't feel right."

"You could ask him what his death-row meal would be, or what weapon he would choose in a zombie apocalypse, or if he would rather get into a death match with a tiger or a ghost."

Nora let some of the tension loosen from her limbs. Jessie always managed to make her laugh, no matter how stressed out she was. "Maybe I'll just stick to current events."

She could only imagine that her friends were grimacing at each other in the silence that followed. "You're kind of…opinionated," Alice said gently.

"Fine, less politics, more cute cat memes. What am I supposed to wear?"

"Little black dress," her friends said in unison.

She got up and hunted in her closet for the cap-sleeved black dress with white polka dots Alice and Jessie had pressured her into buying despite the slightly risqué sweetheart neckline. The swingy, knee-length A-line hem was cute and perfect for the late September weather.

She threw the dress over her head and wrangled herself into it. The doorbell rang just as she was zipping it up. "He's here!"

"Have fun! Do everything I wouldn't," Alice said.

"And everything I wished I could," Jessie added.

She hung up and ran to the door. An itch at her armpit made her stop before she twisted the knob. "Crap." She ripped off the price tag and tamped down the urge to run it over the kitchen garbage, setting it on the hallway table instead. Where it didn't belong.

Relax. You can take care of it later.

She brushed her hand through her hair—not that she cared what her neighbor thought—and opened the door.

Her mouth dropped at the sight. He was wearing a shirt, which shouldn't have been all that shocking considering this wasn't a clothing-optional kind of date. Except it was a worn-looking blue T-shirt with a frayed neckline and a picture of a T-Rex riding a dolphin, matched with cargo shorts and flip-flops.

She looked down at her fancy dress and back at him, then closed her eyes out of embarrassment. Whoever said the LBD worked in any situation had clearly not been in *this* situation.

"Hi," he said, shoving his hands in his pockets. "You look really nice."

The awkwardness between them was so thick, she could have spread it around like peanut butter. "You didn't tell me to dress casual." She hated feeling unprepared and disorganized. Careful preparation and planning was vital to her self-confidence. "I'm completely overdressed for whatever you have planned, and you look like you washed up from a surfing video."

"First of all, I was aiming for artistically tousled, and second, you look great. Like Audrey Hepburn. Except more scowly. Like if Audrey Hepburn were blond and a dominatrix." His lips twisted into a half-grin. "And third, I was going to take you to Rusty's Roadhouse Grill. Best ribs in town."

She cut him a hard glare, which only made him grin wider.

"Everyone in Shadow Creek has to eat at Rusty's at least once. It's a tradition."

Two minutes in, and they'd already stumbled into completely disparate planes of existence. "This is pointless. If our date starts this badly, it's only going to end worse. We're obviously not compatible—"

He stepped inside and pressed his finger against her mouth to keep her from saying anymore. She was too shocked to react, too flustered by the heat of his skin against her lips to do anything but stand there like a fool. "This date isn't pointless and we're not cancelling it. Give me two minutes."

He walked out without any further explanation. Nora shut the door behind him and counted to one hundred and twenty. When he didn't return, she headed to her kitchen and contemplated whether ice cream or potato chips were the more appropriate I'm-so-incompatible-with-all-of-mankind-my-date-ended-before-it-even-started comfort food.

Both. The answer was always both. She tucked a Pringles can beneath her arm and shoved a spoon inside the Chocolate Cherry Garcia before licking it clean. By the time she chased her fourth bite of ice cream with a crispy barbecue chip, another knock sounded at the door. She considered ignoring it. Ben, Jerry, and the creepy mustached Pringles Can Guy had never let her down on a Saturday night before. Maybe she needed to stick to what worked.

"Open the door, Nora, or I'm just going to go play with my weed whacker until you do!"

"Go home, Humperdinck. This was a mistake. Let's be grateful we figured this out before it ended in tears and broken power tools."

"I've got a snow blower, too, Princess. Enough lithium battery power to go all night."

Dammit. With a groan, she returned her snacks to their homes and opened the door. "Oh."

"I know it's not perfect, but it should do," he said, running his hand down the front of the charcoal gray suit jacket.

"No, it's fine," she mustered in spite of the dryness in her throat. It didn't matter if he was in a suit or nothing at all. The man was gorgeous. And she kind of hated him for that. "But this doesn't change the fact we're both overdressed for Rusty's now."

"Don't worry about that. I've got a new plan."

Following him out the door was probably as smart as walking naked into a snowstorm, but she did it anyway.

His truck was in his driveway, covered in mud, sawdust, and probably every other kind of dirt imaginable. She managed to hide her grimace but hesitated before opening the passenger door. He came around and opened it for her, looking almost embarrassed—despite seeming like the kind of guy who never got embarrassed. "Yeah, sorry. I haven't had a chance to wash it with all the work I've been doing. But it's clean inside. I promise."

"It's not that," she lied. Just looking at the dirt made her skin itch. But there was something else she needed to do. She pointed to the back of the truck. "Can you stand there for a second?"

He gave her a curious look but complied. She pulled out her phone and snapped a photo.

"It's a bit presumptive to be sending brag photos before we've even had dinner."

She rolled her eyes and headed back to the passenger side. "I'm sending my best friends a photo of you next to your license plate so they can call the cops in case I don't check in by ten o'clock." At least he wasn't lying about the fact it was pristine on the inside. She wasn't exactly a germaphobe, but she'd paid a lot of money and waited more than a few years for an excuse to wear this dress, and she'd like to make it at least five minutes without getting it covered with mud.

He came around the driver's side and hopped in. "The old 'what if he's a serial killer' photo."

"It's nothing personal."

"No worries. I sent one of you to my friends earlier, too."

She laughed. "Yeah, right. When could you possibly have gotten a photo of me?"

He reversed the truck onto the road and headed north. "Not telling. It's one of my super-secret serial killer stalking techniques."

"Hate to break it to you, but insisting someone go out with you in front of a bunch of witnesses is pretty amateur for a serial killer."

"Or so amateur it's actually brilliant." He winked at her before casting his eyes back on the road.

"I should not be laughing right now."

"Why?" He shifted gears smoothly as they pulled onto the highway, merging seamlessly in between the fast moving cars. How was it fair that even the way he drove was sexy? "Scared you'll actually have a good time tonight?"

"Hardly. We have nothing in common. And—"*And you only asked me out as a pity date.* She cleared her throat. "So, what would your mad genius serial killer name be?"

"The Weed Whacker Whacker, of course."

She shook her head, trying not to laugh. "That's not too bad."

"I was going to go with Sex Machine Killer, but I'm pretty sure it's already trademarked. But Death Stare Slayer is up for grabs."

She responded with said infamous stare. "My resting bitch face is not that bad."

"Only because you've never been on the other end of it."

"That's because I don't blast music at one in the morning!"

He ran his hand along the back of his neck. "Yeah, sorry about that. The woman who's renting you the house was super hard of hearing. I've been having trouble sleeping lately and kind of forgot someone new was living next door."

"That excuses you for the first time, but not for the dozens of times that followed."

"Maybe I liked being on the receiving end of that sexy little death stare of yours."

Nora's insides lit up like a flare. Was he flirting with her? No way. Not possible. He was just being a goof. She wasn't even sure they'd gotten to the point where they stopped hating each other, much less progressed to actually liking each other.

"But I promise to not wake you up any more, okay?"

"Thanks."

They drove a few more minutes on the highway. He kept to the speed limit, which helped her relax a little more and actually enjoy the view of the evergreen-covered hills in the distance. She hadn't realized where they were headed until he pulled the truck into the Black Onyx, one of the swankiest restaurants in Shadow Creek—something she only knew because Rose had mentioned it was her favorite place. Instead of Rusty's, he was taking her to the most expensive restaurant in town, all because she'd dressed wrong.

"I could have changed my clothes," she said quietly as he switched off the ignition.

"Nah, you look too pretty in that dress."

He came around to her side as she was stepping out, and held out his hand. She was tempted to bypass the offer, but even though she was wearing simple ballet flats, she was scared of falling on her face. Electricity jolted in her palm when it met his, tingling right through every limb. She stumbled on the ledge, landing gracelessly in his arms.

She looked up with her breath locked firmly in her lungs. His lips, pulled into a hard line, were too close to hers. The fresh, masculine scent of his skin invaded her senses. The hand on her waist tightened a fraction and she nearly melted into him.

She backed up before she let herself get carried away and cleared her throat. "Listen, Humperdinck. This is just a date. The kind that ends with us saying goodnight with a wave from our respective porches before we go back to ignoring each other, okay?"

The corners of his lips quirked upwards, like he found her amusing.

"What?"

"You don't know my name, do you?"

"I—" Panic seeped into her chest. Holy hell. She'd been calling him Humperdinck for so long, she didn't know his actual name. How was that possible? "Maybe I just prefer to call you Humperdinck."

"Sure you do." His grip on her waist loosened, but he didn't take his hand off her. Instead, he slid it around to the small of her back and led her to the restaurant's entrance. "Come on, let's see if we can charm our way into getting a table at the last minute."

To her surprise, they did manage to get seated almost immediately, but it was a small, cramped table tucked into an inconvenient corner near the bathrooms, far from the sweeping ocean views. Her knees bumped against his under the maroon tablecloth when she sat down. She ignored the explosion of tingles working though her body, and spread her napkin neatly over her lap. She snuck a dab of hand sani-tizer from her purse and quickly inspected her cutlery for watermarks and caked-on food.

"Find anything interesting on that knife?"

"No, but you've got what looks like yesterday's Bolognese dried onto yours."

He picked up the utensil and inspected it with a shrug before wiping with his napkin, then dunked it right into the butter tray. Disgust curdled her stomach as he slathered the butter onto one of the complimentary slices of bread. He offered it to her, but she shook her head with a shudder.

The server came to the table for their orders. She picked up her menu and nearly choked on the prices. "I think we need a few more moments to decide, but could we get some clean cutlery for my friend?"

The server snatched both of their sets of cutlery with a sneer. "Consider the special. It's a mint- and panko-crusted halibut," he said before spinning on his heel and walking off.

"It was really nice of you to bring me here, especially when you had something else planned, but I feel like I should warn you that we're not compatible before you spend fifty dollars on the lamb," she said with her eyes fixed on the menu when the waiter finally left.

"You don't know that. We've barely even gotten to know each other. By the end of the date, you might be begging me for another."

"I know that I'm way less comfortable with germs than you are and that we do not overlap in our taste in music."

"Sure, but you don't know my name."

She narrowed her eyes, but couldn't maintain her annoyance. He was dangerously adept at disarming her with that crooked smile. She needed to remind herself to keep her brain in charge of her decisions tonight and keep every other part of her anatomy out of it. "Your name is irrelevant. It has no bearing on the success of this date."

"Unless my last name is Bora. Or Snora. Or Von Spackledick."

She sipped her water, trying not to laugh. "We're not getting married, and even if we did, I wouldn't change my last name."

"Why? What's your last name?"

"Pitts."

He grimaced.

"It's not that bad."

"Keep telling yourself that, Pitts."

"I'm a chemistry professor and I've published a lot under my own name. I didn't change my name after my first marriage, and I won't change it if I ever get married again. It would be like erasing all of my past accomplishments, and I've worked too hard to do that."

She instantly regretted the sharply spoken outburst. Her refusal to change her name had always been a sore spot between her and Gavin, but the last thing she'd meant to do was bring up her divorce on a first date.

He leaned back in his chair and ran his hand along his jaw. "Wow. Hate to break it to you, Nora Pitts, but we have something big in common."

"What?" She braced herself for the inevitable awful discussion about their past breakups. God, why was she so bad at this?

"Master's of Chemistry from U-Dub."

"No way." She didn't even try to hide her surprise.

"Yep. I was going to finish up with a PhD before my friend Jake and I decided to open a brewery instead. How about you? Are you working at Shadow Creek College?"

She took a deep breath, trying to work up some pride in her voice. "Sure am."

The server appeared again. "Have you decided?"

Shoot. She'd gotten caught up in the conversation and forgot to look at the menu. The pressure flustered her. She scanned the menu quickly. "I'll have the peppercorn steak, medium, but could you replace the green beans with the seasonal vegetables and go light on the gravy? Actually, gravy on the side, please."

The server didn't even try to hide his annoyed sigh. She legitimately was allergic to green beans, and maybe the gravy on the side thing was annoying, but so was paying fifty dollars for a steak while sitting at a table next to the bathroom.

"I'll have the steak as well, rare, with the green beans, and give me all the damn gravy you've got," Humperdinck said.

"You wouldn't be the first person to tell me I'm overly picky," she said when the server left.

He leaned forward, resting his elbows against the table. His ankles brushed against hers. "You know, they say opposites attract for a reason. Maybe you just need someone like me to help you loosen up."

Like she'd never heard *that* from a man before. "And what would you be getting out of this?"

"A good time."

She rolled her eyes. "Exactly. Opposites might attract for one night, but opposites don't make sustainable, happy relationships."

"Jumping ahead a little bit, are we?"

"No, I'm not, and that's the point. I'm not a one-night stand kind of woman. You might be fine with asking a pathetic stranger out as a joke just to get a little action on the side, but I'm not. I only said yes because I wanted Gemma and Rose to choke on their insults and shut the hell up for once. And the fact is, the next date I go on will be with someone who's actually interested in a second and third date."

He leaned back and crossed his arms, ubiquitous grin replaced by a scowl. "So you know all there is to know about me. Is that it?"

"I know what I need to know for the purpose of this date," she answered in a small voice.

"First impressions aren't everything. If they were, I never would have asked out a woman who's wound so tight, she explodes like a goddamn missile every time someone tries to live their life in a way that doesn't abide by her perfectly ordered plans."

She gasped. Tears prickled her eyes when she realized everyone in in the restaurant was watching them.

"Shit, I'm sorry. I didn't mean that."

She adjusted her cutlery so it lined up perfectly with the edges of the table. "You did. And that's okay because it's true."

"It's not." He extended his hand halfway across the table before closing his fist and pulling it back, as though he was about to reach for her then decided better.

Silence frosted the air between them while they waited for their food. Her heart thundered in her chest like it was trying to escape the embarrassment, but her shoulders curved downward, trapping it and the remaining tatters of her dignity deep inside her. They didn't speak or make eye contact while they waited for their food, which fortunately didn't take long.

She cut her steak open, not surprised to see she'd been given a rare piece of meat instead of what she ordered. *Just suck it up. It's not going to kill you.* She popped a bite in her mouth and almost gagged on it from surprise. It wasn't just rare, it was practically raw, and still cold in the middle. Not to mention salted like it was being cured. Spitting out the bite she'd taken would only fuel his conviction that she was an uptight brat, so she chewed it slowly, willing herself not to make a face. After a few disgusting minutes, she managed to crunch through the cold meat long enough to made it bearable to swallow.

"Something wrong with your food?"

She shook her head quickly and took a huge sip of water.

"Bullshit." He reached across the table and jabbed his fork into one of the pieces she'd pre-cut, and shoved it in his mouth before spitting it right out. "Ugh. You can't eat that."

"It's fine," she whispered.

"It's not." He signaled to the server. "My date's food is ice cold and tastes like a salt lick."

The server widened his eyes in affront. "Our chef is one of the best in the city. I assure you, the food is cooked to perfection."

"Sure, if he was trying to cook a hockey puck." He picked up the slab of meat and let it drop against the plate with a clatter that proved how rock solid it was.

"I'm sorry," the server said, aghast. "It's honestly a mistake. Your meal is on us and we'll bring you out a replacement right away."

"Thank you," she said, grateful for the quick resolution.

"We're not staying." Humperdinck pulled out his wallet and slapped a couple bills on the table. "I know this isn't your fault, and we appreciate the offer, but we're going to finish our dinner somewhere else."

He got up, grabbed her hand, and tugged her out of the restaurant. "Where are we going?"

He didn't answer until they were both inside the truck. "How do you feel about Red Top Burgers?"

She wanted to tell him to just bring her home, but he actually sounded earnest. After how terribly this date had been going, he still wanted to see it through. How could she say no? "I don't know, but I'm willing to try."

"Good."

Fifteen minutes later, they'd pulled up to a bluff overlooking the valley with a bucket of fries, a chiliburger with everything on it, and a cheeseburger—hold the onions and lettuce and mustard. He laid out a musty old blanket from the cab of his truck on the grass and sat across from her with the food in the middle.

Her neighbor was a very confusing man. "You could have just taken me home."

"Believe it or not, I'm not trying to go down as the worst date in history. And I didn't ask you out as joke, either. I asked you out because you looked like someone who needed a friend. A real one. Not like those women you hang out with on Friday nights. Now pass me that hand sanitizer."

Her heart twisted with an inexplicable emotion. She pulled the travel-sized bottle from her purse and squirted some in her hand before passing it to him, then laid out her napkin over her lap. "Thank you. It's not easy making friends in a new city. I joined the book club to meet people, but it's not going so well."

He unwrapped one of the burgers and peeked inside the bun, then handed it to her. "Why don't you come by my bar sometime? There's lots of nice people there."

"Maybe I will," she said before taking a quick bite of her cheeseburger.

He returned her smile with a sweet one of his own, captivating her with that lingering gaze. Their date may have been an epic failure, but for the first time, she started to believe that maybe they could actually become friends. Or friendlier. Or at least maybe she'd stop wanting to throttle him every time he blasted his music at odd hours.

He cleared his throat, and even though they only had the headlights from his truck to illuminate their picnic, she was pretty sure there was a hint of blush on his cheeks. "You good with ketchup on the fries?"

She nodded, and then watched in horror as he ripped open the little package and squirted it all over the fries. "I should have figured you're the kind of person who eats fries with ketchup splattered all over the place."

She picked up one fry that was relatively unscathed by the condiment explosion and popped it in her mouth with a tiny moan of pleasure. Curly fries beat out an expensive steak any day.

"Let me guess, you only like your ketchup if it comes in one of those waxy little cups so that you don't have to get your hands dirty." He grabbed a fry and shoved into his mouth, spilling a glob of ketchup onto his finger.

"Exactly." He licked his finger clean, which was gross, yet there was no denying the shiver that rolled down her spine. "I'm starting to think that maybe you're right that we are complete opposites. Morning or night?"

"Morning." She didn't even have to ask which he preferred. "Cats or dogs?"

"Dogs," he answered quickly. "You?"

She bit her lip, holding back another smile.

"Oh, come on. You can't be serious."

She shrugged and stole another fry. "Cats are independent and smart. What's not to love?"

He shook his head, laughing. "They're also vicious."

"Do you believe it's important to wash your feet in the shower?"

He gave her an incredulous look. "Really? That's one of your first date questions?"

"It's a very important question determining compatibility."

"Sure, but it's also the kind of thing you're supposed to find out firsthand the morning after a mind-blowing night together, not through a pop quiz."

A flash of heat blazed through her body.

"But the answer is no. Only if you pee in the shower first. Otherwise, why do what the water and soap running down your body will do for you?"

"Ew."

"Hey, you're the one that asked."

"Not the first bad decision I've made in my life."

"What's the worst?"

She paused with her burger poised at her lips. "I don't know. I guess everything that led me to move here."

"Why? Shadow Creek is great. You've got ocean and mountains and parks. Great restaurants. Good people. What more could you want?"

"All that stuff if great if you have people to enjoy it with. Otherwise, it's just a reminder of how lonely life can be." She sealed her lips together. She might not be a dating expert, but she knew no one wanted to hear about her sad-sack story.

"Then why did you leave?"

"My divorce," she answered honestly. "I had a tenure-track position at one of the universities back east, but when things ended, it was too hard to keep working there. Professorships in my field don't come up often, and this seemed like the kind of job where I could have a little more balance, so here I am. It just didn't turn out to be exactly what I thought it would."

"Do you regret it?"

She contemplated her answer while swallowing another bite of her cheeseburger. "Sometimes. Most of the time. But I'm pretty stubborn."

The truth was, most of her regrets were for what she didn't do in Boston. She'd been so determined to prove herself professionally that she didn't leave room for anything else. If she hadn't spent every minute of life working, she might have actually made some friends to help her deal with the divorce. Heck, maybe Gavin wouldn't have cheated on her in the first place, though she hated herself for even entertaining that thought.

"Stubborn, huh?" He grinned and she smacked him lightly on the shoulder. "Ouch. Stubborn and vicious."

"I'm pretty sure that's what my yearbook caption said about me."

"Probably because you were giving that sexy death stare in your photo instead of smiling."

She laughed. "No comment. But yes, I've always been stubborn. Moving here was one of the first impulsive decisions I've made in my life and I don't want to give up just because it's not going the way I hoped. I'm determined to make it work, even if it kills me."

"Didn't you say you made the decision to move here because you wanted balance?"

"Yes, but I also said I wasn't any good at balance. What about you? I've been talking about myself all night and I barely know anything about you."

"Like my name?"

She sucked in her breath, then exhaled with a growl. "Fine. I admit it. I don't know your name. Please just tell me and put me out of my misery."

"Nope. You have to earn that privilege."

"And how do I do that?"

He kicked off his loafer and wriggled his toes, the biggest of which was poking through a hole in his blue-and-yellow striped sock. "A foot massage might get you the first letter."

"After what you told me about your shower habits? Not a chance."

"I guess I'll just have to charm you with my wit instead."

"Actually, you haven't done such a bad job in that regard."

"So you're admitting this isn't the worst date ever?"

The truth was, this was probably her best date in a long time. He'd made her laugh. Made her feel a little less alone. "In some ways the worst, in some ways the best."

"Good thing I'm an optimist." He leaned across the blanket until his face was so close to hers she could feel his breath against her skin. His easy grin was intoxicating from this distance, making her heartbeat speed up until she could feel it thrumming in her chest. Would it really be so bad if he kissed her right now?

He crept another inch closer and bit the French fry she was holding right out of her hand. "Damn, these things are good."

"Hey! That was the last one."

"Then we'll have to do this again sometime. Told you I was an optimist."

"I'm still a pessimist, but I think we could make that happen. As friends, though."

"Whatever you need to tell yourself to keep that glass half-empty, sweetheart." He cleaned up their garbage and tossed it all into a plastic bag. "Ready to head home?"

"Sure," she answered cheerily, though disappointment twisted in her gut. She was attracted to him and the idea of losing herself in a passionate kiss was damn appealing. But impulses led to regrets. There was no point starting something romantic with him when they weren't meant to be, but there was a real chance they could be friends. As long as they kept their hands to themselves.

The drive home was quick, which was unsurprising considering the size of Shadow Creek, and she was at her doorstep before dusk had completely darkened the sky. He insisted on walking her to her porch.

She unlocked her door and turned around before going inside. "Are you going to tell me your name now? It's going to drive me crazy all night if you don't."

He rubbed his fingers along his jaw. "That depends. Are you going to let me finish this date properly?"

She raised her eyebrow. "What do you mean?"

He cupped her cheek, tilting her head upward. Anticipation thundered like a million butterflies fluttering in her belly as he tugged softly at the corner of her mouth with his thumb, and she parted her lips on command.

He pressed his lips to her cheek with a gentle touch that made her skin tingle. He grazed his way to her mouth, leaving a trail of fire in his wake, and sucked on her bottom lip. Her entire body arched toward his, hands pressed against his chest. She hadn't expected a kiss this tender. She hadn't known tender could electrify every inch of her skin.

His tongue finally slid against hers, teasing and tempting her as he deepened the kiss. Blood thrummed against her core, leaving her with an ache that could only be remedied one way. All she had to do was invite him in...

He broke away, leaving her breathless and raw. "Too bad we're not compatible, huh?" He trotted down the steps and headed back to his place while she stood frozen on the spot.

He opened his door, but stopped before going inside. "Nora?"

"Yeah?"

"When you crawl under the covers and touch yourself while thinking about that kiss, make sure to call out the name Eli Hardin."

3

"*S*o..." Jake drew out the single syllable like a bridge over the Pacific.

Eli grabbed another pint glass and scrubbed it clean. "So what?"

"This is normally when you spill a few nasty details about last night's date that make me want to cover my ears at the same time I call you my hero, and then you come up with a million excuses why you'll never see the woman again."

Eli tossed his friend a dishtowel. "No, this is normally when I tell you to quit cleaning that same stain on the bar that's been there for the last three years. It's never coming off."

"Actually," Julia said, coming from the back office, and pulling up a stool at the bar. She dropped her chin into her hand with a grin. "This is usually the time when we discuss the upcoming season's events schedule, but you haven't been on a date in a long time and I'm in the mood for some gossip. Spill it, big brother."

He filled three sleeves with his Spiritual Imperial Porter, figuring it would be easier to give in to the inevitable than to keep fighting it. The truth was, he loved these quiet moments with just the three of them at the Holy Grale. It was easier to appreciate the beauty of the old church-turned-brewpub in these early, empty hours before they opened to the public. He'd initially thought Jake was nuts for suggesting they buy this place, but it only took one step inside to see the potential of the high vaulted ceilings, exposed brick walls, and colorful stained-glass windows.

He sipped his porter, unashamed of appreciating his own work. The bold flavors of caramel and roasted malt danced a perfect tango in his mouth. "The date was fine. We decided it made more sense to be friends."

Julia and Jake exchanged a look. "You sound like a sad greeting card," his sister said.

"I'm serious."

"So am I. You usually sound a lot happier when a date ends without a second one."

"That's because he's usually the one spouting the 'let's be friends' line," Jake said. "I'm guessing this time around your neighbor did the rejecting. And judging by your mood, you didn't have that conversation this morning."

Eli set his beer down and looked at the other two. Jake and Julia were the people who knew him best in the world. His business partners. His family. The people he would throw himself in front of a bus for, no questions asked. And yet they were talking about him like they didn't know him at all. He hadn't been on a date in almost a year, much less messed around with one-night stands. Yeah, he'd acted out after his mom's death for a few years, but that was a long time ago. He'd matured a hell of a lot since then.

Enough to know that a woman like Nora was a whole lot more special than he initially realized, and enough to know that he had to respect her when she told him she wasn't interested in more after their date.

He reached for his sister's clipboard on the bar and spun it around. "Back to business. I'd like to introduce a new wheat beer into our lineup. Maybe a session ale, too."

Jake frowned. "Our current wheat ale is selling really well. In fact, all of our beers are doing amazing. I think we should limit ourselves to one seasonal brew."

"We need to keep things interesting. If we're stagnant, customers are going to go to any of the other dozens of brewpubs in this town."

"I'm not saying we shouldn't shake things up, but we don't want to mess with perfection, either. Financially, it doesn't make sense to do more than one seasonal brew."

Eli glanced at Julia, hoping for a little sibling solidarity. She winced apologetically.

"So what am I supposed to do? Sit at home being useless while you two run this place? Watch infomercials all day and yell at the television to pass time while I wait around for the mailman to show up?"

Fuck. He knew he sounded like an immature asshole as soon as the words left his mouth, but he couldn't squelch the frustration churning inside of him. Yeah, the Holy Grale was a business, but creating beer was his passion. For the last three years, he'd slaved away in the brewery perfecting the recipes that would make their brewpub completely irresistible amidst a sea of competition. But now they were on the other side of the curve. Disasters were a rarity now instead of a daily occurrence. Their customers were loyal and thirsty. But most importantly, Jake was right when he said their beer was perfect. Eli was basically useless at this point.

"Well, you could just stay home and come up with more ways to torment your neighbor," Jake said, barely holding back a chuckle.

"Not funny."

Julia slammed her clipboard onto the counter. "Wait, back up a minute. Did you...like her? Like, actually really like her? I thought you hated her."

He ran his hand through his hair, feeling more exhausted than he should have considering how early he'd gone to bed last night. "Fine. Yes, I liked her. She's smart, funny, and pretty. We had a nice date but she's not interested in more. Now, can we please talk about business?"

"When I told you this date would backfire, I didn't think it would be because you'd fall for her and then get rejected," Jake said before clapping him on the shoulder. "Her loss, buddy."

Eli tapped the clipboard. "The SPCA fundraiser. Why is there a big red 'X' next to it?"

"Because I don't think we can take it on," Julia said. "Their outreach coordinator decided to retire early, and they haven't found anyone to replace her yet. I thought about volunteering to do it all myself, but our events schedule is so busy this fall, I just don't have the time. I know business is still tight, but I was hoping we could make a donation on behalf of the Holy Grale to the organization, at the very least."

"I think that's reasonable," Jake said, before looking to Eli for confirmation.

"Yeah, make a donation. But we can still host the fundraiser. I'll organize it."

His sister's mouth fell open before twisting into a confused pucker. "You?"

Why did he always say shit without thinking it through first? "Why not? I'm not a kid. I'm a responsible adult and, technically, your boss. I can handle this."

"I know you can handle it, but you've got a lot going on right now. Do you want to take this on?"

He shrugged. "I don't want those animals to suffer because no one else was willing to do it. Besides, we've hosted the event before. How hard can it be?"

"Give him a chance," Jake said.

"All right," Julia said slowly, sounding anything but convinced. "I'll get the files from last year's event."

"You know," Jake said as soon as Julia went back to her office, "if you were looking for a distraction from your neighbor, you could have just gotten a subscription to Netflix."

Maybe Jake did know him a little better than he thought, because Nora had been on his mind a lot more than he'd expected since last night. The taste of her lips. The strange but adorable dimple that formed at the top of her right cheek when she smiled. The way she'd made him laugh and forget everything that had been going on for the last few weeks. She'd been right they didn't have much in common. Hell, even he could agree they weren't right for each other. But that didn't change the fact he'd liked her. A lot.

"It's not just her. I've got a lot on my mind lately, and not a lot to occupy my time since my best buddy moved out."

"What can I say? Clem's a lot more fun to wake up with."

"Too bad for her you're a grumpy SOB who doesn't know the meaning of the words 'lazy Sunday morning.'"

"Make fun of me all you want, as long as you're sure you're not taking on more than you can handle."

"I'm fine."

"You're my best friend, Eli. We've been like two burrs stuck to a donkey's ass since we met fifteen years ago. I know how you get when you're stressed about something. Do you remember that time in undergrad when you were worried about your student loan papers and decided to organize the midnight toga party? You nearly got us arrested after we were the only two idiots standing in the quad practically butt-naked after you forgot to distribute the invitations."

"This is different. It's a fundraiser. We'll sell some tickets, cook some burgers, and have a good time while helping out a good cause. It's not going to be that hard." Eli lined up the last of the glasses and inspected the shelf for dust.

"Okay, here it is," Julia announced as she came out from the back office. She dropped a folder three inches thick on the bar.

"What is this?"

"The file for the SPCA fundraiser. Everything you need to pull it off."

He sucked in a breath. Yeah, he really needed to start thinking before opening his mouth.

"Get your purse. We're going out."

Nora looked at the three women standing at her front door, still not quite comprehending why they were there. "We are?"

"Yes, silly," Gemma said with a harsh laugh. "We need to hear all about your date last night."

Nora bit back the urge to ask Gemma to repeat herself. She'd heard the words just fine—she just couldn't understand why they were coming out of her biggest frenemy's mouth. Gemma and Rose had been outright cruel to her two nights ago at their last book club meeting. Nora had been practically in tears after the whole incident with Eli, and barely spoke for the rest of the evening. Why would they show up here out the blue now?

Maybe they really did want to hear about her date, she reasoned. What was the harm in saying yes? *You need friends.* "Sure. Just let me change first."

A few minutes later, she was in the back of Annie's VW Golf with a clean sweater and her blond hair pulled back in a neat ponytail. Her stomach lurched with unease when they drove up to an old church, but one quick glance at the sign in parking lot assuaged her paranoia.

The Holy Grale. Clever name for a pub.

"I've been wanting to try this place for a while," Annie said as they stepped inside the impressive space. Huge stained-glass windows lined the walls, but the warm wood décor made the space feel inviting instead of intimidating.

"It might be quieter on the second floor," Nora said while they scanned the busy room for a table.

Gemma shook her head. "Nah, let's stay down here where all the action is."

"There's a spot," Rose said, pointing to a high, round table near the back.

The conversation started off fine, not that Nora contributed much. They were talking about a superhero movie that had just come out and she hadn't had the chance to see it yet. She hated watching movies in the theatre with the soda-slicked floors and God-knows-what fluids and bacteria festering in the seats. It was so much easier to watch them at home where she could cozy up on her clean couch with her fresh, air-popped popcorn with real butter, and a big mug of tea. No interruptions. No kids throwing candy or kicking the seat behind her. Just a nice, lonely way to have a night of fun.

Yeah, she was going to have to work on her no-movie-theatre stance.

She scanned the menu while Gemma went on about the size of the star's biceps. Beer. Beer. More beer. Nerves made her left leg shake like a jackhammer against her stool. Usually she could find something else to drink, but this place was entirely beer. Even the food menu was mostly beer-based. Yam-and-ale enchiladas. Chocolate stout cake. Before she finished reading the menu, the server had come by for their order.

"Let's just get a round of the lemon ginger radlers," Rose insisted. "I bet they're delicious."

Nora was too grateful to have the decision taken off her hands to argue. She had no idea what a radler was, but she liked lemon ginger tea, so it couldn't be that bad.

As soon as Gemma gathered up the menus and handed them to the server, they all zeroed in on Nora. "Okay, time to spill. How was the date?"

"It was nice. Eli's more of a gentleman than I expected."

"Hmm. A gentleman in the streets, but how was he in the sheets?" Gemma waggled her eyebrows while the others laughed.

She knew the question was coming the minute she answered her door, but it still galled her. "It wasn't that kind of date, but even so, those aren't the kinds of details I'm comfortable sharing."

"Borrrring," Rose said.

The server came by at that moment and set a pint glass filled with a pale gold liquid in front of each of them.

Annie leaned over the table, cupping her hot-pink-tipped fingers around her glass. "I can't believe you had a chance to do it with your hot neighbor and you didn't take it."

She needed to come up with a new topic of conversation. *Think of something interesting, Nora. Anything.* "Did you know that the graphite in a pencil is made entirely of carbon, just like a diamond?"

Her comment ricocheted off their blank stares like a bullet. Okay, maybe her favorite Chemistry 101 factoid wasn't the best conversation piece. She grabbed her drink and took a sip to mask her embarrassment.

"I did not know that," Gemma finally said. "But I do know that when a man is showing all signs of being hung like a horse, you need to cowgirl-up and ride him."

Nora coughed and spit out the sip of beer she'd just taken.

Gemma laughed. "Not much of a cowgirl, are you?"

"No," Nora said between coughs. The strangely sweet, tangy flavor still invaded her mouth. Was this really what craft beer was supposed to taste like? "This is really awful."

"So you don't like his body, and you don't like his beer. Does that mean he's up for grabs?"

Nora looked at Gemma, feeling one step behind the plot, and the smirk on her face only made the sinking feeling in Nora's stomach worse. She followed the line of their gazes to the bar and—

Oh shit.

Eli.

∼

Even in his own bar, there was no way to not feel creepy while standing outside of the women's washroom, but Eli hunkered down with his back against the wall and waited. Nora had gone in there almost ten minutes ago. He had to admit the strangled, panicked look on her face when she finally caught his eye had dented his self-esteem just a little. And the way she'd almost choked on her first taste of his radler? Yeah, that wasn't doing his ego any favors either.

He almost couldn't believe his eyes when she walked in here. It wasn't the first time a woman he'd gone out with the night before had come in the next day angling for a second date, but Nora had been more than clear she wasn't interested. Of course, seeing her with those women from her book club explained some of the confusion. He'd told Nora he worked at a brewpub, but there were more than a half-dozen scattered around this town. She'd been set up.

The door finally swung open and Nora came out looking pale.

"Of all the brewpubs in this town, you've got to walk into mine, huh?"

She gasped and stuttered to a stop. "I didn't know—"

"I know."

She looked at her feet. "I should go back—"

"I told them to get lost and that you'd found another ride home tonight."

This time she actually looked up at him. "Why?"

"Because it's clear you didn't know they were bringing you to my pub. What isn't clear is why you agreed to go anywhere with them."

"I don't know. I thought maybe they were sincere when they wanted to know how our date went. I didn't know they were going to bring me here so I would look like some crazy stalker." She let out a rush of breath. "God, this is so embarrassing."

"No, what's embarrassing is the way you spit out a perfectly good radler."

He enjoyed the way her cheeks pinkened. "I'm not much of a beer drinker. I wasn't expecting it to be so sweet."

"I'm going to let you in on a little secret. Radlers aren't exactly beer. They're beer mixed with a citrus-based soda. I think they're disgusting, but they *are* popular, so I've created a perfect one and allowed it on the menu."

"A little full of yourself, huh?" That was the grin he was hoping for. The one that made her cheeks bunch up like little apples and the corner of her eyes crinkle.

"I'm overcompensating after a harsh but understandable rejection by a beautiful woman last night."

"We're still friends, right?" Her eyes met his like it was the gravest question in the world.

He sighed exaggeratedly. "I don't know. Can I really be friends with a heathen who doesn't like beer?"

"Hey, if I can be friends with someone who listens to weird disco from the seventies, I think you can put my drinking habits aside."

"Deal. But for the record, I only listen to that stuff because my mom loved it. It reminds me of her."

"Oh." The smile drifted off her lips, leaving a behind a look of pity.

Shit. What was it about her that made him say stuff like that? The stuff that was supposed to stay quiet? "Want a tour? I'll show you all the off-limits stuff."

"Yes, please!"

Instinct almost made him reach for her hand, but he wasn't going to be the jerk who didn't take no for an answer. She'd been clear that last night's date had been nothing but an experiment. A failed one. Instead, he led her toward the back rooms with the lightest touch on the back.

"Hey, Eli?" Julia popped her head out of the hallway as he and Nora walked by. "Oh."

"Julia, this is my neighbor, Nora. Nora, this is my sister, Julia. Also known as the one responsible for all the décor and event listings you see around here."

"It's very nice to meet you." Nora offered her hand. Julia shook it firmly.

"I'm just giving Nora a tour of the brewery."

Julia's eyebrows shot up. "Interesting."

He shook his head and ushered Nora forward.

She glanced at him over her shoulder as they walked, curiosity lighting up her pretty eyes. "What's interesting?"

"I wasn't lying when I said the brewery is off-limits to the public."

"So why am I getting special treatment?"

Because you're goddamn special. "Because I'm in the mood to break some rules today. Welcome to my lab." He pushed open the door and led her through.

"Whoa."

Consternation pulled his jaw tight. "I can't tell if that's a good whoa or a bad whoa, so you're going to have to spell it out for me, Princess."

"It's just so…so clean."

He laughed, though it wasn't exactly joy-filled. "I might not be a clean-freak like you, but that doesn't make me a slob. There's a few more shades of gray on that scale."

She sighed. "You're right. I'm sorry."

He nudged her shoulder with his. "Relax, I didn't bring you here to make you feel bad. I came here to show you my brewery."

Her eyes lit up. "Dear God, I love big machines."

"You know that's fucking sexy, right?"

She blushed so hard, he worried it might actually be physically painful.

"Sorry, it's just that there aren't a lot of people who appreciate this end of the business. All the glory is out front when people take that first sip of a perfectly crisp, cold beer surrounded by their friends in the bar, but to me, this is where the magic happens."

"I get it. Most people think chemistry is all about mixing chemicals and big explosions, but my favorite part is characterizing all the materials with the machines. It's why I specialized in materials science."

He nodded, understanding completely. "I guess you don't have as much equipment at Shadow Creek College as you did at your old school."

She laughed, though there was something rueful in the sound. "A bit of an understatement. I can work with what I've got, but I miss having all that power and state-of-the-art technology at my fingertips." She ran her hand along the pristine, stainless steel cylinder wall of the fermentation tank.

He explained the function of the machines and the brewing process as he walked her through the large space, admiring her with the same keen interest she did the machines. It was nice to explain the chemical processes and techniques to someone who could actually understand what he was saying. Someone who could grasp the importance of precision and experimentation that went into crafting the perfect beer—even if she didn't actually like said beer.

When they finished the tour, he drove her home. She paused in the passenger seat of his truck before getting out. "Thank you so much for tonight. This is the second time in a row that a night out has gone in a completely unanticipated direction for me, thanks to you."

"A good direction?"

She smiled. "Definitely."

"Maybe one of these days I'll surprise you again by finding a beer you'll actually like to drink."

She gave him another smile and opened the door. "Goodnight, Eli. Thank you for the ride."

He watched her walk to her front porch, wondering if she realized just how much she'd thrown his whole life in a completely unanticipated direction, too.

4

*N*ora stood at the third shelf in the supply room and frowned. "Doug, where's the sodium borohydride?"

"Uh, I think we're out."

"That can't be right. I ordered some three weeks ago." She turned to see her student standing in the doorway with ratty old Birkenstocks strapped to his hairy feet and a steaming mug of coffee in his hand. "Are you trying to kill yourself?"

Her assistant grinned sheepishly and took a step back into the hallway. "Relax. I've got a proper pair of shoes in my office. I just haven't changed yet."

She set her hands on her hips. "Closed-toed shoes before you step inside the building. The last thing I need is an accident at the lab." She'd barely managed any significant breakthroughs in the six months she'd been here. A burned hobbit toe was not the way she intended for her research to make a splash in the world of materials science.

"Okay, but I just came to tell you about that experiment I ran last night. It, uh, worked."

Nora scoured the shelves for the sodium borohydride, eventually finding it misplaced on the far side of the stock room with the extra beakers. "Aha! Found it. Wait, what did you just say?"

"The lithium aluminum hydride worked."

She bit her lip. Doug's experiment had been a random idea that popped into her brain last week, and she'd delegated it to him as a way to get him out of her hair for a couple days, not because she thought it would actually work. "Show me."

Ten minutes later, she was at his desk with eyes wide and a wriggling coil of excitement inside her chest. The plot was a thing of beauty, perfectly peaked to show the particle formation. "Did you run it through the SEM?"

"Right here." Doug clicked on the file, and her heart nearly doubled over on itself.

"Doug, you're incredible!" He might be disorganized and scatterbrained, but he was a genius when it came to the wet work.

He blushed and ran his hand through his hair so that the mess stood straight up. "Shucks."

"Can you run a few more samples by tomorrow? The deadline for the Pacific Chemical Conference is 4 p.m. and I'd really love to submit this."

"It's going to be tight, but I can do it."

"Thank you!" Excitement spooled in her belly. She had a small conference budget that she hadn't had any reason to use yet, and this was a great opportunity to present her work. Work untouched by Gavin's dirty hands. Her ideas, her experiments. Sure, it was still in the preliminary stages, but it had the potential to be a great breakthrough, and a fantastic chance for Doug to get a much-deserved publication to his name.

Pride beamed like a sunray in her chest. This was why she loved her job. That moment of pure discovery was why she wanted to be a chemistry professor in the first place.

Maybe she'd even get the chance to connect with some scientists in the area. Colleagues. People she had something in common with. People she might be able to make friends with. God, she hadn't realized how much she needed this.

She spent the rest of the afternoon writing her abstract submission and prepping lesson plans. She buried herself in work until she'd completely lost track of time. Her stomach growled a few times, reminding her she'd forgotten to eat her lunch, but the drive to accomplish something was too strong to stop. It wasn't until a knock came at her door that she looked up and realized the entire day had passed.

Doug stepped into her office with a grin. "I ran another sample. The results hold up, but I can run them a few more times tonight if you want..." His voice trailed off, and she bit back the temptation to ask him to stay even later and triple-check everything. Despite her social awkwardness, she could tell he wanted to get going somewhere.

"No, that's okay. You deserve to cut out early." She glanced at the time on her computer and winced. It was already 6 p.m. "Um, well, tomorrow you can take off early. But you should go home now. We have most of what we need and we have tomorrow to finish up."

"Thanks! I'm going to go celebrate with some of the grad students. You want to come with us?"

She could tell it was a pity invite by the way he looked at her, but she realized that maybe she kind of did want to go with them. She hadn't had much interaction with the handful of Master's students in the department other than Doug. Not because she was a snob, but because every time she was around them, they seemed to be talking about sports or videogames or something else she didn't have the first clue about. Still, it couldn't be worse than hanging out with her book club. "Where are you heading?"

"Paintballing!"

Her excitement drained out of her like a sad, popped balloon. "No thanks. Have fun, though. You deserve it."

He left her with a goofy salute.

She finished up a few last tasks and headed home for the night. When she pulled up to her driveway, Eli's lights were on. She thought about going over to see him to share her good news, but hesitated. She'd been so tempted last night to cross a line—a line she'd been the one to set. Seeing him now would just complicate things even more.

Would that be so bad?

Loneliness propelled her in his direction. The sound of a power-saw rumbling stopped her before she reached his sidewalk.

She dropped her head down with a sigh, then turned around and walked back to her house.

Eli was in over his damn head in every possible way. He'd opened the files for the SPCA fundraiser and realized he had no idea what to do. There were clear plans for advertising and ordering food in the exact same way they'd done last year, but they hadn't raised a whole lot of money doing it that way. Plus, they'd held the event upstairs on the mezzanine level, keeping the lower level open to the public. It was a good idea in theory, since having regular patrons there should increase the traffic for the fundraiser, but that hadn't happened last year. There was nothing to draw the regulars upstairs.

He needed to make this a bigger event. One that drew people in and got them opening up their wallets for a good cause. The problem was, he had no idea how to do that. He also had no idea how to get Jane, the new outreach coordinator, to decide whether hotdogs, hamburgers, or something completely different should be on the menu, or whether they wanted to do a silent auction, or make any other kind of decision. Jane was completely overwhelmed in the new job and seemed to panic over every decision he asked her to make.

After a few hours of poring through the permits and invoices and everything else in Julia's binders, he'd gotten so frustrated, he decided to deal with it by not dealing with it at all. Instead, he dove headfirst into his bathroom reno. Tearing down the old tile in the shower had been a pretty great distraction until he'd discovered the moldy drywall. The pipes were rusty, too—something he'd discovered while inspecting the mold and accidentally causing a huge leak. It was like going to a cinema to watch a Disney movie, only to find out he'd actually stumbled into a horror film.

So now, instead of clearing his mind, he was scrambling to find the water shut-off valve before he destroyed the new floors in his hallway.

He found it quickly in the basement laundry room, then searched for towels and whatever he could find to mop up the mess before it leaked onto the new hardwood he'd installed in the hall last week.

Luckily, he caught the worst of it before there was too much damage. He tossed the last soaking wet towel into the tub and sat down on the edge, exhausted. He dropped his head into his hands and laughed. God, he was an idiot for starting a project like this so late on a Tuesday night, but fortunately the hardware stores were open for another hour. If he measured quickly and accurately enough, he could still salvage some of the repair tonight. At least get the pipe replaced so he could turn the water back on before the morning. He sighed and got up to look for his measuring tape.

His cell phone rang from the other room before he'd made it back to the basement where he kept his tools. He ignored it, letting it go to voicemail. But when it started ringing again before he even got up the stairs, he figured he'd better answer it.

The number on the call display was the landline from the Holy Grale. He swore under his breath and hit *answer*. "Yeah?"

"Hey, Eli," Tom, his brewery assistant, said with a nervous, squeaky voice. "Sorry to bother you when you're off, but we've got a problem."

"What?"

"I thought it would help if I prepared the spent grains for pickup tomorrow and—"

Eli cut him off with a curse. He knew exactly where this was headed. "How big is the spill?"

"Pretty big."

He cursed again. "Fine. I'll be right over."

5

*E*li's skin had never itched so badly in his life. The spent grains covered his body, and his hands were too cramped from shoveling up the mess to do anything about it. It had taken him, Jake, and Tom two hours to deal with the worst of it, and another three to disinfect the surfaces and recalibrate the machines. The new batch of IPA he'd been working on was spoiled, along with the money they'd put into it. The only thing that had gone right was the fact he'd managed to keep his cool when Tom apologized to him for the screw up. Eli hadn't yelled at the kid, despite wanting to rip the little shit's head off for the stupidity. The fact was, mistakes happened, and Eli had made his own share in the beginning. Tom had more than pulled his weight in the cleanup. He would learn and do better next time.

Eli walked straight to his bathroom when he got home, not even stopping to kick off his shoes. He needed a shower, desperately. He let out a string of curses as soon as he flicked on the light. The bathroom wasn't finished. The water wasn't back on. And he couldn't fucking shower until he finished the job.

Frustration roared in his chest. He needed a break. One little fucking break.

It was after midnight, and there was no way he could do what needed to be done without waking Nora and everyone else on the block. He walked back outside, figuring a run was the only way to kill his aggravation at this hour, even though the mix of sweat and brewery dust would probably leave him with a painful, full-body rash.

Nora's living room light was on. He'd respected her wishes since their date, even though the kiss between them was the only thing he could think about for the last week. Her soft lips and eager tongue. The way she'd melted against him when he slid his hand into her hair. They were complete opposites, but she was the only one who had a problem with that fact.

So yeah. Only one date. But at least they were on better terms now. Friends, even.

He was at her door before he'd even realized his feet were moving in that direction. He knocked quietly, in case she'd fallen asleep with the light on, but she opened it within seconds. Her blond hair was wet, like she'd just come out of the shower, and slicked back off her face. She was dressed in a little silk robe that exposed just a hint of cleavage and more than enough of her thighs to make the blood from his head rush straight to his cock. Damn, she was beautiful.

"Eli? What happened? You're a mess."

He swallowed before answering, suddenly nervous. She hated messes, and here he was at her doorstep covered in the stickiest, grimiest shit in the world. "A little mishap with the spent grains at the Holy Grale. I was working on my bathroom this afternoon before I found out, and now I don't have a working shower, and my water's turned off and—" Her face scrunched as she took in the sight of him, making him feel even more like a jerk. Just because he'd had a shitty night didn't mean he had the right to ruin hers, too. "Can I just borrow your garden hose to rinse off?"

"Don't be ridiculous." She grabbed his arm and pulled him inside. "You can shower here."

"I'm a mess. I know you hate that."

"I do, but that's why I have a mop. The bathroom's just on the right." She led him down the hall. Her house was nearly identical in layout to his, but the décor was completely different—soft gray walls and a stark white kitchen that was open to the living room. Mrs. Kocilowicz had put a lot of work into the place when she decided to rent it out and spend the rest of her retirement in Palm Springs—it was one of the reasons he'd thought to fix his own place up—but he hadn't realized it was this nice inside.

He stopped at the door and turned to face her. "Thanks."

She smiled. "Honestly, you smell so bad, it's almost like you're doing me a favor by cleaning yourself up."

The edges of her robe drifted open, revealing the swell of her breast. His gaze drifted along the gentle slope and creamy skin, studying the hint of perfection beneath that blue silk.

Her eyes widened and she tugged her robe shut. "Um, let me know if you need anything."

He nodded, knowing that the one thing he really needed right now was the only thing he couldn't ask for.

Nora hadn't been sure if Eli or a yeti had shown up at her door on first glance. A strange brown dust covered his hair and skin, and even though the thought of having that stuff all over her house revolted her, her sympathy for the man was a million times stronger. But that reaction still paled in comparison to the way she felt when his brown eyes scorched her skin with a look of desire moments ago.

The responsible thing would be to change into full-length flannel pajamas—the kind that screamed "no one but my teddy bear gets to see me naked"—but she needed to sweep the floors first. Cleaning would help distract her from the strange feeling of intimacy of knowing he was in her shower, using her soap, her shampoo, her towels.

Oh crap. The only towel in there was the one she'd just used. It was completely damp and utterly unacceptable for a guest.

She dashed to her laundry room and pulled out a fresh towel from her dryer. The water was still running when she came to the bathroom door and pressed her ear against it. She knocked quietly once, then a little louder. She called out his name, but there was no answer. It was a small bathroom. Maybe she could slip inside quickly and leave the towel for him on the counter. The shower curtain was opaque, so it wasn't like she was going to see anything.

Unease filled her as she twisted the knob, but she couldn't stop thinking about him using her wet towel. *In and out, Nora. Nice and quick.* Holding her breath, she stepped inside.

The water shut off with a click. The curtain flew back a split second later, filling the rest of the room with steam. Eli's eyes were still closed as he ran his hands up his face and over his thick hair, but everything else was completely uncovered for her to see. The lean muscles and strong thighs. The black trail of hair beneath his navel. And his…

Nope, not even in her own internal thoughts could she refer to something that thick and long and perfect by the scientifically correct term of *penis*. It was not just another random part of his anatomy—it was a cock. A terrifyingly huge cock that made every part of her body light up with craven desire.

She needed to back out before he opened his eyes.

Too late.

He did a double-take when he spotted her standing like a fool with her arms reached out, as though the fluffy white terrycloth was some kind of invisibility shield. He raised his eyebrows and stepped toward her. She backed up, bumping into the door. It slammed shut behind her, trapping her in the tight space.

"That for me?"

She nodded.

With his eyes locked on hers, he plucked the towel from her hands and ran it along his chest, soaking up the beads of water trickling down his skin. "It's okay to look, Nora."

She sucked in her breath. He dropped his hands to the side and let her take her fill of his body.

"It's okay to touch, too."

Her exhalation came out in a rush. Her body reacted like his permission was an unbreakable command. Slowly, she reached her shaky hand out and pressed her fingertips to his chest. His sharp intake of breath emboldened her. She traced those hard planes and ridges she'd admired from afar for months, reveling in the way they contracted beneath her touch.

She bit her lip, not recognizing herself in this moment. She wasn't wild or wanton, or the kind of woman who would dip her hand lower to the cut-lines of his hips just to see how his body would react.

His cock hardened. She wanted to wrap her hand around him and hear him struggle for breath. And yet...

"This is crazy. We've already kissed and there was no chemistry." The lie was a feeble last-ditch attempt at defense.

He raised his hand and tucked it against her cheek, brushing her lips with his thumb. "Maybe we just kissed each other in the wrong spot."

A burst of raw, wild heat exploded in her belly. "I...suppose it would be scientifically prudent to test that hypothesis."

He slid his hand into her hair and curled his fingers in the wet strands. He eased her head to the side and brought his lips to her neck, so gently at first, it felt like a whispered promise of what was to come. Her knees buckled and turned to warm marshmallows as he opened his mouth and pressed his hot tongue to her skin like a brand.

He pulled back, Adam's apple bobbing against his throat. "Results?"

"A noticeable increase in effect. Let's see if it's replicable." With a daring she didn't recognize, she leaned forward and kissed his throat. His skin was hot and rough, with the barest hint of stubble. It had been so long since she'd felt the hard planes of a man's chest beneath her fingers. She'd forgotten how delicious it could be. His erection pressed into her belly and a small moan escaped his lips.

"Definitely an improvement," he said in a raw, gruff voice.

"Let's try another," she whispered against his skin. She brushed her lips down his chest and licked his small, flat nipple. His shudder sent an intoxicating thrill through her body.

He pulled her head back with enough force to make her gasp. The fire in his eyes was almost frightening, yet there she was, ready to fuel it until they both combusted.

"Better?"

"Only one way to tell." He unfastened the knot of her robe. The silk parted like water sluicing over her body, and she straightened her back, resisting the urge cover herself. Nerves prickled her skin as his gaze travelled down her naked body. "Damn, Nora. You're beautiful. Everywhere."

He cupped her breast, plumping it up and brushing his thumb across her nipple, making it ache with need. She leaned into him, practically begging for more. He didn't make her wait. He sucked her nipple into his hot, eager mouth.

She dropped the back of her head against the door and whimpered. "Statistical significance, definitely," she managed to grit out as he moved to her other breast. His mouth was somehow hungry yet gentle, lavishing her until she was dizzy with arousal.

"Not good enough." He kissed his way down her ribs, steadying himself with his hands on her waist as he went to his knees.

Her heartbeat hammered so loudly, she could almost hear it echoing in the small room, and her breath came hard and fast, like she'd just run a marathon. He kissed her belly, then her hip bone. And then he pressed his mouth to her pussy.

"Oh God."

"You're still confused, Princess." He flicked his tongue against her clit. "My name's Eli."

He swirled her tight little bud with quick, focused swipes of the tongue until she couldn't remember her own name. Beads of perspiration formed along her forehead but did little to cool her off. Her body was on fire. He dragged his tongue through her folds with a long, indulgent lick that made her groan with pleasure. Her brain could barely fathom that Eli—the man who'd spent the last six months annoying her to death—was the one making her writhe with desire.

It had been so long since she'd experienced this kind of electric pleasure, she reacted like a firecracker, exploding from the tiniest spark. He sucked her clit and it sent her right over the edge. She cried out and buried her hand in his hair as her orgasm ripped through her.

When the shudders finally slowed down enough to let her catch her breath, he rose to his feet and brushed back the strands of wet hair that had fallen into her face. His satisfied grin was both adorable and sexy, even though she was the one who'd just come on his face. "I think we proved our hypothesis. Maybe we're a little compatible after all."

She shook her head. "Not yet. Reproducibility is the key to good chemistry."

He raised his eyebrow, and she responded by sliding down to her knees and circling her fingers around his cock. She didn't care if she and Eli had any chemistry. Didn't care if anything about this moment made sense. She needed this. Needed to feel desirable and in control of her sexuality for the first time since moving here.

She twirled her tongue around the head of his cock, savoring the clean taste of his skin.

A string of curses slipped from his mouth. She squeezed her slick thighs together and took him deep into her throat, suctioning her lips around him. He leaned forward against the door, sliding his cock deeper into her mouth, but she didn't care. Hell, she wanted it. Wanted him to lose control just like she had. She sucked and licked and savored him until her knees hurt from resting against the hard tile beneath her, but it wasn't enough to make her stop. Not when he was repeating her name like a prayer between rushed breaths. The words turned to desperate grunts and she could feel him thicken in her mouth.

He tugged her hair until she popped off his cock. "Not like this. Not here."

She nodded. "Hang on." She brushed past him and rummaged in her vanity for a condom from the unopened box buried behind the neatly stacked rolls of toilet paper and cleaning products. "Expiry date is still good."

"Thank fucking God, because I need to be inside you. Now." He took her by the wrist and led her to the bedroom, which wasn't hard to find in the little bungalow.

Her room was pristine, just like always, but for the first time in her thirty-two years, that made her worry. Would he think she was weird or uptight for not having any signs of life? No creases in her perfectly laid out comforter. No clothes in a laundry hamper waiting to be washed. Gavin used to give her grief about her neat freak tendencies, always telling her it ruined the mood when the bedroom felt like a sterile hospital room.

He paused at the bed and cupped her cheeks. "Hey, you're thinking too hard right now. We can stop if you want."

"No! I'm just thinking about my laundry."

He winced. "Was I that bad?"

Her eyes widened. "No! You were great. It's just...does it bother you that my room is so clean?"

He cupped her pussy and slid his fingers through the slickness, teasing her. "Your room is pristine now, but I intend to make a huge mess of it. And you. And after that, we can clean it all up. Army corners and all. Sound good?"

Her throat was too full of whimpers to answer, so she nodded. He delved his finger inside her and the air rushed out of her lungs. She braced herself on his shoulders while her knees turned to jelly. The way he watched her lose all her composure shouldn't have turned her on so much, but she couldn't stop herself from wanting to give him every moan, every shudder, every reaction he was seeking.

Before she knew it, he had her on the bed and was rolling the condom down his cock. "Ready?"

She scooted back and parted her legs, inviting him in. He entered her slowly, letting her adjust to the feel of his hard length inside her. God, this felt so good. It had been so long since she'd had this kind of intimacy and connection. She clung to his shoulders as his mouth found hers, kissing her with the kind of urgency she'd never experienced before. The kind where she could lose herself in him forever.

"What do you need, Princess?" he whispered against her lips. She nudged her knee upwards, and he responded with a delicious grin. "As you wish."

He flipped her legs over his shoulders, letting his cock surge deep inside her to the spot that always made her scream. She pressed her palms against the headboard, bracing herself to feel the full impact of his thrusts. He moved faster, harder, filling her with even more aching need. It was raw and primal and exactly what she'd needed to lose herself in him. And just when the onslaught of sensations became too much to bear, a powerful orgasm crashed over her, tightening every limb of her body before giving her the sweetest relief.

He lowered himself against her, pressing her into the mattress with his delicious weight until her hamstrings stretched, and quickened his pace. He came soon after, like he'd been holding back until he'd assured her pleasure first. He let her legs fall off his shoulders when it was over and brushed back her now messy strands of hair, looking down at her with a warm, satisfied smile.

And then he kissed her—so tenderly and slow, it made her whole body shiver. His hands and tongue had explored almost every inch of her body, but somehow this kiss felt even more intimate and sensual.

It was over too soon. "That was incredible," he mumbled into her hair.

She hummed her agreement, still blissed out from the moment and trailing her fingers down his spine. She could have lain here forever like this.

He rolled off her and climbed out of bed. "I need to clean myself up."

She nodded and shamelessly watched him as he walked naked back to the bathroom. Eli was just as gorgeous from the backside as he was from the front. But he was also funny, smart, and heck of a lot kinder than she'd assumed.

Don't get carried away, Nora. He's not for you. Incredible sex was one thing, but that didn't change the fact they were completely wrong for each other in every other way. He was too relaxed, too easygoing for someone like her. They had the kind of differences that would drive each other crazy in the long run. She'd seen it with her parents. She'd grown up with that type of tension and resentment and watched how it could destroy two people who were supposed to be in love.

She grabbed her robe off the ground and scurried off to the bathroom to pee as soon as he was done, and when she came back to the room, a part of her was surprised to see he hadn't left. He'd crawled under the covers, leaving them halfway pulled back for her. She hesitated at the door.

"Is this okay? I've had a really shitty day until now and I'd rather not sleep alone tonight."

She'd never heard him sound so unsure. So vulnerable.

"Of course," she lied. "But that's my side of the bed."

He rolled over and she climbed in beside him. He tucked her into his chest, curling his arm around her body.

She hated being touched when she slept. Didn't like cuddling either. And yet, something so wrong had never felt so right.

---

6

*E*li woke up without a nasty headache pounding his skull for the first time in months. His retinas didn't burn from the first hint of sunlight, and there was no kink in his neck. There was, however, a perfectly palm-sized breast in his hand. He squeezed it gently, rolling the nipple between his fingers.

"Good morning," Nora said with a deliciously soft moan. "What time is it?"

"Time for you to close your eyes and let me finish what I'm starting."

She arched into him, pressing her butt to his hardened cock, but then a chime rang out. She rolled away from him and grabbed her phone off her nightstand. "Crap! I need to get ready for work."

"Can't you go in a little late? Call in sick?"

"No. I have a class to teach at 8:30. If I'm not there on time, the students will leave, and then how will they learn about stoichiometry?"

"Go shower, I'll make you breakfast."

She turned toward him, pulling the sheet up to cover her chest, then smiled sweetly. "Thank you."

He didn't want to turn away, but he had enough self-preservation instincts to know she wanted a little modesty this morning. He averted his eyes as she skittered out of the room, focusing instead on the picture on her nightstand of her and two other women hugging and smiling in front of the Eiffel Tower. She was almost unrecognizable behind those big shades, with sunlight dancing over her freckles, and a smile so wide, it felt like a kick in the gut. Somehow, he knew she hadn't smiled like that since she'd moved here.

He needed to do something about that.

He picked up the bright pink paperback sitting in front of the photo and flicked through the pages as he headed to her kitchen. After last night, he shouldn't be surprised that his quiet little neighbor indulged in some steamier literature, but the notion still entertained him. No doubt she had more secrets lurking beneath that tightly coiled exterior, and he planned to uncover every one of them. But first, breakfast.

Her fridge was stocked more neatly than a pharmacy, with every jar and bottle turned to face out like a grocery store shelf, every vegetable neatly chopped inside a Tupperware container with clearly printed labels and dates, and not a stain or speck of dirt anywhere. He was almost scared to touch anything inside it, but he didn't want to be the next-day dirtbag who couldn't even feed the woman he'd just spent the night with.

Regardless, whatever he made was going to have to be quick, because he'd left a trail of spent grains all over her floor. He started the coffee, popped a couple slices of bread into the toaster, hunted down a broom in the closet, and got to work.

Twenty minutes later, Nora came into the kitchen with her hair pulled back in a severe bun, sensible slacks, and a jaw that hung wide open. "You're naked!"

Eli laughed. "I've just swept your floors and a made a meal for you, and that's what you focus on? I feel so objectified right now."

"It looks like the only thing you feel is that cool breeze coming through the window."

"Evil, evil woman. Have a seat and eat your toast so you're not so hangry."

He led her to the stool butting up to the raised counter. She grabbed the mug as soon as she sat down and drained half of it in one long sip. "Okay. I feel a little better. So let's get back to the question. Why are you cooking me breakfast completely buck naked?"

"Other than giving you the kind of sexual fantasy that will keep you satisfied for the rest of your days? My clothes are still a mess and I'm not sure we're at the stage where you'd be cool with me slipping on a pair of your lacy little panties for my walk of shame, short as it is."

He didn't miss the tiny flush that trickled across her cheeks just now. "I can run back to your place and grab you something before I leave for work if you like. But after I eat."

"Enjoy." He slid the plate with two slices of toast topped with something she didn't recognize toward her.

She took a bite, making the kind of face he'd come to appreciate so much last night. "This is delicious. What is it?"

"Toast with ricotta and honey. My mom used to make this for my sister and me when we were kids. I would have made you something fancier, but the truth is I don't really know how to cook, and frying up some bacon in the buff didn't seem like a good idea."

Her eyes flashed down his body before becoming unnaturally interested in her coffee mug. "Um, maybe we should talk about last night. It's probably not a good idea—"

He pushed her paperback across the counter. "We can talk about that later. Right now, we need to talk about this."

She crossed her arms defiantly. "You have a problem with the fact I'm reading a romance novel?"

"No. I have a problem with the fact you've been in the world's shittiest book club all this time when you could be in the best one. My sister started a Books and Brews club at the Holy Grale, and this just happens to be the book they're reading this month."

"Really?"

"Yes, really. Trust me, it's bad enough having to listen to a half-dozen of my favorite customers going on and on about how Talon Brookside is their newest book boyfriend, but the other day I overheard my sister call him a hot hunk of pure domination." He shuddered at the memory. It wasn't that he didn't want Julia to have a nice, healthy sex life. He just didn't want to hear anything about it. Ever. "The next meeting is on Sunday at eight. You should come."

She bit her lip, looking a whole lot less excited than he anticipated.

"It doesn't have to mean anything more than what it is. A book club for people who like to read whatever they want without being self-indulgent pricks about it. Just think about it, okay?"

Finally, a reluctant smile appeared on her pretty face. "Okay. I'll think about it."

Nora had never seen so many eggplant emojis or smiley faces light up her phone. There was no logic to the texts. And apparently no end, either. It was like Alice and Jessie were in a competition to out-emoji each other. Just when she was about to set her phone down and refresh her email on her office computer, another text popped up.

You slept with Humperdinck???? OMG!!!!

She had to give Jessie credit for using actual words, but that didn't make this group text any less uncomfortable to read while at work. Then again, she wasn't able to think about anything else all day, which was why she'd told her friends about sleeping with Eli in the first place. She'd never experienced anything that explosive before. Her whole body still tingled from the memory of his lips on her skin.

A moment of weakness, she typed back. *And his name is Eli.*

Did you find that out before or after you slept with him? Alice interjected.

Before!!! Nora added an angry face just for good measure. She wasn't that irresponsible.

Then again, she barely recognized herself since she met him. She'd never had a one-night stand before. Never gave her brain over to her body with such reckless abandon in a fit of desire. Sleeping with someone she didn't belong with was foolish. Absurd, even. And yet it still felt so right, she had to squeeze her thighs together just thinking about him.

A text from Alice popped up next. *Neighbors with benefits? Awesome.*

Nora: *Or a disaster waiting to happen.*

Alice: *You already hated each other. At least this way you get a little action out of it before you go back to driving each other mad.*

Jessie: *And maybe it's meant to be.*

Nora: *Maybe it's not.*

She understood why Jessie, a romantic who'd married her high school sweetheart, jumped to that conclusion, but Nora knew better. It didn't matter how much he made her laugh on their date, how amazing he made her feel last night. They weren't right for each other. One step inside his house this morning to grab him clean clothes had confirmed that belief. The place wasn't just messy, it was a catastrophe. It looked like he'd started a million home renovation projects and abandoned them all halfway through. Nora had nearly developed hives in the two minutes she'd been in there.

But the promise of one more incredible night like that was almost enough to convince her to ignore the mess. She sighed and typed one last message, not wanting to end the conversation on such a negative note. *He made me breakfast.*

Alice: *Omelet? Everyone knows an omelet means he wants to do it again.*

Jessie: *But if he gives you cereal, run like wind!*

Nora shook her head and laughed. *Lunch break's over. Love you guys.*

She put down her phone and refreshed her email for the thirtieth time that day. This time, the email she'd been waiting for finally appeared. Her pulse immediately went into overdrive as she clicked it open. "Dear Dr. Pitts, we are happy to inform you that your abstract has been accepted…"

She twirled around in her desk chair and cheered.

Doug poked his head inside her door. "Everything all right?"

"Our abstract was accepted. That means a weekend away in Portland two months from now. You want to come? There are a couple travel grants we can apply for and it would be great for your CV."

He scrunched his face and ran his hand through his unruly hair.

"Weekends are when my disc-golf league meets. But, uh, you have fun."

She smiled, knowing she would. Two months from now, she'd be hanging out with people who cared about the same things as her. People she was comfortable with. And with any luck, she'd find some new inspiration to rejuvenate her after months of feeling lost.

Nora's streak of luck lasted throughout the rest of the workday. The letter of intent she'd submitted to a grant agency a few months ago was accepted, meaning she actually had a chance at getting some real funding for next year, and she had a full classroom today. Not one single student was absent—a first in her time here. It had been a while since she'd had so many things go right, so she decided to go out for sushi to celebrate. Maybe it was a bit indulgent, but it was almost eight o'clock by the time she wrapped everything up and she didn't feel like dealing with cooking and dishes tonight.

And maybe she was avoiding going back home to deal with the fact she'd just slept with her neighbor. She had no idea how to act after a one-night-stand. If she was too aloof, it might jeopardize the tenuous détente they'd just established. But if she was too friendly, he might think she wanted more from him.

But you do want more...

Ugh. Why was this so complicated? Eli wasn't the first man she'd been with, but she still felt just as awkward and unsure of herself as she did twelve years ago when she got partnered with Mike Sweeney in lab the day after he walked away with her virginity and her favorite pair of panties.

There was a long wait for tables in the tiny restaurant when she arrived. She should have made a reservation on a Friday night, but it hadn't occurred to her in time, so she contented herself with examining the menu while she waited.

"Nora! What are you doing here?"

She whipped her head around to see Annie, Gemma, and Rose coming into the small entryway behind her. "Oh, I just came for take-out," she stammered, because apparently she was a grown woman who was suddenly embarrassed to be caught dining out alone.

"I didn't know you liked this place," Annie said. "We could have invited you to join us tonight."

"It's actually my first time checking it out," Nora answered. She waited with a mix of curiosity and insecurity to see if they would actually invite her to join them.

"What are you ordering?" Gemma said, filling the awkward silence.

"Probably just the California roll dinner special."

"Oh, no. Don't do that. This place makes excellent sashimi. And you haven't lived until you've tried the unagi."

"I'm sure it's good, but I like California rolls."

"That's so sad," Gemma said with a mock frown. "Japanese food is a culinary wonder."

"I know, I just..." *Like to order the same thing at every sushi restaurant because I can't break my routines no matter how hard I try.* Embarrassment crept on her cheeks and the little paper menu crinkled in her tight grip. She managed a small shrug. "I'm just in the mood for something simple tonight."

"Hey, you never told us how your date went," Annie jumped in.

"It was fine."

Rose laughed. "I knew it would be a disaster."

Her words hit Nora like a sucker punch. "Actually, it went great. In fact, I'm bringing him dinner tonight."

She brushed past the women to the hostess table and placed an order for two California Roll specials.

"Oh, that's awesome," Annie said with a smile. Nora didn't know whether to believe the note of sincerity in her voice or not. Annie had always been the nicest of the three, but the fact she was friends with Gemma and Rose was something Nora wasn't sure she could look past.

Three more women Nora didn't recognize came through the door at that moment, though they clearly knew Gemma, Rose, and Annie. Nora made herself scarce as the group greeted each other. Their table for six was called a moment later.

"Bye, Nora, can't wait to hear all about your date with your hunky neighbor at our next book club," Gemma called out with a wave.

Nora gave a pathetic wave back. Thankfully, her food arrived quickly, but those few minutes in the foyer left her with nothing but time to wonder if she wasn't the real problem. Could she blame the others for not inviting her? They had a reservation and this place was too crowded to tuck in another chair. Besides, it was obvious they didn't want to eat with a killjoy who was scared of anything that came with tentacles. Or a person who lied about a follow up date because she was too embarrassed to admit she was eating alone on a Friday night.

She paid for her takeout and wondered what the heck she was going to do with two orders of the California Roll special as she drove home.

You could just see if Eli's hungry. His light was on when she pulled up. She warred with herself while sitting in her driveway, but ultimately, she would have felt too much like a jerk if she didn't at least make the offer.

She got out of her car and walked up to his door.

He answered her knock, wearing a T-shirt, jeans, and a surprised expression. Clothed or not, he was gorgeous enough to steal her breath. "Hey, Nora. What's up?" The question was almost cautious, like she was a spooked deer who might run away at any moment, instead of a woman who'd showed up at his door with a bento box and cup of miso soup.

"I've got some extra takeout and I thought you might be hungry."

His brows pulled together, consternation reflecting in in his eyes. "I thought we weren't doing a second date."

She straightened her back and clutched the Styrofoam containers more tightly. "This isn't a date. I just ordered extra."

He crossed his arms and leaned against the doorframe with a grin. "Admit it. This is totally a second a date."

"It's a neighborly act."

"So you brought takeout for Mr. and Mrs. Arnolds, too?" He took the bag of food from her hand and let her into the house.

"No," she said, following him. "I *may* have ordered you food because I ran into the women from my book club at the restaurant and told them we had a second date tonight."

"So, totally a date, huh?" He led her to the kitchen, where a couple dishes were left in the sink and a giant stack of papers scattered across the counter, but at least the place looked ten times cleaner than it had this morning. He must have been working hard to make headway on his renovations.

"Fine," she conceded as he pulled a bottle of soy sauce out of the fridge. "It's a date. An accidental one, but that still doesn't change the fact we're not each other's type."

He set two plates on the table, then stepped in front of her and cupped her cheek with one hand. "Hate to break it to you, but a woman who brings me sushi on a random Friday night is exactly my type. But you can pretend it's not a date all you want."

He pressed his lips to her forehead in a quick kiss that sent tingles down right to her toes. He'd had his mouth on every part of her body last night and yet this simple touch electrified her. The scariest part was that she was starting to think he was exactly her type, too. "It looks like you've been busy in here."

"Yeah, the renos are taking longer than I wanted but it's getting there."

Nora carefully split her wooden chopsticks and ran them together to remove any slivers. "Are you planning on selling?"

He shook his head and dunked a roll in his soy sauce. "No, I just figured it was time to grow up and make this a real home. My mom left Julia and me a bit of money when she died. I used half of it to start the Holy Grale with Jake and then other half to buy this place. My mom was big on having a nice, presentable home. All the chores and cleaning used to drive me crazy when I was young, but I appreciate the work ethic she instilled in us. We're doing this remembrance thing for the ten-year anniversary of her death in a couple months, and it feels wrong not having my house fixed up when I know it would bug her if she were still alive." He frowned, dangling his roll in the air while the excess sauce dripped off. "That sounds kind of stupid when I say it out loud."

She reached her hand across the table to his, and he responded instantly, interlocking their fingers. "No, it doesn't. You want her to be proud of you. I get it. It's just..." She glanced around the room. "It's a lot to take on for one person. Have you thought about hiring someone to do some of the work?"

He popped the roll in his mouth, looking at their entwined hands as he ate. "I kind of like having something to occupy my time. I get antsy if I don't have a project on the go, but I have a bad habit of jumping in headfirst and figuring stuff out as I go. It's gotten a bit out of hand lately."

A couple weeks ago, she might have agreed he was in over his head, but the new wood floors looked amazing, and the mess of boxes and laundry and everything else from this morning was already dealt with. "You're making headway. You just need to figure out how to organize things a little better. I could help."

"Sounds like you're gunning for a third date."

"We're friends now. Friends help each other."

He squeezed her hand before letting it go and diving back into his food. "So how's work going?"

It took her a moment to process the question when all she could think about was how empty her hand suddenly felt without his. He was respecting her wishes, she quietly realized. If only her traitorous body could do the same. "Pretty good, finally. I feel like I've been floundering for a while, but we just made a big breakthrough this week and I'm going to present the results at a conference in a couple months, which gives me something to look forward to. I'm hoping it leads to more breakthroughs and hopefully a publication down the line."

"That's awesome. When is it?"

"The first week in November."

Something flickered across his face, almost like disappointment, but it disappeared just as quick. "I have to say, though, conferences were my least favorite part of grad school."

"Really? I love them. Organizing all my thoughts and results into a twelve-minute PowerPoint is like a perfect celebration of everything I've accomplished."

He dropped his chopsticks onto his plate and stared at her with an inscrutable expression.

"What?"

He laughed. "You're a huge nerd!"

"Am not!"

"It's not an insult. I think it's sexy as hell."

"Oh." Her cheeks hurt from the smile she was fighting.

"The little love notes you left in my mailbox were fun, but now I'm wondering what I need to do get a full PowerPoint out of you."

"They weren't love notes! They were hate notes."

"And this isn't our second date." He stole one of her tempura sweet potatoes.

She narrowed her eyes. "Steal any more of my food, Humperdinck, and there won't be a third."

"At least I got you to admit it's a date."

If he kept flirting with her, she'd be doing a lot more than admitting things she didn't want to. She cleared her throat and leaned back in her chair. "So, what part of grad school did you like?"

"I liked being in the lab. The freedom of experimenting and trying something new. But the actual writing-my-thesis part sucked. I've never been good at organizing my thoughts like that."

"Why do I get the impression you're hard on yourself?"

"Nah, I'm just realistic. Besides, I've already got my sister to be hard on me."

"What do you mean?"

He shrugged. "Julia's always been the organized one. A total type A personality, kind of like you. She's planning the remembrance ceremony for our mom, and no matter what I do or suggest, everything's wrong. I think she'd be happy if I did nothing but show up."

"If she's anything like me, she's probably obsessed with getting every last detail right and forgetting about how she's coming across to the people she cares about."

"Or she still blames me for Mom's death."

The quiet hurt in his voice made her suck in her breath. "Why would you say that?"

There was a long pause, and for a moment Nora wondered if he was going to say anything at all. "I got into a fight with my Mom right before she died. I'd called to tell her I was thinking about quitting school and she lost it on me. She was a single mom. She told me she worked too hard to put Julia and me through school for me to quit. A couple hours later, I got a phone call saying she was in a car crash. The last thing she said to me was to grow up and stop screwing up my life." Emotion choked his last words.

Nora had no idea what she could possibly say to him, so she did the only thing she knew how. She jumped out of her chair and wrapped her arms around him. He tugged her onto his lap and buried his face in her hair. She stroked the back of his head while he held her. It might have been a decade ago, but it was obvious he'd carried the guilt around with him all this time. Her parents regularly drove her crazy, but she couldn't imagine the pain of losing one of them like that.

"Sorry," he mumbled, dropping his hand to her thigh with a possessive touch that made her most sensitive parts sing with desire. "I think I just killed my chances of a third date."

"Friends are supposed to talk about this kind of stuff."

"Then you're a good friend. I've never really talked about this before with anyone."

He held her gaze with an intensity that made her melt. All the reasons she was supposed to resist him evaporated from her brain. She licked her bottom lip, keenly aware of the closeness of their bodies, the hardness of his thighs beneath her legs, and the way he touched her like he never wanted to let go.

He laughed ruefully. "I can't believe I'm saying this, Princess, but you need to stop looking at me like that."

"Why?" She crawled off him.

"I need to head into work tonight. And even though I'm giving you a hard time about this date, I don't really think you came here for what's running through my mind right at this moment. Come on, I'll walk you home on my way out."

True to his word, he walked her to her stoop, even though it was right next door.

"Thanks for dinner."

"No problem." She stood there, fumbling with her keys in her hand, wondering if he was going to kiss her again. "Hey, when is the remembrance ceremony? I'd like to come if that's okay."

"First Sunday in November."

"Oh." Same date as her conference.

"What's the matter?"

"I'm presenting at a conference in Portland that weekend."

He offered a smile that didn't come close to reaching his eyes. "That's great."

"Thank you."

The silence that followed was so awkward, it made her stomach hurt.

He ran his hand along the back of his neck. "Listen, I'm going to be working all day tomorrow, but you're coming the Brews and Book Club night on Sunday, right?"

She stifled a groan. As much as she needed to make some friends in this town, the idea of walking into a loud brewpub with a bunch of strangers was terrifying. Then again, it wasn't like it could go worse than her original book club.

"Sure. I'll see you there."

7

*B*y the time Sunday evening rolled around, Nora finally realized why she'd allowed herself to be so easily bullied by Gemma, Rose, and Annie into hosting book club every month. As bad as it was, at least she was in her comfort zone. Her home, her food, her control. But tonight was a whole other story. Nothing was in her control. She didn't know any of the people at the Books and Brews club. What if she wore the wrong outfit? What if the people at this book club were just as standoffish? What if she didn't fit in?

Even the idea of a book club at a bar sounded so absurd, she had trouble believing it was a real thing.

This was ridiculous. She was an adult with excellent hygiene, above average intelligence, and proper manners. And she actually loved the book the group was discussing.

But what if they thought her questions were silly? Hell, what if it was the wrong book? She groaned and fell back on her mattress. She was relying entirely on Eli's recollection that the pink cover with looping writing and a happy couple locked in embrace was the same one that the book club happened to be reading.

The knots in her stomach tightened until they ached. This past week had been full of too many ups and downs to handle another disappointment. This event might go wonderfully, but it also might turn out to be another disaster, and she just couldn't handle that tonight. She was tired, and all she wanted to do was crawl into her sweatpants and eat her weight in kettle corn. She could always go next month. Maybe she'd grow enough confidence by then.

She changed into her favorite sweats and resigned herself to a coward's way out. Her doorbell rang just as she was about to settle onto her couch with her e-reader. Reluctantly, she dragged herself to the door and opened it.

"Eli? What are you doing here? I thought you were working."

"I was, but I figured you'd feel better about going to the book club meeting if I gave you a ride." His eyes scaled up and down the length of her body. "Um, I can't believe I'm asking this, but is that really what you're wearing? I mean, I'm all for being comfortable, but it looks like you've been using those clothes as a target practice in a meatball throwing competition."

"They're my lounging on the couch clothes. I've had these since high school." She gestured to the school logo on the side of her pants.

"You were an athlete?"

"A cheerleader. At least I was in my junior year. I gave it up to focus on my studies."

He winced and clutched his hands to his heart. "A nerdy cheer-leader. I swear you are trying to kill me with that image. Seventeen-year-old emo soccer-playing me would have been all over you in high school."

"Probably not. I had acne and non-ironic oversized glasses, and my teenage hormones only made my perfectionist streak a million times more intense and overbearing. But I could do a mean splits." She turned and walked into her kitchen where her earl grey was still steeping, knowing he would follow her.

"Nope. I guarantee teenage me would have found a brainiac teenage you super hot, but I can't promise the old sweats are going to have the same effect on the folks showing up to the Books and Brews meeting tonight."

"That's the problem." She pulled the teabag out of the steaming mug and tossed it into the compost bin. He watched her with his arms crossed and an expression that made it clear he was prepared to wait however long it took for an answer. "I've already made an embarrassment of myself the last time I was at your brewpub. What if nothing I wear is right? What if go there and I don't fit in again? What if I sit down in someone's special spot? It's not easy walking into a room full of strangers and hoping that they like me."

"You're overthinking this."

She cupped her hands around the mug and dropped her head. "That's what I do. I get anxious and stressed and uptight, and I over-think things until I suck the fun out of life."

"Or maybe you're just someone who gives a shit. There's nothing wrong with that. But there is something wrong with missing out on a good opportunity because you're scared, especially when I'm here to help."

"How?"

"You like to be prepared for new situations, right?"

She nodded slowly.

"So let me prepare you. Books and Brews is meant to be a causal event and there's usually a few drop-ins, but I know most of the regulars. My sister, Julia, is always there. I've already told you she's organized, and that means she always asks the same questions. First, if you could ask the author any question about the book, what would it be? Second, how believable were the character arcs? And third, how hot was the sex?"

Nora's head jerked up so fast, her brain reverberated against her skull. "Uh…"

He grinned. "Yeah, they pretty much only read romance novels."

"Just romance? Seriously?"

"Sometimes mystery or sci-fi and that kind of stuff, but I'm pretty sure they only choose those books if there's hot sex in it."

"So no highbrow discussion about stodgy books that make me want to poke myself in the eyeball with a rusty fork?"

"I can't promise you that, but I know they laugh a lot. Clem is pretty serious about books, but she's not a snob. Just the opposite.

She's a little awkward and shy, but she's the nicest person you'll ever meet, and she likes to ask things like 'how did this book make you feel?'"

Nora nodded. This sounded like something she could handle. Maybe even get excited about.

"And then there's Lorenzo, who sneaks in chocolate to all the meetings and only likes to ask who in Hollywood would play the characters in a movie version of the book."

Her stomach sank again. She wasn't a visual reader. She had no idea who she would cast as Talon and Genevieve. Heck, even if she could think of a rugged, blond, six-foot-four man and a tattooed woman with bright pink hair, that wouldn't mean they had the right energies for the characters. And even if she could come up with a name, what if the others at the meeting thought it was totally wrong?

He leaned across the counter and cupped his hands around hers, pressing them into the warm mug. "I don't know where you just went right now, but I know it wasn't good. All you need to do is relax, drink one of my delicious beers, and talk about a book. Or just sit there and drink one of my delicious beers."

She groaned. "That's another problem. I've never tasted a beer I liked."

"Because you haven't tasted my beer."

"I did!"

He shook his head with an expression of disgust. "You've tasted my radler, which is the best radler in town, but you haven't tasted my *beer*. Grain, hops, yeast, water, and my magic touch. Nothing else."

"Maybe," she conceded, though she was doubtful. "I don't know anything about beer. At all. What if I sound stupid when I try to order? What if I order something that I don't like?" Saying her fears out loud only made them sound silly, yet just the fact Eli was here, listening to her like she was making sense, soothed her anxiety more than any list or pep talk.

"You don't have to drink beer if you don't like it, even if my beers are fantastic."

"I know, but...I want to like it."

"Why?"

"Because you like it, and we're friends, so I should learn to like it."

She wasn't sure if she'd said the wrong thing because he looked at her like he was just noticing her for the first time. "All right. If you want to learn more, I can give you a crash course right now." He checked his watch quickly. "We have just enough time for what I have in mind."

"Which is?"

He grinned. "Do you trust me?"

The answer that came straight from her gut surprised her. "Yes. I do."

"Good. I'll be back in a couple minutes."

She walked him to the door, curiosity beating in her veins.

He paused quickly on her stoop, then turned around and planted a quick peck on her lips. "One more thing, Princess. This lesson is going to work a lot better if you're naked when I come back."

Eli carefully selected three bottles from his fridge and jogged back over to Nora's place. He knew the complicated beauty of beer better than most people, but that didn't mean there was any reason to be afraid of it. Drinking beer was about relaxing and savoring life. Enjoying the people you were drinking with. He just needed to show her that. He'd never met a person he couldn't find the right beer for. He just had to open her mind to the experience.

He stumbled to a halt in her living room. She wasn't exactly naked, but she was damn near close. Her tiny, soft blue robe covered her arms and upper thighs, but the loosely tied knot let the fabric drift apart at her chest, hinting at the swell of those small but perfect breasts beneath.

"I gotta admit, I didn't really expect you to be naked."

Her eyes widened. "But you said—"

"I know what I said. I just didn't know that you would listen.

Hoped. Prayed. Offered the devil my firstborn son. What changed your mind?"

She laughed. "I didn't change my mind. I just haven't figure out what I should wear yet and I figured this robe was better than actually being...naked."

Biting his tongue went against every smartass, flirtatious instinct he had, but someone needed to stop using the word *naked* in this conversation. Besides, he didn't want to make her uncomfortable. "Ready for your lesson, professor?"

She bit her lower lip and nodded, absentmindedly running her fingers up and down the edge of her robe. "No, but I do trust you and I really want tonight to go well, so if you think you can help, I'm willing to try."

God, he had no idea if she knew just how sexy she was. He led her to her couch and set the beers on the coffee table. She winced and pulled out a set of coasters from the storage space below the table and slipped them beneath each of the bottles.

"Right, sorry. Okay, there are two basic types of beer," he said, using the same professional tone he used on the rare occasions he gave tours of the brewery even though he found himself oddly nervous. "Lagers and ales. The big difference is that lagers are bottom fermented, and ales are top fermented. Lagers are the most popular type of beer in the country, and tend to be simple and easy-drinking. Lagers should be crisp. Refreshing. The kind of beer you reach for on a hot day."

"Does that mean less respectable?"

He grabbed the bottle of his Lord's Work Lager and handed it to her. "Nope. There are many ways to enjoy beer and I'm not going to shit on anyone's experience. Besides, my lager is fucking fantastic."

She winced and fought back a cough at the first taste, but he'd been in this business long enough not to take it personally.

"You don't like it?"

"I don't *not* like it. I'm just...not used to it." She took another sip and swallowed it like her esophagus was actively repelling the drink.

She hated it. No matter how much she tried to deny it, her face looked like she'd sucked on a lemon instead of the beer he'd spent over a year of his life perfecting.

"Maybe you need something with more character." He uncapped an American IPA next. "Ales, as we currently think of them, have been around for thousands of years, and there's a huge amount of diversity in how they're made, but you can expect a bit more complex flavor in this one. A little bit fruity. A lot more bitter. The hops are more noticeable in this style of beer. Some people find them too bitter, but the way I see it, it's kind of like music. No one wants to listen to a happy song when they're sad. The perfect bitter beer can create the most beautiful harmony with an equally bitter mood."

"I can't decide if that sounds delicious or terrible."

"Don't judge it by the description. Judge it based on how it tastes."

She straightened her shoulders like she was readying herself for battle, and took a sip, then sputtered, which turned into a coughing fit. She set the bottle back on the coaster, eyeing it like it was a giant bug. "It's not...bad."

Eli rubbed the back of his neck, wondering how much worse this could go. "Okay, last one. This is a porter. It's thick and rich, but not quite as bitter as the IPA. Don't be put off by the heaviness. It has notes of caramel and coffee, and should be smooth on the tongue."

She picked up the bottle and took the tiniest sip he'd ever seen. "This one's okay," she said with a forced smile.

He shook his head. "You need a real taste. Hang on." He dashed back to her kitchen and came back with a tall glass. He poured the beer, letting a small layer of foam settle at the top. "Try it now."

She did, taking only a slighter bigger sip this time, though still looking like she was forcing the dark liquid past her protesting lips.

"Porters have a different mouthfeel than the other beers. You have to let it wash through your entire mouth before you swallow."

"Mouthfeel?"

"The tactile feel of the beer in your mouth." He turned toward her and stroked her cheek with his thumb. "You need to relax your jaw to let the flavor in and appreciate the structure."

She leaned into his touch and he couldn't bring himself to pull away, even though he knew he should. "I'm trying, but it's not working."

He kept running his thumb along her soft skin, trying to ease some of the tension locking her body so tight. She let out a deep breath and met his eyes. Electricity sparked between them at that moment, surrounding them in a heavy, charged air. Her gaze dropped to his lips at the same time her hand went to his knee.

She leaned forward and placed a quick, tentative kiss on his mouth. He kissed her back gently, feathering his lips against hers. Giving her time to change her mind. She didn't pull away. Instead, her hand crept higher up his thigh until she was nearly on top of him.

He tugged her closer until she was straddling his lap, and deepened the kiss. His tongue swept through her mouth, dancing against hers until he felt the tension finally disappear from her jaw. She grabbed his hands and brought them to the tie of her robe, and he nearly exploded with desire. He wanted her so bad, it felt like a dream to be touching her again. He parted her robe and ran his hands along her curves.

She pulled the robe off her shoulders, letting fall to the ground, and unhooked her bra. He broke the kiss and watched in complete awe as she dragged the straps down her arms and tossed the bra onto the ground. He could have stared at her perfect, creamy skin for hours, but he wasn't a complete fool. He kissed her sternum, taking his time exploring the delicate expanse of skin.

She leaned forward, arching into him and pressing against his hardened cock. Her fingers coiled in his hair like she never wanted to let go. For a woman who guarded herself so fiercely, it was shocking how she opened herself to him so generously.

He moved to her breast, taking her pink nipple into his mouth. The rough sound of her breath was more beautiful than any music. Everything about her drove him crazy with desire.

"Condom," she whispered into his ear.

He pulled one out of his front pocket—the one he'd put there earlier in the faintest of faint hopes, even though he knew it made him a douchebag to keep hoping when she'd turned him down before. She fumbled with his fly at the same time he cupped his hand over her lace-covered sex, stroking and readying her. She kissed him hungrily, moaning into his mouth as her panties grew wetter against his fingers. Finally, she managed to free his cock and it was his turn to lose himself in the ecstasy of her touch.

She rolled the condom down his length.

"You sure, Princess? Not too late to change your mind."

"Definitely sure. Don't make me wait."

He pulled her panties aside and slid into her. She cried out and clung to his shoulders as she used her thighs to ride him at a fast pace. Watching her take her pleasure from him like this was hotter than anything he'd ever experienced. He cupped her breasts and pinched her nipples, rapt by the unguarded sensations playing out on her beautiful face.

She came fast and hard. Her body slammed against his, head buried in his neck as she cried out. He gripped her hips and took over the rhythm, wrenching out as much pleasure as he could until he came with a growl.

She slumped against him, breathing heavily. He had no idea if this changed anything. Sex—even incredible sex—was so simple. Just bodies moving and thrusting and claiming. But there was nothing simple about the snarled, twisted feelings inside his chest as he stroked his hand up and down her spine.

"So," he finally found the energy to say. "Feeling relaxed enough for the Books and Brews meeting?"

"More than relaxed. Boneless."

"Oh, I'd say you were thoroughly boned."

She giggled—a sweet, soft sound that reverberated down his spine.

"See? It's impossible to be nervous when you're thinking about me naked."

"I don't think that's how it's supposed to work."

"I never said I was a conventional guy."

She tilted her head back and looked him curiously. "No, you haven't. I'm just finally starting to understand a little better what that means."

He glanced at the old farmhouse clock on her wall. "We should probably get going if we're going to make it on time."

Her lips twisted into a frown. "I'm going to feel weird going out in public after what we just did. Especially without showering first."

"There's no reason to worry. I promise they're going to love you as much as..." Fuck. He stopped himself before he said anything too stupid.

The silence that followed stretched on too long. She slid off him and retied her robe around her. "I'll be right back."

A few seconds later, he heard the shower turn on. True to her word, she was only gone for a couple minutes before the water turned off and he heard the sound of her footsteps scurrying to her bedroom. "All yours," she called out from her bedroom.

That was his cue to clean up. He made a quick trip to the bathroom, and when he came out, she was dressed in jeans and a blue sweater. She'd pulled her hair back into the tight ponytail she always wore, but the red flush on her cheeks and spark in her eyes were new, and damn if that didn't fill him with pride.

"You never did tell me what you thought about the porter," he said as they stepped outside her front door.

She bit her lip again. "Um, it wasn't bad..."

He laughed. What else could he do? God help him, he was falling for a woman who hated beer.

---

8

*E*very time Nora's nerves threatened to flood her with self-doubt during the ride to the Holy Grale, all she had to do was sneak a glance at Eli. Just looking at that man filled her with the kind of serenity that was only supposed to be felt on tropical beaches and massage tables. It was a strange puzzle she couldn't quite tease out. Just a few weeks ago, she was plotting ways to make his stereo spontaneously combust in the middle of the night. Now, he was the person who'd made her feel safe. Calm. Loved.

Nope. Not going there. Good sex was not love. It wasn't even a precursor to love.

She toyed with the seatbelt strap across her chest that suddenly felt too tight, running her fingers along the rough, sharp edge. God, what was she doing? Sleeping with Eli again was a dumb decision, no matter how good he made her feel. It didn't change the fact they had next to nothing in common, it just made that truth harder to see.

She'd watched her parents' marriage dissolve around the same time her own had fallen apart. If anything, she ought to be grateful that a man as demanding and dedicated to his work as her dad and a woman who couldn't hold an interest longer than the length of a single television commercial lasted for thirty-five years before calling it quits. Her mom had put her foot down and insisted her dad retire within twelve months so they could travel the world like she'd always wanted to. When that deadline came and went, she cheated on him and then she left. Now she was living on a boat somewhere on the West Coast of Canada, signing up for silent yoga retreats and communing with the orcas, while her dad spent so much time in his office, he was starting to fuse to his leather chair.

Nora had promised herself she wouldn't make the same mistake of falling for a guy she wasn't compatible with.

He must have sensed her barreling thoughts, because he reached over the console and squeezed her hand. Calmness instantly settled over her and quieted the errant thoughts.

They pulled into the parking lot. "Ready?"

"No, but I think I'll survive."

He came around to help her out of the high truck. She slung her purse over her shoulder and took his hand. He pulled her against him as soon as her feet hit the ground, sliding his arm around her waist.

"Eli, it's just—"

He let her go. "I get it. I promised you I'd teach you about beer and help you relax for tonight. What happened earlier doesn't have to mean anything other than that. You didn't promise me anything. It's okay."

She exhaled the heavy breath in her chest. "Thank you."

He led her inside and up the stairway to the mezzanine level she'd admired before. The place was just as busy as it was the other night, with groups of friends, families, and Seahawks fans gathered around the wooden tables. The view from the upstairs was even more incredible, with exposed beams and huge windows, but even though the noise was more muted up here, it was still too loud to carry on a proper conversation.

Was she going to have to scream her points across the table just to be heard?

Pushing that thought out of her mind, she silently recited the information Eli had given her about the people who attended the book club, trying to remember all the thoughts and ideas she had about the book.

Eli dipped his head toward hers, lips almost brushing her ear. "It's back here. We've got a couple of private rooms upstairs for events, including one specifically for book clubs."

"Seriously?" She'd never heard of anything like that before.

"Yeah, Jake's girlfriend is a big reader, so he built her a library room so she'd always feel welcome here."

"A library? Geez, that's a pretty special gift."

He nodded. "Some people are worth it. You'll see what I mean when you meet Clem."

Her throat tightened. She couldn't imagine the kind of love that would inspire a gift like that. The nicest thing Gavin had ever done for her was order pizza every Friday so she wasn't stuck with the dishes. Heck, everything Eli had done for her since their first date—from the picnic under the stars to teaching her how to order beer without making a fool of herself—was a million times kinder and sweeter than anything Gavin ever did.

As soon as Eli opened the door, she realized just how much she'd underestimated the size of the gesture. There were books everywhere. Packed shelves lined the walls. Even the windowsills had books perched haphazardly on them. Her heart sang the moment she stepped inside. This was happiness—pure, unbelievable happiness packaged into one perfect little room.

Two sets of leather wingback chairs flanked round coffee tables at either corner of the room, and a long eight-person dining table sat in the middle.

Julia jumped up to greet them. "I'm so glad you made it." She linked her arm through Nora's and led her to the big table where a half-dozen people sat.

"All good?" Eli asked.

Julia waved him off. "Relax, big brother. She's safe with us."

Nora nodded, surprised by how much she believed Julia was telling the truth. There was a warmth and friendliness that seemed to radiate through the room. The copies of the book in various cover styles and states of wear and tear—instead of the anguish porn she'd grown accustomed to with her last book club—helped, too. But it was the tray of gorgeous cupcakes iced with little mini-fondant books that really screamed "safe, happy place."

"Okay, I'll be back with your drinks soon, and to act out any of the sexy scenes requiring a strong, handsome man, as needed," Eli said.

"So," Julia said as soon Nora sat down between her and a woman with dark curly hair. "You and my brother seem to be getting along a lot better than before."

Nora clutched her copy of the paperback more tightly, certain that her cheeks had just heated enough to match the fuchsia color on the cover. "We figured out how to get over our differences and become friends. Just friends," she added quickly when Julia's eyebrows shot up. *Friends who happen to enjoy getting naked with each other.*

"Well, I should probably start with introductions," Julia said. "Next to you is Clem, the inspiration for this room." The woman with the dark curly hair offered a friendly smile.

"And across from you is—"

One of the two blond women across the table reached over and shook Nora's hand with a force and enthusiasm that nearly pulled her clear across the table. "Clover. And this is Chastity. We're Clem's older and wiser sisters. It's so nice to meet you!"

"You're going to love this book club. It's a blast. And I'm not just saying that because we get to leave our kids at home," Chastity added.

"Well, maybe it's a little bit about leaving the kids behind." Clover laughed. "My twins are kind of a handful. This is actually my second copy of this book. The girls got ahold of the first one and covered a bunch of pages with the sparkle glue my mom bought them for Christmas. It was like they knew exactly how to find and ruin the good parts, too. I was about to read the scene where Talon and Gen bang each other for the first time on the sailboat, and bam! The pages were completely stuck together." She blew a blond curl off her forehead with an exasperated giggle. Nora didn't blame her for sounding exhausted. She was tired from just hearing that story.

"I'm Lisa," said a woman next to Chastity. She was wearing a blue silk scarf that gave Nora a desperate case of envy. "It's my first time here, too. Clem and I know each other from the library, and she finally convinced me to come."

Nora smiled warmly, intimately recognizing the hint of nervousness in Lisa's voice.

"And I'm Lorenzo," said the last person—a big guy with a shaggy black beard, tattoos up his arms and neck, and super kind eyes behind thick black frames.

"Oh, right! The one who always asks what Hollywood stars would be cast as the main characters in a movie version?"

He let out a hearty chuckle. "Of all the things to gain a reputation over, I didn't think it would be that."

She winced. "Sorry. I just like to be prepared."

"Hey, no one's judging. Preparedness is next to godliness," Julia said. "I'm obsessed with bullet journals and preplan my entire schedule six months ahead of time. And Clem usually has a hundred quotes and notes tucked away in her e-reader."

Clem paused long enough from unwrapping a cupcake to say, "More like five hundred. Can you blame me? Talon's dialogue is so swoon-worthy."

There was something oddly familiar about the woman's deep, raspy voice, though Nora couldn't quite figure out what it was. "That's impressive."

"Don't let her scare you," Chastity said. "Our little sister has an unfair advantage."

Nora had no clue what she meant by that, but the tension peeled off her shoulders. She settled into her seat and pulled her paperback and notebook out of her purse. These were the kind of people she'd been hoping to find when she moved to Shadow Creek—people who loved books and probably wouldn't bat an eyelash at her quirks.

Who'd have thought the man who'd been driving her crazy since the first day she moved here would be the one to give her this gift?

"Okay, let's get started," Julia said. "Talon going down on Gen when he was all sweaty and dirty after the ATV ride. Hot or ewww?"

It turned out that talking sex scenes with a room full of strangers was actually a pretty good way to break the ice. With a vote of five to two, they agreed that sweaty and dirty was only good on paper. In real life, it would be a no-go, with Clem and Clover casting the dissenting votes. When was the last time Nora had laughed this much? Not since she was back in Toronto hanging out with Alice and Jessie.

The door opened. Nora turned her neck to see Eli walking in with a tray full of drinks. "First round's on the house tonight, folks, but tips are always welcome."

"Don't eat the yellow snow," Julia said.

"Always looking out for your big brother, huh?" Eli kissed his sister's forehead with a loud smack before setting her beer down. He circled around the table in the opposite direction, leaving Nora's drink last.

He surprised her by setting down a glass of red wine in front of her. She looked up, confused. Eli squeezed her shoulder, running his thumb along the back of her neck. "Hope you don't mind—I swiped a bottle of merlot from your wine rack when you were in the shower," he whispered. "No one drinks something they don't like in my establishment."

Her cheeks heated as he walked out of the room, remembering exactly why she'd been in the shower.

"So," Clover said with a giggle. "Is this a good time to talk about the use of sexual tension in the book?"

Nora was pretty sure everyone laughed at her expense after that, but there was nothing mean-spirited about it. She took a sip of wine to clear her throat. "I loved how the tension revealed the characters' insecurities about love."

"I know, right?" Lisa said before diving into a thoughtful analysis of the way the characters' backgrounds intersected to create conflict in the story. After that, Nora got lost in the discussion. Some of it was silly, some of it was intense, but all of it was completely engrossing, leaving her with a burning desire to reread the book all over again.

"Oh my goodness," Julia said after setting down her empty glass and sneaking a glance at her phone. "I can't believe how much we've been talking. This is one of the best discussions we've had yet. Should we do one more question?"

Clem nodded vigorously, clutching her e-reader to her chest. "I just need to know...how did this book make you feel?" Her eyes landed on Nora.

"Safe," Nora answered instinctively. "Like no matter what kind of day I've had or how bad things get in the real world, there's always a guarantee of love at the end. The characters in this book went through so much. They're such opposites, it's like they were on different planets. Different universes. There were so many obstacles to them falling in love—" She sucked in a breath. Everything she loved about this book was an excuse she'd given to Eli why they couldn't be together. "But at least in this book, they get to be happy."

"Sometimes it works out that way in real life, too," Clem said.

Nora set her glass on the table. "Oh my god. I recognize your voice!"

Holy heck. It had taken her brain a while to catch up, but she finally realized where she'd heard Clem's distinctive rasp before. She was a book narrator. Nora had listened to her on her morning commutes, in the lab, and a million other places while trying to keep up with all the books she wanted to read.

Clem smiled shyly.

"Don't bother asking her for spoilers," Chastity said. "She won't even give them up to her sisters."

"Wait, does that mean you narrated this series, too?"

Clem nodded.

"And The Red Zephyr books," Julia added.

"Damn, I love those books," Lorenzo said, running his hand through his beard. "I can't believe I didn't know that."

Nora was a natural blusher, but her fair skin had never come close to the deep crimson flush on Clem's cheeks. "I'm probably the only person in the world who's never read that series," Nora said, hoping to relieve some of the pressure on Clem before the poor woman burst.

Clover gaped. "But you've watched the show, right?"

"Everyone's watched the TV show," Julia said.

Nora shook her head. "It's hard to find the time to keep up with TV with my late nights in the lab."

"Well, that is a terrible shame," Julia said. "And we have to fix it."

"Fix what?" The door opened, and Eli came into the room.

Nora's heart did a little stutter-step when he set his gorgeous smile right on her. Man, she could get used to seeing that reaction on his face every day. Which goes to show how poor her instincts were, even after having her life implode six months ago. The last thing she needed was to get caught up in a man, especially one who lived right next door.

Julia flung her arm in Nora's direction. "Nora's never watched *The Red Zephyr*. She has three seasons to catch up on before the next viewing party."

He crossed his arms and leaned against the door. "Well, neighbor, think you can fit a little Netflix and chilling into your weekend?"

She should say no. She needed to say no.

"Yeah, I think I can."

9

"*I*f you miss cleaning this damn place so much, you could move back in."

Jake ignored Eli's quip and swept the last pile of dust into the pan. "If you needed help, you could've asked."

Eli ran the dust rag over the top of his windowsill. "I did. You just didn't notice all those longing glances across the bar. The way I pleaded for help with my fluttering lashes that day we had to unplug the toilet after those college kids made a bet they could each eat five blue cheese and bacon hamburgers. That was my heart telling you I needed you, Jake."

Jake stopped sweeping long enough to send an unimpressed glare Eli's way.

"Hey, man. Those bedroom eyes might work on Clem, but I'm immune to your charms." A sponge sailed across the room, rebounding off Eli's chest. He chuckled and finished wiping down the rest of the coffee table. "But, um, thanks. I really appreciate your help today."

He might not be great at asking for help, but the instant he'd hinted to Jake he needed a hand finishing up this reno, his best friend was there for him. In one grueling afternoon, they'd finished installing the new vanity in the bathroom, laid the last of the flooring in the spare bedroom, and were now cleaning every last inch of the place.

"Can't say I understand how a pristine house is supposed to convince Nora to fall in love with you, but at least you'll be able to walk around without tripping over these boxes and shit."

"I'm not—" He frowned. "She doesn't like messes."

Jake grinned.

Eli rolled his eyes.

He'd never been the most disciplined person in the world. He relied on passion and sheer stubbornness to get him through the harder situations that came his way. The rest? Life was too short to worry about the details. Except when it came to Nora.

He liked her. Really fucking liked her. Too much to screw things up with her. And despite every instinct in his body screaming at him to go knock on her door every night, he forced himself to play it cool. Even though she'd given her body to him twice now, she'd kept her heart and her mind firmly guarded. He understood why. She was focused on making friends, not finding a lover. And after he'd caught glimpses of her laughing and enjoying herself at the Books and Brews club the other night, he couldn't blame her. She'd spent the drive home with a wide, unbridled smile.

So instead of inviting Nora back to his place that night, he walked her to her door and left her with a chaste kiss and a promise to come by on the weekend.

"After all this work, I'm kinda thinking I should ask for a retroactive discount on the rent I paid you."

"You didn't pay me any rent."

"Then you could just give me some cash."

Eli laughed. Jake was born rich as fuck, but his parents had cut him off after he and his ex-fiancée decided they were in love with other people. Unfortunately, that family drama had occurred after Jake had borrowed a shit-ton of money to get their brewpub off the ground. Jake sold his house to pay back the money and moved in with him to get back on his feet.

Eli wasn't great at admitting his feelings, but he'd liked having Jake around. They'd been roommates for most of their adult lives, ever since the first day of college. They'd become more than friends in that time. Jake was family.

"I'll pay you in hugs. Big, sloppy bear hugs."

"Don't think I won't take you up on that. Clem likes when I'm in touch with my feelings."

"You're a lucky bastard. You know that, right?"

"I am, and hopefully you'll be one, too, soon. If renovating your entire house doesn't get Nora's attention, then I don't know what would. But at least it looks great."

"I didn't renovate to get a woman's attention," Eli grumbled. "That was just a happy by-product of all the noise from my circular saw."

The shitty side of it all was that Nora had gotten pretty damn set in her opinion of him as a slob. He wasn't. The fact that he and Jake were both tidy by nature was one of the reasons they'd never wanted to throttle each other in all the years they lived together, but there was no way to renovate without first creating a giant mess.

He took a moment to glance around the room and take in the finished product. The house was small, but it looked damn good.

His chest tightened. Maybe one day he'd be able to celebrate his accomplishments without the bittersweet coating in his throat. He wanted to believe his mom would be proud of this place. She'd worked herself to the bone to make sure he and Julia never had to go without, and keep them living in a nice home. He wanted provide the same for his family one day.

Jake laughed. "Only you could land a date with a woman by annoying her half to death."

"It's a talent."

"It's fucking weird."

Eli didn't add that he hadn't exactly landed Nora. She was still determined to believe they were too different. Too unlikely. But at least she was giving him a chance at friendship. Nora had turned him completely upside down, and the weirdest part was he didn't even hate it. He'd never felt this way about a woman before, but that didn't mean he couldn't recognize a good thing when it moved into the house next door. He just had to find a way to make her see that.

"Almost done. There's just one thing left." Jake pointed to the stack of files piled on his kitchen counter.

Eli rubbed the back of his neck. "Uh, yeah. There's still a little more work to do for the SPCA fundraiser."

"How much more work?"

"All of it." He'd considered lying, but there was no point. Jake's bullshit meter was finely attuned to Eli's tics whenever he lied.

Jake let out a breath. "Julia's going to kill you."

"When isn't she?" It wasn't like he hadn't been trying. The new outreach coordinator at the SPCA was even less organized than he was, giving Eli no clue where to start. And sure, he could just copy what his sister had done last year, but they hadn't exactly knocked the event out of the park, not that he would say that to Julia's face. There was so much more they could do. The problem was figuring out where to start. "Don't worry about it. It'll get done. I always come through."

Jake should his head. "All right, I'm heading out. Good luck tonight."

Eli laughed. "Good luck? Why don't you just douse me in Joop! cologne and shove a couple of blueberry-flavored condoms in my pocket."

Jake put his hand on Eli's shoulder. "Dude. Never go for flavored condoms. Only ribbed for her pleasure."

Eli shuddered. "You sound like my creepy fifth grade sex-ed teacher. Now please leave before Nora overhears the next thing out of your mouth."

He swung the door open, but froze before shoving Jake out.

"Too late," Nora said, standing on his front stoop. "But I can guarantee your sex-ed teacher had nothing on mine. Mr. Niemeyer used to eat the banana in front of us after using it to demonstrate putting on a condom. Said that wasting food was a sin."

Eli cleared his throat. "Jake?"

His friend nodded. "Getting lost as we speak." He smiled at Nora before sneaking out the door.

Nora waited until the door was shut behind her before speaking. "It looks amazing in here." She slipped off her shoes. "You've been working hard the last few days, huh?"

"Yeah. Hope the noise wasn't too much."

"Funny enough, I seem to be getting used to that."

"Careful, Princess. By the end of the year, you might start confusing the sound of my weed whacker with a lullaby."

"About as likely as you getting used to my boot in your nuts."

He shook his head with a laugh. "Such a tease."

His doorbell rang before she could respond.

"Pizza's here." He opened the door, paid a hefty tip to the delivery guy, and brought the steaming pie to his kitchen. Nora had already pulled plates out of his cupboard and was holding them up to the light, inspecting for dirt. With anyone else, he might have been insulted, but he wasn't bothered. It meant she was making herself comfortable in his home. Getting used to him. He knew she wasn't going to change something so fundamental about who she was, and he didn't expect her to. He wanted her to feel comfortable in her own skin when she was around him. He wanted every quirk, every oddity, every wish—just not the shame and embarrassment that accompanied it.

She set the plates down and inhaled. "That smells so good."

"Yeah, Emilio's Pizza is the best in town. I hope you don't mind I ordered for us."

She bit her lip.

"Relax, I ordered pepperoni and mushroom. Everyone likes pepperoni and mushroom." The way her mouth pulled into a wide grimace made him question just how surefire his surefire bet really was. "Crap. You don't like mushrooms, do you?"

"No," she answered too quickly. "I love mushrooms."

He raised his eyebrows. "Truth?"

"Yes, they're amazing fungi. Full of vitamins and minerals. And even the non-edible, parasitic kinds are the source for some of the world's most important medicines. And most of all, they're delicious."

He ran his hand through his hair and laughed. "Oh my god. You don't like pepperoni? I figured I needed to stay away from olives and onions and pineapple. But pepperoni? They're like little round circles of happiness for your mouth." Never in his entire thirty-two years had he met a non-vegetarian who didn't like pepperoni on their pizza.

She winced. "They're weird and greasy and sometimes you get those hard little gristly bits in them and..." She shuddered.

He sighed and flipped the pizza box open.

"What are you doing?"

"Taking off every last bit of pepperoni from your half of the pie."

She tilted her head to the side, tension easing from her face. "Thank you."

"No, thank you. It means I get double on my side."

"There's one more thing I have to warn you about. I—"

He pressed his finger to her lips. "No. Don't say it."

"It's true," she mumbled against his hand. "I told you we're opposites."

He groaned and opened his cutlery drawer. "I can't believe I'm allowing this abomination in my home."

"When you see how much cleaner it is this way, you'll come over to my side."

"The dark side."

She accepted the knife and fork, then grabbed a slice and carried it all to the living room. He reminded himself it was too early to kiss the ridiculous out of her right now. Instead, he did something that made his skin curl with disgust.

He grabbed another knife and fork, and followed her to the living room, shaking his head the entire time.

"You don't have to do that just for me."

"One of these days, you're going to understand how wrong you are."

A pink flush swept across her cheeks. "So, this isn't the kind of show that's going to give me nightmares, is it?"

Eli settled next to her on the couch, giving her just enough space to keep her comfortable. "There's a reason I've developed these arms into perfect love cushions for cuddling."

She rolled her eyes, but by the third episode, she'd drifted over to his side of the couch and curled into his chest with a warm fleece blanket draped over them. It was a good thing he'd seen every episode before, because he couldn't concentrate on anything but the scent of her hair filling his nose, and the press of her fingers against his stomach that deepened every time a battle scene came across the screen. He settled his hand on her hip, holding her like they'd done this a million times before. Every little gasp and breathy sigh she uttered was a direct signal to his cock, but he didn't move other than to rub small circles onto the thin strip of skin between her T-shirt and jeans. He needed her to see there was more than just sexual chemistry between them.

And, if he was being honest with himself, he needed this, too. The comfort of a warm, soft body next to his on a quiet Friday night.

The credits rolled on the fourth episode. "It's late—do you want to take a break?"

No answer.

He brushed the blond hair from her face. She was asleep. He shut off the TV, pulled the blanket over her shoulders, and closed his eyes.

When Eli woke, he knew instantly that Nora wasn't there. His instinct for her was deeper than his consciousness. But she wasn't far. Her scent was still fresh in the morning air. Early morning air, judging by the darkness streaming through the windows. He rose to his feet and stretched his right shoulder, which was still numb from serving as a pillow for her all night. He found her in the kitchen with a steaming mug of coffee in her hands and a binder in front of her, flipping carefully through the pages.

"Sleep okay?"

She looked up at him with a grin that almost masked the tired bags beneath her eyes. "Not too bad, but your biceps are way too hard to be pillows."

"Compliment accepted." He flexed his muscles for good measure, making her laugh. He poured a mug of coffee and sat down across from her at the small, round table. "Riveting stuff, huh?"

"You didn't mention you're planning an event. I thought this was Julia's area of expertise."

"She didn't have time to plan it, so I said I'd do it."

"When's the event?"

"Three weeks from now."

She winced. "How far along are you?"

He took a long sip of coffee. It was hot enough to scald his tongue —which was just the way he liked it. "Not far at all."

She pursed her lips like she was unsure whether or not to speak. "You know, I could help you with this."

Jesus, she wasn't making it easy to not fall for her. "That's okay. I know you're good at this stuff, but the problem is my contact at the SPCA is in over her head and can't make any decisions, so I can't move forward with the planning. Every time I ask her to make a simple decision about hamburgers or hotdogs, she panics."

Her lips twisted to a wry grin. "You know that's exactly the kind of thing I could help you with."

Now she had his attention. "How?"

"It's simple, really. You have to stop asking indecisive people what they want and start telling them."

He looked at her intently until she turned away with a soft blush. If only it were that easy. "Okay, then tell me how I do that."

"What do you want this event to be?"

He took a moment—not because he needed to think about it, but because he was so used to everything he suggested being shot down as stupid.

"Honestly," she added.

He sucked in a breath. "Honestly? I want to have a big, family event with burgers and beer and juice boxes. And I want the animals there. Otherwise it's just another generic fundraiser—like the kind we do all the time for local sports teams and stuff. But at least with those fundraisers, there's a built-in group of parents and friends and coworkers who show up to support each other. With this kind of thing, we need a reason to draw new people in. And, frankly, new people coming to our brewpub is how we benefit from all this."

To his surprise, she didn't laugh or roll her eyes. "I totally get what you're saying. Nothing makes people open their wallets faster than an adorable pet. But I'm guessing the bylaws don't allow that."

He shook his head.

"Then we'll follow up with the bylaw office later and find a way to make it work. If you want it badly enough, you'll find a way to make it happen. For now, let's come up with an estimated number of guests and plan for everything that needs to be ordered. We'll put it together in a simple one-page summary for your SPCA contact to sign off on. Sound good?"

He looked at her in awe. "Sounds perfect."

Just like her, he thought. And that was exactly the problem.

10

"*I*t's a microwave, Dad. It's not trying to kill you." Nora cradled her phone against her ear with one hand and flung through the clothes hanging in her closet with the other.

"Says the person who isn't eating a dinner of chicken with a side of salmonella. How am I supposed to figure out all these fancy knobs and buttons?"

She dropped her head against the closet doorframe. The man was a prestigious professor of economics who could explain game theory in his sleep, but a simple kitchen appliance turned him into a toddler having a tantrum. "You shouldn't be cooking raw chicken in the microwave in the first place."

"I was working late and don't have time to bake a goddamn chicken breast for an hour. If you still lived here, you could be cooking dinner for me."

If you ever left the office before eight o'clock at night, you'd have all the time you needed. "If I still lived in Toronto, I would be slaving away at the office, too, and griping about how there's no one to cook dinner for me, either. Besides, I moved out when I was eighteen, remember?"

She pulled out a green sweater and held it up against her chest while her dad grumbled on the other end of the line. He'd never been much of a cook. Nora had done most of the cooking growing up, and after she left, her mom had taken over that duty. But since her parents separated, her dad acted like feeding himself was some dangerous, *Lord of the Rings*-style quest instead of a mundane task that a fully functioning fifty-nine-year-old man should have figured out by now.

She hung the sweater back up in its designated space in her perfectly color-coded arrangement, and grabbed a blue blouse she normally considered work attire. Nope. Too formal. God, why was it so hard to figure out an appropriate outfit for a night out with people she hardly knew? "Dad, have you tried getting out more? Lots of people your age have success with internet dating."

"I'm still married."

"I know." No way was she revisiting the question of why the divorce papers still weren't signed. That was one equation her brain couldn't handle no matter how many times her folks tried to explain it. "What about a poker league or softball team?"

Another grumble. "I'm too old and too busy for that kind of thing. Why aren't *you* doing any of that?"

"Because I'm exactly like you. Except I know how cook."

"You got that from your mother. And your pretty blond hair."

But my tendency to work myself to death and avoid all notion of balance from you.

His wistful voice broke her heart all over again, even though she knew it was silly. Her mom was the one who'd cheated, but he was the one to push her to it with his exacting personality and endless late nights at work. They were such opposites, it was amazing they'd even stayed together as long as they did. "Why don't you just order in tonight, okay?"

Her doorbell rang, muffling the sound of her dad's rumbles. She ended the call with the same niggling worry about him she'd always had, but reminded herself he was an adult. Babying the man hadn't done him any favors while he was with her mom, and it wasn't going to help now.

She grabbed the first sweater she'd tried on half an hour ago and raced to the door. "Hi!"

Julia and Clem stood on her doorstep beneath a pair of umbrellas. Julia shook the rain from her hair and smiled. "Ready to go?"

"Yep," Nora said, grabbing her own pink-and-white polka-dotted umbrella and trench coat. She followed the two women to Clem's SUV waiting in the driveway and hopped into the backseat.

"I'm so glad you were free tonight," Clem said as she backed out onto the street. "I've been wanting to try this for ages, and it's going to be way more fun with friends."

"My Saturday nights haven't exactly been jam-packed since I moved here," Nora answered.

Julia craned her head from the passenger seat to look at her. "Hmm. And here I thought you were the reason my brother's been taking off a bunch of Saturday nights lately."

"We're friends," she said weakly.

"I hope he won't mind that he's going to have some competition for your weekends now," Julia said. "Because I'm already planning next week's outing to a new brunch spot downtown."

Nora nerves settled a little bit more and she allowed herself to smile giddily, knowing the darkness of the evening would hide it from view. This was exactly what she'd been hoping for since the day she arrived here—a connection with other women with similar interests and values. The feeling that she was finally fitting in.

Never would she have thought she would have her loud neighbor to thank for this.

They stopped in a neighborhood closer to downtown to pick up Lisa, who looked just as excited as Nora to be getting out on a Saturday night. A short while later, they'd arrived at the Dark Side, a beautiful little chocolate shop that turned out to be anything but dark on the inside. White counters matched the gleaming floors, topped with clear glass displays, all of which were highlighted by gorgeous industrial-style rubbed-bronze pendant lamps. It was pristine and bursting with the aroma of chocolate. Heaven.

Lorenzo came out from the back room, wearing a blue-and-white striped apron that somehow looked impressively regal rather than silly on him. "I'm so glad you could come! I've got everything prepared for you in the tasting room."

He brought them to a small, private room off the back kitchen that had a long white marble counter in the middle of the room, flanked by half a dozen high-backed stools. Three trays of differently colored chocolate pieces sat on the counter with plates of apple slices and glasses of lemon water.

"The first rule of chocolate tasting is that white chocolate is not chocolate," Lorenzo said solemnly.

"Tell that to half the clients booking weddings at the Holy Grale lately," Julia said with a laugh. "Everyone wants white chocolate wedding cakes this year."

Lorenzo scoffed. "That's because I happen to make the greatest white chocolate ganache on the West Coast. Delicious, creamy, and perfectly smooth, but *not* chocolate. I've prepared a selection of different chocolates for you to try today. The second rule of chocolate tasting is to have fun and relax. Chocolate is purely about pleasure and indulgence. We like what we like, and there's no point in being snobby or insecure about it."

Nora raised her eyebrows, and Lorenzo laughed. "Okay, fine. A little snobbiness about white chocolate is allowed."

He ran them through the series of chocolates from different parts of the worlds, explaining the variations in flavors of the cocoa bean and effects on the final product. At Lorenzo's urging, they each picked up a piece of buttery smooth Tanzanian dark chocolate and sniffed.

"Now rub a little bit between your thumb and forefinger to release the aroma," Lorenzo said.

Nora looked around, stomach lurching at the idea of getting a mess of chocolate on her fingers. Clem had already managed to get it all over hand and even a dab on her nose.

Relax, it's just chocolate, she told herself, but the prickling feeling she always got when uncomfortable rose up her neck and cheeks, no doubt leaving a splotch of red in its wake.

"Hey," Lorenzo said over her shoulder. She clenched her stomach, steeling herself for his reproach at her rudeness. "Remember how I said this is about having fun? Don't worry about following instructions if you don't want to."

Relief loosened her stomach. She relaxed and sniffed the chocolate without making a mess on her fingertips. She wasn't quite sure she could discern the hints of vanilla and orange Lorenzo described, but her mouth was already watering.

"Next, let the chocolate melt on your tongue to awaken the flavor. No chewing."

Nora and everyone else did as told. This time the full effect of the flavor hit her tongue in an explosion of taste.

"Oh my God," Clem said between her moans—a sound that struck Nora as almost sexual because of the woman's husky voice—then snuck another taste from the remnants on the plate. "I don't care if I choke on this stuff. It would be a worthwhile death."

"Agreed," Lisa said.

"Actually, it would be terrible if any of you died before you sampled the stuff from Papua New Guinea," Lorenzo said, handing them each a warm, wet towel to clean their hands.

They sampled each of the chocolates in turn, using the lemon water and apple slices in between as a palate cleanser. It turned out Nora and Clem were both partial to the Tanzanian, whereas Lisa liked the Ecuadorian stuff and Julia was the lone vote for the smoky, spicy Papua New Guinean chocolate.

"Is this the part where we get to buy a whole bunch of chocolate now that we are properly educated on how to eat it?" Lisa asked. "Because I'm ready to stuff my face with slightly bitter Ecuadorian chocolate with notes of coffee and molasses, thank you very much."

Lorenzo crossed his beefy arms with a soft chuckle. "Not yet. We've still got the best part to get to."

"There's something better than eating chocolate?" Clem asked before sneaking another piece from the tray in front of her.

Lorenzo grinned. "Making it. I'll be back in few minutes with the supplies."

Nora looked to Julia as soon as Lorenzo left. "Are all your girls' nights out this amazing?"

Julia shrugged, but Clem answered for her. "Yep. Whether it's a wedding, book club, or night out, Julia is the best event planner in town."

"How'd you end up in that line of work? I've never heard of an event planner working at a brewpub," Nora said.

Lisa laughed. "I've never heard of a brewpub in a church, either."

"You can blame Eli and Jake for the Holy Grale. As for me, I thought about wedding planning, but it's a tough market with a lot of competition in L.A. After Eli and Jake bought this place, I figured it was as good an opportunity as any to get my foot in the business."

"It's a long way to go for a job," Nora said.

"After Mom died, there wasn't much keeping me in L.A. Eli's the only family I have left, so it made sense to come here," Julia said

"How about you?" Clem asked, looking at Nora. "What brought you to Shadow Creek? Do you have family out here?"

She shook her head, suddenly wondering if her dad had managed to get a decent meal for himself tonight, or if her mom was remembering to get enough sleep. "No family. Just a job opportunity at the college here."

Before anyone could ask any more questions, Lorenzo came out with more supplies, including—Nora noticed gratefully—clear plastic gloves. He poured liquid chocolate directly onto the counter and demonstrated how to temper it with his huge, square metal spatula, swirling the chocolate with a gentleness that was utterly captivating.

He'd obviously been making it look easy, though, because a few minutes in, the white marble countertop looked like a battlefield with sticky brown chocolate smeared everywhere.

"There, you're getting the hang of it," Lorenzo said to Lisa as he leaned over her shoulder and demonstrated the technique once more.

"Sure, and if you keep doing this for me, it'll be perfect," she answered with a bright laugh.

"I'm pretty sure I'm a lost cause, so I'm just going to eat," Clem said as she snuck another taste off her plastic-covered fingertip. As much as it grossed Nora out, she couldn't blame Clem. Chocolate covered most of her hands and not an insubstantial amount of her clothing and face, too.

Julia messed around valiantly with her spatula before looking across the table at Nora. "Hey, how come you've got the hang of this while the rest of us suck?"

Nora examined her chocolate. It was much neater than anyone else's, and thickening nicely, though nowhere close to Lorenzo's expert craftsmanship. "It helps to be an overbearing perfectionist." She cringed the moment she uttered the self-deprecating words.

"Hey, you say that like it's a bad thing. Around here, overbearing perfectionist is a compliment," Julia said with a wink. She looked at Clem. "Same with messy, quiet introverts."

"How about slightly paranoid, hopeless romantics with a serious case of klutziness?" Lisa asked.

"Obviously," Julia said. "We welcome everyone in this group, as long as you love chocolate."

"And books," Clem added.

Nora smiled.

They moved on to setting the chocolate into molds, adding bits of nuts and caramel and other confections. The conversation halted for a bit because of the concentration required for this task, but there were a few laughs. They finished up their chocolates by wrapping them in beautiful cellophane packages tied with ribbons. All things considered, Nora was rather proud of her effort.

Clem slid her package across the table to Nora. "I give up. Please help."

With a small chuckle, she knotted the gold ribbon and curled then ends with a pair of scissors, then added an extra blue ribbon to make it prettier and slid it back to her. "Here you go. Perfect."

"You know, at first I was worried about Eli taking on the SPCA fundraiser," Julia said. "But then he told me you were helping and I'm starting to believe he'll pull it off after all."

"He's doing a really good job. I think you'll be really impressed"

Julia snort-laughed. "Because you're doing it all for him? I love my brother, but he's not the most organized person I've ever met."

She crossed her arms, frowning. She really liked Julia, but it was a bit shocking to hear her speak about Eli like that. "Actually, he's been doing everything on his own and he's working really hard to prove to you that he can do this. I'm really just a sounding board."

Julia leaned back in her seat, looking a little surprised. "Huh. Maybe I am a little hard on him. Either way, I'm glad you're his friend." She added a warm smile that reassured Nora there were no hard feelings.

"And ours, too," Clem said.

They packed up their chocolates and thanked Lorenzo with words and hugs, and by buying a truckload of his chocolates, too. By the time they left and reached Nora's door, they'd already made plans for their next outing.

She was so elated from the great evening, she practically skipped to her door, barely aware of her surroundings.

"Hey."

She jumped back with a gasp, grabbing the railing to steady herself. "Eli! I didn't see you."

"Oh man, I thought the light from these sconces highlighted my handsome jaw and soulful eyes. I had no idea it actually made me disappear."

She rolled her eyes, trying really hard to hold back a laugh. "I meant I was distracted in my thoughts."

"One day you're going to really notice me, Nora. And when you do..." he said wistfully before using his hands to mime an explosion in front of his face. "Bam! You won't know what hit you. You'll be begging for the chance to glance upon this handsomeness."

This time, she really did laugh. "Trust me, you're too loud not to notice." *And far too gorgeous.* Her body practically buzzed whenever he was near.

"That mean I can come in?"

Her stomach tightened.

"I just want to share some good news." He flashed her a grin that made it impossible to say no.

"Sure."

"Great, but you might want to let Julia know I'm not the big bad monster here."

"Oh!" Nora turned quickly and waved to Julia, signaling all was okay. She pulled her keys out of her purse and let Eli in.

She hung up her purse and jacket on the coat rack at the entrance, then headed to the kitchen to put her chocolates on the counter.

"Do I get to try one of those?"

"Of course." She unwrapped the package and turned it toward him.

He picked up one of the dark little squares and popped it into his mouth, then made a sound that sent a happy shiver down her spine. She loved the way he dove into even the smallest parts of life and held nothing back.

He reached for another, but she slapped his hand lightly. "I said one."

He laughed. "Evil temptress."

She handed him one more, then tucked the chocolates safely in her fridge.

He grinned and shoved it into his mouth before she could change her mind. "Does this mean you had a good time tonight?"

"Yeah. It was really lovely."

He crossed his arms and gave her a look.

"What?"

"I'm waiting to hear you say it."

"Say what?"

He leaned across the peninsula, meeting her eyes. "I'll give you a hint. It starts with 'Dearest handsome Eli', and ends with 'you were right.'"

She laughed. "Fine. You were right. I'm very glad you introduced me to your sister and her friends."

"That's awesome, because now I get to say it to you."

Her eyebrows knitted together. "I don't have a sister."

He grinned and came around the counter, setting his hands on her upper arms. "I mean you were right."

"About?"

"The bylaw office. They're letting us bring the animals to the fundraiser. It's going to be awesome."

"That's incredible!" She instinctively pulled him into a big hug, pressing her chest to his. He responded instantly, tightening his grip until their entire bodies were flush. God, it felt good to be in his arms.

He tilted his head back slightly to look at her, cupping her cheeks in his hands. "You're incredible."

The fire in his eyes burned so hot, she felt like kindling ready to be ignited. He kissed her so deeply and passionately that she didn't have time to think before the desire overcame her. She buried her fingers in his hair, parting her lips and urging him on. She could taste the lingering chocolate on his lips before he moved his mouth to her jaw, her chin, her neck. Every inch of her skin was ablaze, begging to be the next spot where his hot tongue made contact. He dropped his hands to her ass, and her knees went weak when she felt his erection press into her.

She wanted this—wanted him—so badly, she could barely breathe. But she couldn't do this.

She pulled back. He released her mouth instantly, but didn't let her go. He dropped his forehead to hers, breathing heavy. "Sorry, I got a little carried away."

"It's okay. So did I," she whispered.

"But?"

She inhaled deeply. "But I can't do this. I really like you, Eli, but I'm finally feeling like I'm fitting in with a group of women in this town. What if we do this and things don't work out?"

"What if they do?"

Her heart leapt like he'd sent a jolt of electricity directly to it. She wanted to believe it so badly, but she couldn't. Not if she wanted to protect her heart. "Your friendship means a lot to me, too."

He exhaled long and slow and brushed the now messy strands of hair off her face before planting a gentle kiss on her forehead. "Same."

She wanted to explain more. Tell him about her parents. About her divorce. About how damn hard it was to lose everything when a relationship inevitably went sour. But he let her go, respecting her choice without making her spell it out, and walked to the door.

He set his hand on the knob, then turned around. "We're still on for season two of *The Red Zephyr* tomorrow, right?"

She forced a smile, though her heart was trying to escape her chest at that moment. "Wouldn't miss it."

11

"*W*hat's that smell?"

Eli brushed his hands against his jeans and turned to look at Julia, who'd just come into the brewery. He'd barely heard her over the sound of the bar patrons laughing and talking in the background, but he knew what had drawn her here. "Bourbon."

She frowned, letting the door close behind her and leaning against it. "I'm not sure we've talked about expanding our operations to include hard liquor."

"I'm not making bourbon. I bought a bourbon barrel. And chips. Check it out." He waved her in, urging her to sniff the aroma from the aged wood.

She inhaled deeply, then looked at him. "Okay, it smells good, but I'm still not following. How is this supposed to be not crazy?"

"I never said it wasn't crazy. It is, however, going to be delicious. Bourbon barrel-aged stout. I don't have a good name for it yet."

She didn't look displeased, which he considered a win given everything he did lately seemed to fall short of her expectations, but she did look confused. "I thought we decided no more seasonal brews. How are you going to maintain a supply of that for the customers with only one barrel?"

"I'm not planning on serving this at the Holy Grale. It's for the remembrance ceremony."

He braced himself, waiting for her reaction. Julia's shoulders fell slightly as the air left her lungs in a slow, measured exhalation. She looked tired suddenly, like she no longer had the energy to hold up the mask of cheerful perfection she always wore. He hated that he had that effect on his sister. Since they were little kids, they'd always had each other's backs in a way that was impossible to describe to someone who didn't have a sibling. But ever since they'd been planning this ceremony, there's been too many bad memories dug up. Too much unspoken hurt buried for too long.

"Mom hated beer."

"But she loved bourbon."

Julia looked to him. Her lips curved ever so slightly upward. "Yeah. She did. And she would have been proud of what we're doing here."

He nodded, unsure how to deal with the relief that made his chest feel like it had been filled with helium.

"Do I get to try it?"

"It won't be ready for a few weeks, but you'll be the first to try it when it is."

She walked all the way into the room, but instead of heading to the barrel, she went directly to Eli and hugged him. "I'm sorry I've been hard on you."

"Nah," he said, hugging her back. "I probably deserve it."

She let him go and brushed the non-existent wrinkles out of her sweater. "Nora says you're doing a good job with the SPCA fundraiser."

He couldn't help but grin now. Everything was coming together even better than he could have imagined thanks to Nora's help. "Yeah. I think you'll like the surprise I have planned."

She raised an eyebrow. "She's a good influence on you. I like her."

He opened his mouth to say he liked her, too, but stopped himself. It wasn't Julia's fault Nora had basically chosen her over him. He understood her reasons, even if he didn't like them, because he'd rather have her as a friend than not at all. She'd come over again last night to binge watch *The Red Zephyr* episodes. More than once, he'd found himself reaching for her hand—for just the slightest bit of physical connection—but he'd stopped himself before he came off like a creep. "Thanks for taking her out the other night. She needs good friends here."

Julia nodded. "Hey, I was thinking…"

It was his turn to raise his eyebrows. "Try not to hurt yourself, sis."

She smacked him on the chest. "I was thinking we could go to the storage facility where all of Mom's stuff is and find some things to use at the ceremony. Remember that little round table with the tile mosaic on top?"

He laughed and ran a hand along his jaw. "Hell yeah—how could anyone forget her tile mosaic phase? I think we spent the entire summer driving around to discount home reno stores looking for the perfect tiles for all her projects." Every light switch, mirror, and flat surface in the house was tiled over thanks to their mom's newfound obsession with crafting.

"But you've got to admit smashing the tiles into tiny pieces was fun."

"Says the person who didn't end up at the hospital getting stitches in her thumb."

Julia's eyes widened. "Do you remember when Mom tried to make a picture of a dolphin and it looked like a—"

"Don't say it! It was bad enough watching Mom forever destroy the most beloved creatures of the sea. I can't handle my baby sister saying that word."

"A penis!" She burst into laughter while he groaned.

"You are too young to know what that word is," he grumbled.

"I'm thirty years old, Eli. I took Ms. Cumming's sex-ed class in fifth grade just like you."

He sat down on top of the barrel, chuckling. "No one teaching sex-ed should be named Shirley Cumming."

She bumped his shoulder with her hip until there was enough room for her to perch next to him. "Do you remember Manny the

Masturbating Monkey?" She laughed so hard, she could barely get the words out between gasps of air.

He lost it at that memory, convulsing into a fit of hysterics.

The door swung open once more. Jake stepped inside, frowning. "Everything okay here?"

Eli looked at Julia, and the pair of them burst into more laughter.

Jake picked up a keg, shaking his head as he walked out the door.

"What about this?" Eli unwrapped the newspaper from an ornate crystal vase in the box at his feet and held it up.

Julia smoothed back her ponytail and frowned. "Is that the one we bought from that weird thrift shop for Mother's Day when I was ten?"

He nodded. She came over and took it from him, examining it more closely. "God, we had terrible taste back then."

"Speak for yourself. I think the flower design is classic."

She laughed. "Sure, if you were born in the 1880s. But I know how to use it. Let's set it out front with a couple small flowers by the guestbook."

They continued sorting through the piles of dust-covered furniture and boxes until their backs couldn't take any more bending and lifting. Luckily, they'd found everything they needed for the ceremony. It wasn't the first time they'd had to dig around in this stuff, since they'd moved it up from a storage facility in Los Angeles, but it felt like he was seeing everything again for the first time. The memories hit him hard with each piece of delicately patterned china and lace tablecloth they looked at. It was good to be doing it with Julia. It had been too long since they talked about their mom. She would have wanted them to work together on this.

Still, he couldn't quite shake the feeling that he was the useless cog in all of this. If he disappeared tomorrow, Julia would still pull this ceremony off without a hitch. Just like she did the funeral a decade ago. He was a thirty-two-year-old man and still had no damn clue how to be an adult about his mom's death.

"Oh, there's one more box," Julia said, awkwardly shuffling around the piles of stuff to the back corner of the dark storage space. She struggled to lift it, so he quickly came over to help.

His arms felt like they were going to rip right off his shoulders when he lifted the box. "What's in this thing?" He carried it to the front where there was more light, and opened up the folded cardboard flaps of the box that, from the images on the side, once housed a crate of bananas.

"It's photo albums," Julia whispered, pulling out an ancient burgundy book from the top. She pulled back a sheet of sticky, crackling plastic from the first page and removed a photo. "Look."

It was Eli, round-faced with hair mussed in all directions and a pair of GI Joe pajamas on his skinny body. It was Christmas morning, judging by the decorated tree in the background, and he was holding up a bright red remote-controlled car.

"Oh man, I remember that Christmas. You begged Mom for that car for months and…" Her voice travelled off as soon as her memory led to the same place as his.

A week after he'd opened it, he'd accidentally left it outside and it had been stolen. At the time, he'd had a fit because his mom wouldn't replace it. As an adult, what he felt looking at that old photo was a million times worse. Now he understood how hard his mom had to work to afford the expensive toy. How ungrateful he'd been to be so careless about it. How she'd probably been so much more disappointed than he was in that moment.

His throat went dry and a strange feeling hit him in the chest—like his lungs were a pair of shoes with the laces pulled too tight.

Julia set her hand on his shoulder. "Mom was always great at Christmas presents, huh?"

He nodded. She set the picture back in the plastic and flipped through a few more pages before setting the album back in the box. "Thanks so much for doing this with me."

"Anything for you, sis," he said with as much of his normal good humor as possible. He picked up the box of stuff they were taking with them and headed out of the hallway.

"Hey, I was thinking," Julia said as she trailed after him. "Maybe we could have a photo album at the ceremony. Just a little memory book that the people can flip through. Maybe that's something you could put together?"

He stumbled over a folding chair left on the ground. "Yeah, of course."

She beamed at him. "Great!"

He sucked in a breath and forced a smile onto his face. "Great."

Nora added one extra dash of chopped cilantro to her white chili and examined the effect. It was almost too pretty to eat, really, but her stomach was growling like the unseen monster in a horror movie. She'd skipped lunch, and was now feeling pretty grateful that past Nora was considerate enough to prepare the chili yesterday for her current self.

She laid out her blue-and-silver woven placemat, arranged her cutlery, and poured a glass of cold water from the jug she kept chilled in the fridge. She sat down and picked up her spoon. "Finally." Her stomach growled in agreement.

The doorbell chimed. She was so hungry, she considered ignoring it, but there was only one person who rang her doorbell on a week-night, and only one person who could cause the flutter of excitement in her belly before even seeing him.

She pulled opened the door and grinned. "Hi."

Eli met her smile with one that made her toes curl in her slippers. "Hey. I was in the mood for some company tonight, and instead of breaking down some more walls, I figured I'd see if you were up for some company, too."

If she hadn't spent so much time staring at his face lately, she might have believed this really was a casual visit, but there was a tightness around his eyes. "I'm pretty sure the only untouched walls left are the exterior ones at this point."

"Are you questioning my manly renovation skills?"

"No," she said over her shoulder as she led him down the hall. "Just your sanity."

He smacked her on the butt, causing her to yelp and jump forward.

"Watch it, now." He stopped and sniffed the air. "What is that?"

"White turkey chili. Hungry?"

He looked at her with dark eyes that reminded her of burning embers. "Famished."

Every muscle in her body slackened like she was ready to fall into his arms. Not for the first time, she wondered why she was fighting her attraction to him when they were drawn together like some undiscovered gravitational force. "I—"

The doorbell rang again. Nora frowned. The sound was so unexpected, she was barely able to understand what she was hearing.

"Nora? Sweetie, is this the right house? Oh gosh. Am I in the wrong place? Nora? Nora Pitts?"

Nora squeezed her eyes shut. "Oh no."

"Need me to get rid of whoever that is?"

She shook her head, unwilling to open her eyes yet. "No—"

"Nora? Honey, is this any way to greet your mother? I know it's your house. I recognize the welcome mat."

Eli's hands went to her shoulders, steeling her with his strength. "Unexpected visit?"

"The only kind," she muttered.

He followed her back down the hallway toward the front entrance, where they found her mom having already let herself in and staring at the store-bought print near the front door. Her graying hair fell in long, loose waves over her shoulders. Her clothes had a newly acquired West Coast feel, with a Cowichan sweater and multi-colored, floor-length skirt. Catherine Pitts had always managed to be the kind of woman who looked elegant despite the fact she didn't wear expensive clothing. Nora had figured out long ago that it was probably all the costume jewelry her mother wore, but she was pretty sure she'd never be able to pull off the same look without the extra panache that could only come with age, experience, and just the right amount of kookiness.

"Mom, what on earth are you doing here?"

Catherine ran her finger over the top right corner of the canvas, as though that would make it come alive. "Do you think this is supposed to be a fallopian tube?"

Nora had bought the print six years ago, and Catherine asked that same question every time she'd seen it. No matter how many times they'd looked at it, the tree in the background of the picture was just a tree. "Mom."

Finally, her mom turned around, flashing a brilliant smile that only widened when she saw Eli. "Well, hello. Who are you?"

"Eli Hardin." He took her hand and shook it politely. "The neighbor."

"Neighbor, huh?" She glanced at Nora. "Is that what the kids are calling it these days?"

"Mom!"

Eli let go of her hand. "I should get going."

Nora's heart sank, but it was for the best. "Yeah."

"You're coming to the fundraiser on Saturday, right?"

"Wouldn't miss it."

He smiled before kissing her cheek, then waved to Catherine. Nora waited until he'd shut the door behind him before speaking. "Tea?"

"Jasmine?"

"Of course."

Her mom patted her cheek. They headed back to the kitchen, where Nora's bowl of chili was cooling. She set the kettle to boil on the stove and poured her food into a Tupperware container, having lost her appetite the moment she heard her mom's voice. It was almost bizarre how easily they slipped into their old routine. It was as familiar as an old sweater. Her mom hunted down the mugs in her cupboard while Nora poured the tealeaves into the diffuser. They didn't have much in common, but tea was the rebar in their mother-daughter bond.

Once everything was laid out just right, they sat down on her couch with their mugs. Nora tucked her feet under her and inhaled the delicate, soothing aroma of her tea. "I thought you were at a silent yoga retreat."

Her mom threw her hand in the air. "It turned out to be so boring. Nobody talked at all!"

Nora laughed, but just a little. It was still hard to look at this woman and not be angry at the fact she'd cheated on her dad. What happened in their relationship was technically none of Nora's business, but her parents had always treated her like the adult in the family, the one who made dinners and reminded them when she had soccer practice. She'd been their unwilling sounding board whenever they wanted to complain about each other or their marriage, and it was hard to extricate herself from that role now. "I thought that was the point."

"Don't get me wrong, it's great to do yoga without having to listen to a bunch of twenty-two-year-old human Barbies talk about how hungover they are while looking fresh as daisy puke, only to have them whisper at me that my spine isn't straightened properly while I'm doing downward dog. I just didn't realize there'd be no talking after all the yoga. I mean, it's not natural not to talk to anyone for a month. And the worst part was they confiscated my wine bottles." She paused only to take a cleansing breath and sip her tea. "Anyway, I've decided a trip to Italy would be more civilized, and since I have a couple days before my flight, I thought I'd come see you in your new home."

"That sounds like quite an adventure."

"It's the only way to live."

Nora glanced down at the rogue bits of leaves swirling in her tea like they were trying to tell her something—a message in some kind of code she'd never been able to decipher no matter how many thousands of cups of tea she'd consumed in her life. At least, that's something her mom always liked to believe. Nora wondered how it was possible to love someone so much while resenting them so fiercely at the same time. She couldn't forgive her mom for cheating on her dad and breaking up their marriage, but that didn't mean she loved her any less. This was her mom. The person who'd made her homemade buckwheat waffles whenever she'd had a craving, and read her *The Feminine Mystique* as a bedtime story. Catherine's flightiness and itchy feet had caused her family more than enough headaches growing up, but she was also the person who gave Nora the confidence to move out on her own and follow her dreams.

Her mom leaned over and patted Nora on the knee. "So how's life?"

"It's okay. The college here is a lot smaller than my old school, and I miss having all the research infrastructure, but I managed to get some good results the other day, and I'm going to present at a conference in Portland next month."

"I asked about your life, not your job."

Nora's stomach clenched. She tucked her knees up to her chest, feeling like a child. "My job is my life."

"You're so like your dad."

There was no comfort in the awkward silence that followed. Talking about her dad right now was like squeezing into a favorite pair of jeans that no longer fit.

Her mom cleared her throat and looked away. "So, how is your dad?"

"He's...Dad." It was all she could say. He wasn't fine. He wasn't not fine. He was, as far as she could tell, just existing in the only way he could.

Her mom sighed so softly, Nora almost didn't hear it. For a moment, she wondered if her mom was lonely. She was the kind of woman who attracted people like bugs to a lantern on a warm summer night. It was impossible to toss out the name of a city or country, no matter how far across the globe, in casual conversation without her interrupting to tell you about her friend Bobby from Dublin she met at a poetry slam, or Julissa from Johannesburg who loved ceramics. Now she finally had the freedom to travel and explore and do everything she wanted, and yet she seemed...sad.

Nora didn't want to feel sorry for Catherine, but she couldn't help but wonder if living in her dad's shadow for so long—with his constant grumbling about work every time she suggested a family getaway or that they order takeout other than pizza—hadn't rubbed the glow off her dreams.

"I'm sure he's fine," Catherine finally said, as though speaking the words would somehow make them true. "I'm just glad you're here instead of moping around at home with him. It makes me so happy to see you following your dreams and making nice friends, like that handsome neighbor of yours."

"Mom, if you want to fish for information about my love life, you're going to need better bait."

Her mom grinned. "Ah, but you're admitting you do have one."

Nora wrapped her hands more tightly around her mug and thought about Eli. How close she'd been to abandoning all sense when she saw him tonight. And then where would she be? Because no matter how strong their attraction was, they were still too different. She didn't want to end up like her parents—sad and lonely and filled with regret.

"No. No love life at all."

12

"Mom, you forgot to pack your phone charger." Nora held up the white cord.

Catherine frowned. "That's not mine."

Nora rubbed her forehead. "Yes, it is. You just charged your phone with it an hour ago."

Her mom squinted at the charger. "No, I don't think it is."

Nora huffed and shoved it in her mom's bag. "It is."

"Okay." Her mom patted her on the cheek. "You always were so organized."

It took all of her self-control not to get angry, because being organized was one thing. Staying organized while her mom was here was an entirely different battle. Not only had Catherine been attempting to redecorate Nora's house with colorful items she'd found at antique shops, she'd also been pathologically incapable of putting away dishes or clothes, or anything else.

Nora had spent every free minute sweeping and tidying and scrubbing toothpaste out of the bathroom sink. But trying to maintain a basic standard of cleanliness with her mom around wasn't nearly as hard as dancing around the subject of her infidelity. It was too hard not to draw parallels between her failed marriage and her parents'. Too hard not to be angry.

"Hurry up, Mom. We need to leave soon, or we're going to miss your flight."

"My flight's not until seven o'clock."

"Your flight's at four."

"Are you sure?"

Nora's phone rang just as she was about to scream in frustration. She looked at the call display and sighed. Her dad. Exactly what she needed at this moment. She snuck off to her bedroom to answer the call. "Hi, Dad."

"The internet's not working."

"Did you reset the modem?" Five silent seconds ticked by before she spoke again. "The little black box next to the printer in your office."

She talked him through the process, which wasn't helped by his impatience, but eventually she got him through it. She hung up and sat on the edge of her bed, needing a breather before going back out to deal with her mom.

"Was that your dad?" Nora looked up to see her mom standing in the doorway, expression grim. Nora nodded. "He's a grown man. He shouldn't be relying on you for that kind of stuff. You have your own life to live."

"Seriously?" Nora jumped to her feet, fueled by an uncontrollable rush of anger. "You couldn't even remember my birthday when I was kid! You made the choice to walk away from your marriage. You cheated on Dad. And now you want to act like the moral superior in all of this?"

Her mom gasped. "It's a lot more complicated than you think."

"Really, Mom? I'm pretty sure having sex with a visiting scholar in normative ethics is pretty straightforward. You either do it or you don't. You either care about your marriage or not." Nora's hands shook as she spoke, unleashing all the anger and hurt she'd been holding back for the last ten months. She'd never exploded like this before. She'd always treated her mom with kid gloves, but it had been a long week and she didn't have it in her to soften her edges anymore.

Her mom opened her mouth like she was about to protest, but she didn't say anything. She walked into the room, sat down on the bed, and dropped her head into her hands.

"I'm sorry, Mom. I shouldn't have yelled." Nora sat down beside her and rubbed her mom's back. She'd forgotten how fragile her mom was.

Her mom reached for her hand. "No, I'm sorry. You should never have been put in the middle of this. It's not fair to you."

Nora squeezed her mom's hand. "I've always been in the middle."

"Maybe it's time for that to change. The situation with your father and I...it's complicated. We're all still getting used to what it means."

"Do you...do you miss him?"

Her mom paused for so long, Nora wondered if she'd forgotten the question. "Every day, but what you don't understand is that I missed myself just as much."

"Why didn't you try to work it out? Why couldn't you just compromise a little bit? Wouldn't that be better than throwing away your marriage?"

"I know you're angry at me, but our marriage wasn't working. I've put off all my dreams for thirty-five years—thirty-five amazing years, don't get me wrong—then one day I woke up and realized I was nothing but gray hair and regret. I'm old, sweetheart, but I'm still alive. I can't keep forgetting that. I need to follow my dreams before it's too late. Can you understand that?"

Nora's heart seized. "Yes, I can understand that." *All too well.*

Most days, Eli invited a healthy dose of chaos into his life. It was a good way to keep himself on his toes. Keep his mind from wandering to places it shouldn't go. But the days leading up to the SPCA fundraiser had been absolute hell. Not just because of the millions of calls lighting up his phone, or because he had no idea what the heck he was doing and didn't want to let Julia know that when she'd just started to a have a little faith in him. But because he didn't have Nora.

She was the one person who made him feel calm amid the chaos. The last stitch that kept a seam from ripping apart. The one who would know if he'd forgotten to put out the sign-up lists for the blind auction, or remember to have enough napkins around. But she'd been busy with her mom for the last few days, so instead of relying on her, he'd had to trust in his ability to scramble at the last minute and perform under pressure. No matter how hard he worked to get this fundraiser organized, he was pretty certain there would be something he would forget at the last minute. More likely, many somethings. And the event was starting in half an hour.

The SPCA volunteers were setting up in the parking lot while he'd run back inside to the supply room to grab some extra plastic forks and knives, paranoid that the amount he'd ordered might not be enough. Unfortunately, he had no idea where in this bloody supply room the plastic cutlery was.

"Everything okay?"

Eli, neck-deep in the bottom shelf, didn't bother to turn around. He knew Jake's voice better than his own. "Yep, just looking for more cutlery."

"You ordered four hundred sets of plastic forks."

"What if it's not enough?"

"We're only serving hot dogs and hamburgers. Nobody even uses forks to eat hot dogs and hamburgers."

Eli pulled back onto his heels, accidentally banging his head on the metal shelf. He rubbed his head while Jake chuckled. "I just want to be prepared."

"Things are going to be great. Having the event in the parking lot was genius."

A thread of pride wove through Eli's jittery, nerve-wracked limbs. Jake's opinion, along with Julia's, meant everything to Eli. *Nora's, too...*

He ignored that quiet little voice in his head. "Thanks, man." Out of the corner of his eye, he spotted the bright yellow box of cutlery on the bottom shelf a row over and reached for it triumphantly.

"Hey, I know this is a busy time, but there's something important I need to ask you," Jake said as Eli rose to his feet. Jake stood in front of him with a little velvet box in his hands. Inside was a rose gold ring with a deep blue, oval sapphire in the middle, surrounded by tiny, sparkling diamonds on the band.

Eli gasped and clutched his hand to his heart. "Yes! Yes! A million times yes. I never thought this day would come, but it's true. Best friends do make the best marriages!" He wrapped Jake in a massive bear hug. "I think I'll need to get the ring resized to fit my massive hands."

"You're such an ass," Jake muttered into Eli's ear. When Eli let him go, he could see just how nervous Jake was in spite of his attempt to loosen his mood a little. "Honestly, what do you think?"

"I think I don't know the first thing about rings. It looks beautiful to me, but why aren't you asking Clem's sisters about this?"

Jake rolled his eyes. "I did ask them. Chastity and Clover dragged me to the jeweler, pointed at this ring, and threatened to castrate me if I didn't buy it."

From what Eli knew about Clem's sisters, that sounded about right. "So why do you need my opinion?"

Jake's jaw tightened. "I'm not asking your opinion on the ring. I'm asking your opinion on whether I'm doing the right thing. I've already gotten Clem's family's opinion on everything, but they're her people. You're *my* people."

For once, Eli didn't have a joke or sarcastic remark ready. "You love her," he said simply.

Jake nodded. "Of course I do. But I've screwed up an engagement before. What if it's too soon? What if—"

"You love her," Eli said firmly. "She loves you. I've never known two people more right for each other. You're only feeling nervous because this is the best thing that's ever happened to you. It's normal to feel nervous. But I know Clem, and I know that it doesn't matter how you propose or whether the ring is perfect, because she loves you. And you love her. Some things are simple."

Jake's shoulders loosened, like the tension had unspooled from his body. He gave the ring one last glance before snapping the box shut and sticking it in his pocket. "Thanks, Eli. I mean it."

"Anytime. As long as I get to give the best man speech," Eli said. "I've been saving that story about you dancing naked at that toga party in college for years."

Jake groaned, but his smile was back. "You know I'll get the same revenge on you one day."

"Not a chance. A wild horse can't be tamed," Eli said, but his stomach lurched and in that moment, he'd never hated himself more. The only thing a real friend would be feeling right now was pure happiness, but a sticky, nauseating jealousy had slid beneath his skin, covering him like an oil slick.

Jake shook his head as he turned to leave. "One day, man. I'm telling you, one day."

Eli had never considered the idea of marriage—not because he was against it on principle, but because he'd been so busy working toward his dream of opening the Holy Grale it had never crossed his radar. Plus, there'd never been a woman who made him think of the future. Until Nora.

And she didn't want him.

For the last few weeks, he'd been spending so much time with her, she was as regular a part of his life as breathing. They'd blasted through hours of *The Red Zephyr* on Netflix. Shared dinners almost every night he wasn't working at the Grale. Even worked through the details of tonight's event. As friends. She was a great friend—selfless, kind, and funny. But that would never be enough. He wasn't falling for her. He'd already fallen, like a skydiver without a parachute, and if something didn't change quickly, there was only one way for this to end.

As much as Nora was grateful to have her own space again, she was sad to see her mom go. She'd missed her these last few months. Not that she ever got to see her more than a few times a year, but the resentment she'd had about her mom's role in her parents' separation had added an extra layer of distance. It was good to remember that, for all her kookiness and short attention span, her mom still loved Nora fiercely. She couldn't imagine how hard it was for Eli and Julia to have lost their mom when they did.

Eli. Her heart still did that little stutter step when she thought about him. God, it would be so much easier if she could figure out how to make that go away.

Half the parking lot was covered with a white tent when she arrived at the Holy Grale, so she'd had to park on the street over a block away. But it was worth it. Eli had done a spectacular job. There was a grill and long table full of buns, plates, and condiments near the entrance. Next to that were four huge cages with a handful of people around peering inside. Music blared in the background, kicking up the energy. She didn't even stop to look for Eli after she paid her five-dollar admission fee. Her heart was already completely and utterly fixated on a new object of obsession.

A woman in a bright blue polo shirt opened the cage and pulled out a gray kitten with tiny white paws. "This is Mittens. He was found wandering in a state park all alone two months ago, and no one's come to claim him. Do you want to hold him?"

Nora grinned. "Yes!"

The kitten's fur felt like the softest blanket as he squirmed in her hands, and Nora's heart melted like warm butter. She cooed and petted the little guy as he tried to crawl up her neck.

"You know," the SPCA volunteer said, "he is available for adoption. In fact, all the animals here are ready for new, loving homes."

Nora sighed. "I wish I could, but I'm not allowed pets in my rental." Still, she found it really hard to hand the little guy back to the volunteer. With regret making her arms unnaturally heavy, she passed him over and—

"Puuuuuppiiiiiieeees!"

Nora nearly fell over as two identical blond children flew past her and pressed their faces right against the bottom cage. The volunteer seemed to take it in stride, not even losing her balance as she wrangled the kitten and the kids.

"Girls! We are not getting a puppy!" Nora turned to see Clover looking panicked and running toward the cages.

"I'm calling him Jimmy," one of the girls said.

"No! Her name's Princess SparkleButt," the other said, struggling against her sister for a better view.

Clover tried to pull the girls back, but they clutched the metal wires like their little fingers were handcuffs. Finally, she gave up and sighed. "Oh, hi, Nora."

"These are your girls?" Nora said, too shell-shocked by the whirlwind of action to do anything but state the obvious.

Clover brushed a strand of curly blond hair off her face. "Some days, I'm pretty sure they belong to Satan, but yeah, these are Ellie and Millie."

The girls turned and preened. "Our teacher calls us Little Hellions."

"It's a term of endearment, honey," Clover said with a grimace. "Have you been inside yet? There's a spa trip up for auction that I really want to win, but my mom keeps outbidding me."

Nora laughed. "I guess I'll have to check it out for myself."

She left Clover to pry her girls from the animals, which seemed like a lost cause once the volunteer released the slobbering bulldog for them to pet. After stopping to wash her hands in the bathroom, she explored the silent auction. The spa trip did look appealing, but she liked Clover and didn't want to add to the competition. Plus, after taking care of those kids, Clover deserved it. Instead, Nora wrote her bid down for a beautiful watercolor painting from a local artist.

"Good choice. I painted that myself."

Nora turned at the sound of Eli's voice. "No you didn't. It says right here that Vince Regenery painted it."

"And maybe Eli's not my real name after all." He grinned and she gave him a playful shove. "Okay, fine. I didn't paint it, but I did ask the artist to donate something for the auction. That counts a little, right?"

She laughed. "Sure. Maybe. Either way, you've done a really great job tonight."

His shoulders straightened, and his expression sobered. "Thank you. I couldn't have done it without you."

"Yeah, you could have. You just needed a nudge in the right direction, but the ideas and work were all yours."

He ran his hand against the back of his neck, like he was nervous. It was so odd to see him that way. A part of her wanted to pull him into a hug, but the other part of her knew it wasn't the time or place for that. He had things under control. A little nerves weren't a problem.

"Hey, did you get your free hotdog yet?"

She grimaced. "I'm not hungry."

"Yes, you are. You just don't like eating mass-produced factory foods from a giant shared grill, or using condiment bottles that other people have used."

Her cheeks flushed. "Do you have any idea what goes into a hotdog?"

"Unicorn farts, magical deliciousness, and unnamed animal by-products. But you're not having just any old hotdog. Come on." He took her by the wrist and led her outside.

Any fear of crusty condiment bottles and heavily processed animal by-products faded to the back of her mind at his touch. His fingertips against her wrist felt like a brand. He'd been so respectful of her space and wishes, but she could barely manage to do the same.

In that heartbreaking moment, she realized that these last four days apart weren't enough to quell the desire she had for him. She was going to need even more distance from him if she had any hope of keeping their friendship true. And, God, that sucked.

He led her to the barbecue. Jake, wearing dark aviator shades, was manning the immaculate grill. He looked up at her and gave a quick wave. "Hi, Nora, good to see you again."

"You, too," she answered. She hadn't gotten to know Jake much when he was still living with Eli, but he'd always been friendly and polite, and seemed to have a calming influence on his friend.

"See?" Eli pointed to the grill. "That spot on the upper right corner has not been touched by anything yet."

She had to admit, the grill was meticulously clean and the food smelled delicious, but she wasn't comfortable with picking a wiener or patty from the stacks in the giant aluminum tray countless other people had probably reached into with their bare hands or coughed on.

With a shudder, she snuck her little container of hand sanitizer from her purse and rubbed some between her palms. "It looks great, but I'm really not hungry."

He raised his eyebrows, seeing right through her. "You say that now, but you haven't seen this yet." He bent down to the cooler near Jake's feet and took out a small package wrapped in brown paper.

"What is that?"

"Organic, antibiotic-free turkey dogs with no unnamed animal by-products. But it definitely has some magical deliciousness."

Nora laughed. "Okay. Magical, organic turkey dogs. I'm impressed with the level of quality you're putting out here for a fundraiser."

Eli shook his head. "Nah, everyone else is getting no-name, super-value pack wieners with all the additives and animal by-products. This one's just for you."

"For me?" Her throat was tight and her sudden frown made her regret tying her hair back into such a tight ponytail.

"Of course, for you. Assuming you've got your appetite back."

It was such a sweet gesture, she didn't know what to say. No one had ever been so patient with her. So accepting. In the short time she'd known him, he'd gone from her worst nightmare to the person who made her feel like a queen. And it scared her. "Yes, please."

A few minutes later, she had a fresh bun filled with a delicious turkey dog topped with ketchup and mustard that came from little white individual packets. Sadly, she'd had to forgo the sauerkraut because it was only available from a large communal jar.

"Hey, Nora!" Julia, standing with Clem, Lisa, and Lorenzo, was waving to her from across the lot.

"Looks like you're being summoned," Eli said. "Go on, but we need to talk later. Okay?"

She nodded, unsure what was so important that they needed to talk about but too distracted by Julia's increasingly eager hand gestures to ask. With a small wave to Jake and Eli, she made her way over to her friends with a ridiculously large smile on her face.

The next couple hours passed in a flurry of laughter, good conversation, and more than a little bit of spying on the silent auction. She didn't get the chance to see much of Eli, other than occasional glimpses of him running around and chatting with the SPCA volunteers. And aside from one incident where Clem's nieces accidentally let a guinea pig loose, the event had gone off without a hitch. Luckily, Nutmeg didn't make it very far in her escape attempt before Eli and one of the volunteers managed to collect her in an expertly rigged trap out of a cardboard box and some string.

By the end of it all, Nora didn't really want to leave, but she still had a stack of lab reports waiting for her back home to grade. But she couldn't leave without one last visit to Mittens.

"You're petting that kitten like you're getting ideas," Julia said.

"He's just so soft and sweet," she said with a sigh as Mittens batted at her hair.

"You know, you could say the same thing about my brother."

Nora flattened her lips into a hard line. Julia hadn't pried much into her relationship with Eli before now. "He's a good man."

"I know that. I just wanted to make sure you knew that. The two of you have been spending a lot of time together lately."

Mittens purred and stretched as Nora scratched gently behind his whiskers. Until her mom's impromptu visit, she hadn't realized how dependent she'd come to be on Eli. Casual dinners after work. Netflix marathons. "I care about your brother. A lot. But none of that changes the fact we're not the kind of people who would work out in the long run. We're too different."

"Different isn't always bad. Sometimes, opposites bring out the best in each other."

God, she wanted to believe that. Eli did make her feel calm and special and safe. But her parents had been madly in love once. "And sometimes they destroy each other."

Julia's eyes widened, but she wasn't looking at Nora. "Oh shit."

Nora turned to see Eli behind her, anger flaring in his brown eyes. "That's what you think of me? After all this time, you think I'm going to destroy you?"

He stormed off before her shock had worn off.

"I should go after him," Julia said.

Nora put her arm out to stop her. "No. I will."

She handed Mittens back to SPCA worker and ran after him. She caught up to him just before he stepped into the brewery room. "Eli, wait."

He stopped with his hand on the door. The muscles in his back and shoulders tensed beneath his T-shirt.

"I didn't mean that. Not the way you think."

"How did you mean it?" He didn't turn around, but the low growl of his voice left no doubt about his expression.

"I…" She didn't know what to say. Didn't really know how to defend herself.

He pushed open the door and shut it behind him.

Panic tightened her throat. She wasn't good at confrontations. She didn't know how to make Eli understand. But she couldn't just leave him like this.

She cracked open the door and followed him inside. "Eli, I'm sorry."

He rubbed his forehead, not meeting her eyes. "I know you are. I am, too."

"What do you mean?"

He walked toward her and slid his hand behind her neck, drawing their foreheads together. "I thought I could do this. I thought I could be the guy who understood when you said you wanted to just be friends, but I'm not. I can't do it, Nora. I can't just be your friend when I'm falling for you. It hurts too fucking much."

His breath was warm against her skin. She squeezed her eyes shut. "What are you saying?"

"I'm done. No more cuddling on your couch. No more wondering how your day went. No more going to bed wishing you were with me. I know it makes me an asshole who doesn't understand the word no, but if I can't be with you as your lover, I can't be with you at all. At least not right now. Not until it stops feeling like I've been stabbed in the gut every time I look at you."

Hot, sticky tears slipped down her cheeks. She wanted to scream. Beg him to change his mind. But how could she without making it worse?

He kissed her forehead and let her go, turning his back to her once more. "Just go. Please."

His whispered words were so strong, so certain, they sliced right through her heart. She wiped her cheeks with the back of her hand. All she'd wanted was to keep their misguided romance from tearing them apart, but now she'd lost him anyway.

13

"*D*eath cannot stop true love," Nora mumbled along to her television before shoving another scoop of Chocolate Cherry Garcia in her mouth.

Her phone buzzed and she paused the movie long enough to type a quick *I'm fine* into her phone.

You're watching The Princess Bride *again, aren't you?*

Nora ignored Alice's text, threw her phone onto the couch, and turned the movie back on. Her friends seemed to have a sixth sense for when she was moping in front of the TV watching her favorite movie.

The truth was she had been watching her favorite comfort movie a little more than normal this past week, but tonight she'd only cried at the legitimately sad parts instead of throughout the whole thing. That was progress, as far as she was concerned. Alice and Jessie had been there for her, but lately it felt like the phone calls and texts weren't enough. She wanted them on the couch with her. She wanted to be back home in Toronto. She'd given Shadow Creek a chance, and even though she was just starting to find her place, she'd gone and screwed that up. Maybe she needed to finally accept that coming out here was a failed experiment.

She set down her bowl of ice cream on top of a coaster and picked up the Pringles can.

Empty. Dammit.

Her phone buzzed again, but this time the vibration signaled an email coming through, rather than a text. There was a time in her life that her career was so busy, she would wake to at least a hundred emails every morning, but since moving to Shadow Creek, she rarely got any after five p.m.

She pulled up the email on her phone and sat up straighter. It was from Dr. Lo, the professor she'd studied under for her PhD. It had been ages since Nora had heard from her, but it was the subject line that caught her attention.

Job opportunity for you.

Nora's stomach clenched as she cradled her cell phone like it was a bomb about to go off. Dr. Lo hadn't even bothered with the usual pleasantries—not that Nora blamed her. It had to be a bit of a disappointment that one of her top students had landed a coveted tenure-track position at a top research university, only to wind up at a college in the middle of nowhere that had more coffee kiosks than lab space. Instead, the email jumped right into the job description.

Chief scientific officer for a startup company developing novel materials for green energy applications—in Toronto.

Nora rubbed her temples. This was amazing and terrible all at the same time. It wasn't an academic job, but it was one that would bring her back home.

Following in her parents' footsteps and becoming a professor had been her dream from the time she got her own microscope as a present for her fourth birthday. Sure, teaching had its drawbacks, but once in a while she was able to inspire a student. And as frustrating as it was to write grant proposal after grant proposal, she loved running her own lab and designing her own projects. If she went to work for someone else, she'd lose all that control.

But you'd be home.

Her doorbell rang and she jerked back with a start.

Eli was the only person who came to her door. Without stopping to think, she ran to open it. If he was here, maybe he'd forgiven her. Maybe—

"Clem?" Nora stared blankly at the unexpected face on the other side of her door. "What are you doing here?"

"It's October 22nd," the woman said simply as she reached for Nora's arm.

"What?"

Clem gave her a gentle tug. "*The Red Zephyr* night. The season finale of the fourth season. You were supposed to catch up on the episodes and come to our viewing parties. Tonight's the last one, and you can't miss it."

"But—"

"But what? Julia's waiting in the car and you know she doesn't like to be late."

Nora hesitated. After her fight with Eli, she didn't think she'd ever see Clem and Julia again. But she couldn't bring herself to say that out loud. "I haven't finished catching up on the episodes."

"Then you're going to have to deal with spoilers, because everyone's at my place waiting for you, and you have no idea how hard it is for me to come up here to your door."

Nora frowned. "Because you don't want me to come?"

"No, of course I want you to come. Everyone wants you to come. I meant because I literally had to come up to your door. I wouldn't do that for just anyone." Clem shivered. "So let's get going."

Julia honked from the car and waved.

"We're not taking no for an answer," Clem said.

"Okay," Nora answered, realizing that Eli wouldn't be there if Nora was still invited. The last thing she wanted was to push him away from his friends, but it would make the evening a little less awkward if she didn't have to deal with him. "I'll grab my coat."

It was a short drive over to Clem's place. Unlike the classic sixties bungalows lining Nora's street, Clem's house was a beautiful old craftsman just around the corner from the Holy Grale, with a stately porch and huge elm trees along the yard.

The inside was just as beautiful, with original moldings and hardwood floors. Nora had always appreciated the beauty of houses like this, but could never live in one. She needed the clean, square lines found in her simple home. The kind where dust couldn't hide.

Clem's front living room was filled with people already. Her sisters were there with their husbands, who, to Nora's surprise, were identical twins. Lisa and Lorenzo were chatting amiably on the couch, briefly stopping their conversation to say hi. Jake was laying out snacks on the coffee table.

No one else was here. Nora let out a breath, unclenching her stomach, finally relaxing. A part of her desperately hoped Eli would be here so they could make things right, but the other, bigger part of her was too afraid to confront him. Too afraid of what he would say when she tried to apologize again.

"Who needs a drink?" Clem asked.

Half the people in the room raised their hands or shouted requests.

"I'll help," Nora offered, wanting to be polite, but also secretly wanting to check out Clem's kitchen to make sure it was clean before she dove into the snacks on the coffee table. Nora followed her through the heavy old door off the living room and froze.

Eli was there, dumping a bag of Cool Ranch Doritos into a bowl. "Hey, Clem. Nora."

His voice was so impassive, she didn't know what to say. There wasn't a hint of emotion—happy, sad or angry—to go by.

She swallowed the lump in her throat. "Hi, Eli."

She wanted to ask him if he wanted her to leave, but he picked up the bowl and walked past her into the living room without another word. Like her presence was so insignificant, he didn't even care.

For the next two hours, Nora tried to follow along with the story on the large flat-screen TV, but found herself sneaking so many glances at Eli that she eventually gave up trying to follow the plot. He didn't look at her. Not once.

And the worst part was, this was what she'd wanted. She was the one who wanted distance. To be able to hang out like this with their now mutual friends without it being awkward. He was respecting her wishes still. She just didn't expect it to suck so much.

By the end of the show, everyone around her was abuzz with excitement, talking about the plot twists and surprise ending. Nora tried to play along and act excited, but her heart wasn't in it. She was tired and ready to go home.

"Hey, Eli," Julia called out as she was slinging on her coat. "Can you give Nora a ride home?"

He met Nora's eyes for the first time all evening, and she felt like her heart was going to explode. "Sorry. I'm heading straight to the Holy Grale after this. But I'll see you around."

"Yeah, sure," she said as bravely as she could. "See you around."

"So while the results are still premin...preimin..." Nora took a deep breath and willed her brain to remember the word she'd said out loud a million times before. If she was going to deliver this conference presentation in the ten measly minutes allotted to her, she couldn't trip up over simple words. "Preliminary."

She gave herself a quick thumbs-up in the full-length mirror of her closet door and continued running through her slides. When she reached the final acknowledgement slide, she checked the timer. Twelve minutes and thirteen seconds.

Shoot. She rubbed her forehead and steeled herself to do her tenth run-through of the evening. The conference presentation was still a week away, but she wanted to be prepared. Plus, it wasn't like she had anything else to do on a Friday night anymore except shave off two more minutes from her presentation. She reset her PowerPoint to the beginning slide and set the time on her phone. "Thank you for that lovely introduction, and to my colleagues for their excellent presentations. I'm Dr. Nora Pitts and—"

Her doorbell rang. Excitement flickered in her belly. She was smart enough to know it wasn't Eli, but the only other people to ring her doorbell lately were Julia and Clem, and right now she could use a little cheering up. She shut her laptop and made her way to the front door, but her excitement disappeared the moment she opened it.

It wasn't Eli, and it wasn't Julia or Clem, or anyone else she wanted to see either.

"Well, are you going to let us in?" Gemma dangled a bottle of merlot from her hand like Nora was a puppy being offered a dog treat.

"What are you doing here?" she stammered.

"Book club," Rose, who was standing next to Gemma, said with an exaggerated roll of the eyes. "We're reading The Fountainhead, remember?"

Nora shuddered. Annie, who was standing behind Gemma and Rose did the same. "I told you I'm no longer interested in being part of this book club."

"Oh, come on," Gemma said, stepping into the small foyer. "It's not like you're doing anything else on a Friday night. I'm sure you can whip up something tasty. Don't you have frozen hors d'oeuvres in freezer just in case?"

Nora winced, just long enough for Rose and Annie to follow Gemma inside. "Wait."

When Gemma gave no sign of listening, Nora stuck out her arm to block her. She'd never done something so bold.

"I'm not hosting book club," she said once more, articulating every word in the commanding voice she normally reserved for her lectures. "All you've done from the moment we met was take advantage of my hospitality when it suited you, and treat me like dirt when it didn't."

"You can't possibly be that sensitive," Rose said, though a hint of doubt had softened the normal bite in her tone. "We're doing you a favor. It's not like you have anything else to do tonight. We thought you'd like the company."

It was Nora's turn to roll her eyes. For months, she'd been desperate for these women to like her. Now, she didn't care. Maybe she didn't have the easiest time making friends, but at least she finally knew she deserved more than whatever crumbs they were willing to throw at her. "You thought wrong. Please leave."

"You heard her. You're not welcome here, so go."

Nora's head whipped up at the sound of Eli's voice behind the women. He pushed his way between Gemma and Rose, and set his hand on Nora's shoulder. She was too shocked to say or do anything but stand there like a gargoyle. But despite her frozen exterior, every inch of Nora's skin felt like a lightning rod, crackling with electricity. She was hyperaware of Eli's touch. What the heck was he even doing here?

Rose scoffed and trotted down the porch steps. Gemma smirked before following.

Annie hesitated. She glanced to the red sports car the other women were climbing into before turning back to Nora. "Hey, I'm sorry. I know we haven't been great friends to you and I told Gemma and Rose we shouldn't have come, but they were kind of insistent."

Nora nodded. "Thanks."

Annie offered a tentative smile. "Maybe I'll see you around."

"Maybe."

Eli slammed the door before Nora could say anything else. The instant the women were out of sight, his hand left her shoulder.

"I had that under control," Nora whispered, scared to look at him. Scared that if she did, he would disappear like a figment of her imagination.

"I know."

She finally looked up at him, but his gaze was fixed on the door behind her, as though he were too scared to meet her eyes.

She inhaled deeply. "Then why are you here?"

"I just... I don't like the way they treat you. No matter what's going on with us, I don't want you to forget that."

Emotion welled in her throat. She reached her hand toward his chest. "Eli—"

He stepped back and shook his head. "Where's your phone?"

"What?"

"Your phone," he repeated.

"On the counter," she answered, as confused as ever.

He walked into kitchen and picked up her phone. "Passcode?"

He held the phone out for her to tap in the four digits to unlock the screen. She frowned but complied, then handed it back to him. "Is something wrong?"

He shook his head, but didn't say anything else. Instead, he typed quickly, occasionally pausing to bite his lip. Finally, he handed the phone back. "Here."

An image of a smiling couple with their foreheads pressed together against a teal backdrop appeared on the screen, the words *Summer of Love* written at the top in bright, looping script. "This is a book."

He nodded. "The book you're supposed to be reading for the Books and Brews meeting Sunday night. Julia said you told her you weren't coming."

Nora sighed. She'd told Julia she couldn't make it to the next meeting, claiming she needed to prepare for her conference next week. But that had been nothing but a convenient excuse. She couldn't bring herself to walk back into the Holy Grale when he didn't want her there.

And now he was here, acting like he knew what was best for her when he'd barely spoken a word to her in the last week. A thread of annoyance pierced through all the other emotions swirling inside her. "So you decided to one-click the book on my account?"

"It was three bucks. I'll pay you back, as long as you go to the meeting."

Her shoulders sagged, suddenly feeling too heavy for her body. She reached her hand toward him, wanting to feel him again. Wanting to erase all the anger and hurt between them. "Eli—"

He backed away before her fingers made contact. "I should go."

She dropped her hand, disappointment burning like acid in her lungs. "You don't have to."

He raked his hand through his hair. "Yeah, I do. Things aren't right between us and maybe they'll never be. But that shouldn't keep you from the book club. I don't want to be the reason you lose out on those friendships. Please?"

It was the please that broke her. He still cared about her, in spite of how she'd hurt him, and she didn't know how to make things right. What if she never could? Tears prickled her eyes. "Okay."

"Sunday, then."

"Sunday."

He turned and walked out of her house, and even though she wanted to chase after him and beg him to forgive her, she let him go.

Nora drove past the parking lot entrance of the Holy Grale three times before she finally pulled in. Partly because she'd arrived seventeen minutes early thanks to a nervous overreaction to her fear of being late, but mostly because she still hadn't built up the courage to come back here. Even though she'd gotten to know everyone at the book club, and considered them friends, that had been before things had gone so sour with Eli. She wasn't sure they would welcome her back now.

How had she managed to ruin everything again?

Her stomach danced with nerves as she stepped out of her car and walked along the parking lot. It had been so much easier last time when Eli was here with her, filling her with confidence while he escorted her in. Heat colored her cheeks at the memory of the way he'd managed to make her feel calm.

She tried to switch her thoughts to the book as she stepped inside the Grale. The book had been more intense than the cover suggested. An angst-filled second chance romance about a couple rebuilding a life together after breaking each other's hearts. It had been hard to read, even painful at times, but the exquisite ending had made the journey worth every moment of that stomach churning angst.

The Grale was busy as usual, but not so crowded that she couldn't see through to the bar. Eli wasn't there. Maybe he was in the back, hiding out with his machines. It's what she would do.

She'd seen him last night when she was coming home with an armful of groceries, he was outside talking with Mr. Budd, the guy two doors down who liked to water his plants in his housecoat.

Whether he wore anything beneath that housecoat had been a rather entertaining source of neighborhood gossip.

But she hadn't been worried about what Mr. Budd was or wasn't hiding beneath those frayed terrycloth edges when she'd seen them. All she could see was Eli, looking handsome and relaxed and completely indifferent to her. She'd tripped on the sidewalk and managed to split open her paper bag, sending her fresh Honeycrisp apples spilling everywhere. Mr. Budd had jogged over to help her, revealing the fact he absolutely did not have anything underneath, but Eli had just...ignored her. He walked to his car with only the briefest nod in her direction to acknowledge her presence and drove off. She'd grown so used to him being her hero over the last few weeks that not having him there to rely on felt like a stab in the heart.

But this is what she'd asked for, wasn't it? She wanted to focus on building friendships, not the kind of romantic relationship that could break her heart all over again.

Too late.

She straightened her back and told herself to stop being so silly as she climbed the stairs to the mezzanine. Her faked confidence lasted just long enough to get to the doorway of the room where the book club met. She hesitated again, but the door swung open before she could change her mind.

"Nora!" Julia's smiling face greeted her on the other side. "You made it!"

"Hi," she answered weakly.

Julia slipped her arm through Nora's and drew her inside. In a low whisper, she said, "I'm only going to say this once. You're part of this club, no matter what's happening between you and Eli. We take care of our own. And if you still have doubts, just know that Eli made sure to give me the same speech this week."

Nora's jaw dropped, though really, she shouldn't have been surprised. He'd been taking care of her from the moment they went on their first date. She took her seat at the table and realized a glass of red wine was waiting for her at her spot.

"Great. Now we can get started," Clem said with a grin. She picked up her copy of the book and held it to her chest like a hug. "How did this book make you feel?"

By the time Nora arrived home from the Books and Brews meeting, she'd actually managed to distract herself from her lingering worries about her conference presentation, the job offer in Toronto she still hadn't responded to, and Eli. For two hours, she'd done nothing but talk about a heartbreakingly gorgeous romance novel with people who understood exactly why she'd devoured it in less than a day, only to flip back to the first page and start it all over again. It wasn't just the characters or the passionate love scenes that hooked her. It was the hope that filled every page, in spite of the obstacles thrown at the couple. Nora had needed a little hope right now.

She couldn't help glancing at Eli's house as she walked up her front steps. The lights were out. Julia had said he wasn't at the Holy Grale, and it didn't look like he was home.

Maybe he's on a date.

She didn't know where the thought came from but it felt like a stab in the gut.

You have no right to feel that way, she reminded herself. If she were a real friend, she would be happy for him to move on.

But you don't want to be just friends with him. She sat down on her step and dropped her head into her hands. Why was it so hard to figure out what she wanted?

The sound of a power saw made her head pop up. She jumped up raced along the path leading to her backyard. Eli was in his yard, noise-cancelling headphones on, as he sliced the saw through a block of wood.

She watched him working for a minute, captivated by the way his biceps flexed with his precise movements and the look of determination on his face, before she remembered he'd probably hate it if he knew she was spying on him. With a sharp jab of regret, she backed slowly toward her door, hoping to sneak back inside without being noticed.

His eyes caught hers the instant she took a step backward, like he'd known she was there watching him this entire time.

He pulled off his goggles and noise-cancelling headphones. "Am I bothering you?"

She searched his face for any trace of emotion. Any hint of reaction to her presence. He was like a blank wall, giving nothing away. "No, I was just…curious."

"Don't worry, I'm not renovating anymore. I'm just finishing up this bench and then I'm done."

"Bench?"

He nodded slowly, then motioned behind him to where a half-finished bench sat on the grass behind his work table.

It was a simple bench with a natural-edge back, and though the actual seat was still missing, it looked completely inviting. "It's beautiful."

"Thanks," he said gruffly. For a moment, she thought she'd said too much, but then he added, "I'm making it for my mom. There's a program with the city that lets you donate benches in Heartwood Park in someone's memory."

"That's so wonderful." She wanted to reach for him, but the chain link fence felt like an ocean between them.

He laughed, but there was no humor in it. "It was Julia's idea. Not mine. I'm just the grunt worker."

"But you're building it and that matters—"

"No, it doesn't," he bit out harshly. He walked over to her and set his hands just outside of hers, making her pulse jump. "I don't get to take credit for building things. All I do is destroy, remember?"

"Eli." She reached her hand to his, trying to let her touch say what she kept bungling with her words. His brows furrowed, and for a moment, she thought she was getting through to him. That he would let her explain how she hadn't meant to hurt him. That she missed him.

But he jerked his hand away. "Save it."

He walked back to his worktable, and she tried desperately to snatch the right words out of her brain before it was too late.

"I'm sorry," she called. "I didn't mean it and—"

It didn't matter. He'd already put his noise-cancelling headphones back on.

14

"It's perfect!" Julia ran her hands over the smooth edges of the bench and smiled. After a long day sanding and staining the wood, Eli finally finished the bench just in time for tomorrow's ceremony. This was a lot better than the reaction he'd gotten to the memory book with the photos from their childhood he'd shown her earlier. His sister had hugged him with tears in her eyes, only to harass him two seconds later about whether he'd made sure to track which album the photos came from so they could put them back in perfect order. He'd managed to reassure her that he'd labeled the back of each picture in pencil, but it had hurt more than he wanted to admit when she'd asked him if Nora had helped him figure out how to do that. Because she still didn't trust him.

"It had better be. I broke my nail sanding this thing down." He tried not to let his annoyance show. It wasn't his sister's fault he was in a sour mood. Hell, it wasn't even her fault she was the one to come up with the idea of making a bench. She was always thinking of the right thing to do. The special touches. The logical course of action. He was the screw-up who still hadn't come up with any genuine contribution to the ceremony.

Julia smacked him in the chest. "Be serious."

"Okay, fine," Eli conceded, holding up his hand and showing off his short, ragged nails that had been ravaged from years of working in the brewery and a tendency to act like an overanxious squirrel when he was stressed. "I won't make you pay for my emergency pedicure."

She rolled her eyes. "Manicure. And I should take you for one. Your nails are disgusting."

"How about you buy me a new hand sander instead?"

"Let me see a copy of your speech first, and then we'll see."

He leaned back against the vinyl siding of his house and raised his eyebrows. "What speech?"

She stopped petting the wood and looked up at him. "The speech. The ceremony is tomorrow and you're supposed to give a speech!"

"Julia," he said as calmly as he could. "You told me months ago not to write a speech because you had that covered."

"Because I thought you weren't going to take this whole thing seriously." She groaned and began pacing, which, in any other circumstance would have been amusing with her spiky heels sinking into the grass. But it wasn't funny. It was pissing him off that she was tearing up the lawn he'd worked hard to maintain.

He ran his hand through his hair and took a deep, rough breath. "I *am* taking it seriously."

His patience was stretched so thin, it could snap from a gust of wind, but he was trying to hold it together. Her frustration wasn't just about the stress of the event. It was about stress of the last ten years trying to hold everything together. She'd been a teenager when their mom died. The insurance money had taken care of them financially, but she hadn't had anyone there for her emotionally. Eli had been in a different city, mired in his own emotional tailspin while she'd had to figure out how to put the house up for sale, how to rent an apartment and do her own taxes, and every other complicated thing life threw at her. All of it on her own, because he'd been too self-absorbed to realize she needed help. And in the end, she didn't really need his help. She'd learned it all on her own.

"I know you're taking it seriously now. That's why I thought you were preparing a speech. I didn't think I had to tell you that."

He walked over to her and put his hands on her shoulders, squeezing her reassuringly while still giving her space to breathe. "I'll write something tonight. It will be fine. I do my best work under pressure. You know that."

She blew a strand of her usually perfectly styled hair off her round face. "Okay. Thank you. Oh, and don't talk about that trip to Tijuana when I was seven. I'm already bringing that up."

He smiled, trying to make it seem genuine. "No problem."

She hugged him, burying her face in his chest. "I'm sorry I'm being hard on you. I just...I miss her so much. I want this to be perfect."

His throat felt suddenly raw and painful. "I know. It will be."

Eli had been confident when he'd reassured Julia that he would get a speech done, but it turned out to be another case of him jumping head first into something he couldn't pull off. Every time he set his pen to paper, the words that came out were so hollow, he couldn't imagine bringing himself to read them out loud in front of a small crowd of his friends. Nothing sounded right.

Mom was a special woman...

He balled up the page and threw it across the room. He'd be better off just stealing a bunch of lines from a Hallmark card.

He closed his eyes and thought about the memories that had surfaced when he'd gone through the photo albums. Most of the photos weren't even of her. There were hundreds of him and Julia. The only solo photo of his mom had been a blurry one of her wearing a big artist's smock covered in paint. She'd signed up to take an art class. He must have been about twelve at the time, and he remembered that strange feeling of realizing for the first time his mom had an interest that didn't directly revolve around him or Julia. He hadn't been sure what to make of it at the time, but he knew he resented having to babysit Julia when he wanted to be hanging out with his friends. One night, he'd gotten into a fight with his sister when she stole his Game Boy. He'd called her some mean names, and she'd yelled back that she could do whatever she wanted because Mom had secretly left her in charge since he was too immature to babysit. He knew instantly she wasn't lying, and it had made him explode in anger. He ran off to a local park, and was picked up by the cops a few hours later. His mom had been frantic and stopped going to her lessons.

His eyes burned with the stinging threat of tears. He'd been such a shitty kid back then. But the worst part was, he hadn't changed. Not really. He was still so self-centered, he couldn't even write a damn speech to honor his mom because it hurt too much. He was the reason his mom was dead, and he couldn't even do this one thing for her.

Nora was right. He destroyed everything.

He swiped his arm across the table, knocking the pad of paper, along with the cup of coffee he'd been nursing, onto the floor. The mug landed with a clatter, breaking into a million pieces on the floor and splattering brown liquid everywhere. So many emotions surged through his body, he could barely breathe. He stood up and threw his chair into the wall, but it wasn't enough. He suddenly needed to tear down everything in this house.

Adrenaline pounded so hard in his veins, he couldn't see straight. He was the reason his mom was dead and now he was having a goddamn temper tantrum.

"Get yourself together," he mumbled, as if saying that out loud would force his mind and body to comply. He had to close his eyes and count to fifty before he had calmed down enough to open them again.

He ran his hand through his hair and looked around at the mess. There was a fist-sized hole in the drywall from where the chair had made contact. A pool of coffee was seeping into the seams of his wood floors, and bits of jagged white ceramic were everywhere. He swore out loud and grabbed a dishcloth from the drawer next to his stove. He wiped up the mess and gathered the pieces of broken ceramic into a pile.

"Dammit!" He looked at his hand and saw a thick drop of blood spilling out from a small slice on his palm. What the hell was he doing? He could break everything in his house and every last bone in his body, and it wouldn't help. He needed an entirely different kind of self-destruction.

15

"*H*ave you gone to see a dentist yet?" Nora rolled over in bed and fumbled to turn on her lamp.

"I'm not going to give my money to some hack who'll overcharge me for a bunch of stuff I don't need."

She sighed and rolled out of bed, accepting the fact she wasn't going to be getting back to sleep anytime soon. If her dad was calling her in the middle of the night about a painful tooth, it was probably ten times worse than he was letting on. "You have insurance."

"I'm not going to the dentist. I don't have time. Just tell me what that stuff your mom used to give you is called."

"She gave me a sugar placebo because she doesn't believe in supporting the pharmaceutical industrial complex." She pulled on her robe and headed to the kitchen. "If you have an infected tooth, there's no drug that will help with the pain. You need a root canal. Even Mom would tell you that."

The silence that followed was so painful, Nora had to hold her breath. She wasn't even certain her dad was still on the line until he finally spoke again. "Have you talked to your mom lately?"

Nora pressed her palm against her forehead, wishing this conversation were just a dream. "She was just here for a quick visit before she flew to Italy."

Her dad's heavy exhalation filled the receiver. "I miss her."

It was Nora's turn to not know what to say in that moment. She turned on the kettle and hunted in her drawer for some chamomile tea while searching for her next words. "Do you regret marrying her?"

It was a stupid question, but after everything that had happened with Eli, she needed to hear she wasn't making a terrible decision in pushing him away.

"Never," her dad said swiftly. "I loved her. I know we didn't fit together, but not marrying her would have hurt even more. Plus, I wouldn't have you."

She swallowed the heavy lump that had settled in her throat. "I love you, Dad. Promise me you'll go see a dentist tomorrow."

He grumbled something that sounded like a reluctant acceptance and told her he loved her, too. She pressed her palm against her aching chest and wondered how on earth she was going to fall back asleep after that. She hated that her parents were hurting. Hated that she didn't know who was to blame anymore, or if there even was someone to blame.

Most of all, she hated that she was feeling the same pain every time she thought about Eli. She'd been so busy trying to protect her heart that she'd forgotten he needed to protect his.

Her kettle whistled at the same moment a knock came at her door. It was nearly midnight. Only one person would knock at this hour. Her heart kicked into high gear. She abandoned her tea and dashed to the door.

Eli stood on the other side, but she barely recognized him. His eyes were rimmed with red and body so tense, she gasped. "What's wrong?"

His hands were coiled into fists as he stepped inside. "I need you."

Her pulse thundered in her veins. "What?"

"I know I'm not supposed to be here. I know I've got no right to ask anything of you, and if you tell me to leave, I swear I will. But I need you."

His voice was so raw and anguished, she could feel every rough, unvarnished edge of pain inside him. She knew why he was here. The remembrance ceremony was tomorrow, and he didn't want to be alone. "Okay."

He opened his mouth like he wanted to say more, but no words came out.

She reached for his hand. "Eli, it's okay."

The physical contact unleashed something in him. He met her eyes with a look that would have scared her if she didn't know him as well as she did. He kissed her, deep and hungry, pressing his lips to hers like he was trying to erase the weeks since they'd last done this. It was almost frantic in its urgency. And what could she do but kiss him back? His pain was so big, it filled the entire room. She didn't want to think about the reasons this was wrong. She just wanted to soothe him.

He walked her backwards to her bedroom, hands clutching her robe, pressing his lips to hers. When the back of her knees bumped into her bed, he pulled the robe off her shoulders and feasted on her neck like he was addicted to the taste of her skin, filling her with a sensation that made her knees weak with desire.

Her breath came so rapidly just from his kisses that she could barely make her fingers work as she reached for his T-shirt. He reached back and tugged it over his head before sealing his lips on hers. They struggled to get rid of the rest of their clothes, buttons and straps tangling and disobedient beneath their hands. She barely noticed the sound of her nightgown ripping as he yanked it off her shoulders before they fell against the mattress.

She reached blindly for her bedside drawer, accidentally knocking her paperback onto the floor. For once, she didn't even care if her bookmark fell out or the pages were bent. All she felt was relief when Eli leaned over her and found the condom she'd been looking for. But the grunt of pain when he tried to open the little plastic package did make her worry.

"What's wrong?" As she spoke, she finally noticed the thick bandage across his palm.

He handed the condom to her. "Took out my anger on a coffee mug."

She paused to stroke his cheek before tearing the little package open and rolling the condom on. He kissed her in return, like she was his last breath. She'd never had someone need her like this. Never felt the kind of passion that made her thoughts succumb to pure instinct. He lowered her to the bed and settled between her legs, where she ached for him. He pressed against her entrance, then sucked in a breath.

"Are you…" Another stilted breath. "Is this…okay?" He struggled for the words, but she knew what he was asking. No matter how much anger or pain he felt, he wouldn't do anything to hurt her. Not this way, at least.

"I need this, too," she answered softly.

He exhaled and slid into her, filling her so deeply and perfectly she couldn't understand how she'd denied this for so long. He laced his fingers with hers and slid them over her head. There was nothing gentle about the way he thrust into her or kissed her or held her hands. Their movements were desperate and greedy. She was lost in his scent, his sounds. In him.

"I need you," he whispered between hungry kisses. "I need you."

He repeated those words, driving into her harder and faster until she couldn't focus on anything but the rough, pleading sound of his voice and the feel of their sweat-slicked bodies sliding against each other. She could feel how close he was, and nothing in this moment mattered more than bringing him over the edge. She rocked her hips, reveling in the wild grunt that escaped his lips.

With no warning, he let go of her hands and flipped her legs over his shoulders, driving into her at an angle that sent her careening. She screamed as the strongest orgasm of her life tore through her. He came seconds later, repeating her name and burying his hands in her hair like she was the only thing anchoring him to this earth.

He collapsed on top of her, then rolled off a few seconds later to clean himself up. In those stark, quiet seconds apart, a small thread of panic was able to creep back in to her mind. She had no idea what just happened or what it meant.

When he came back a few minutes later and crawled beneath the covers, the vise around her heart finally loosened enough to breathe.

His hand slid against her hip, fingers pressing deeply into her skin, and his body curled up against hers.

"Eli?"

"Not tonight, okay? Tomorrow we can talk all you want."

"Tomorrow," she agreed. She didn't need words tonight. She just needed him.

Eli didn't want to open his eyes when he woke up the next morning. Fat, heavy raindrops splattered against the window in a rhythmic lullaby. He'd finally had the kind of sleep he didn't want to wake up from. The kind where he wasn't tormented by dreams or nightmares. The kind where he finally felt a little more human when he woke up instead of twice as tired as when he first went to bed.

When he did finally open his eyes, the gray skies made it look like it was still early morning, but the clock on the bedside table clearly stated it was already nine-thirty. Nora wasn't in bed, which was a disappointment but not a surprise. She was probably already on the road to her conference. They needed to talk, but he was grateful for the excuse to postpone that eventuality a little longer. He was in no rush to hear her tell him that last night was a one-off that didn't change anything. Right now, he needed to deal with the day ahead of him.

He got dressed quickly and headed to the bathroom. She'd left out a tube of antibiotic ointment and a box of bandages for his hand on the sink counter. The gash was ugly, but not too deep. He cleaned it up and went to her kitchen, hoping she remembered to leave him a key to lock up with, but instead he found Nora.

She was in the kitchen with her back to him, cell phone tucked against her ear while she cracked an egg with one hand into a bowl.

She must have showered while he was asleep because her hair was damp and pulled into a low ponytail, and she had an adorable red apron with white lace edges that reminded him of a French maid.

He wanted to go to her. Hold her. Kiss the skin below her ear. Instead, he stayed in the doorway, waiting for her to notice him.

"I found a dentist who takes emergency Saturday appointments," she said into the phone, sounding like a frustrated kindergarten teacher. "I've already booked you an appointment for noon today. You need to go."

She dropped her head backward, looking up at the ceiling with a sigh. "Please, Dad? Okay. Thank you. I'll call you later." She ended the call and set her phone on a clean stretch of counter, then turned her attention to a large, hardcover cookbook perched in one of those metal rack thingies that held the pages open.

He cleared his throat and said, "You need a recipe for scrambled eggs?"

She straightened with a small gasp of surprise.

"Sorry. Didn't mean to scare you."

"You didn't," she said, heading to the sink to wash her hands. She wiped her hands dry with a paper towel and turned around. "And for the record, I don't need a recipe, I just prefer to use one."

He smiled, grateful they were finally on neutral ground. He wasn't sure how to act after his outburst of emotion last night. He'd been worried he'd hurt her. That she'd be angry with him. "It's impossible to get scrambled eggs wrong."

Her lips quirked upward in a half-smile. "Sure, but it's not as easy to make the world's best scrambled eggs without Chef Brassard's ultimate scrambled eggs with brie and fresh chives recipe."

"Hard to agree since I've never tasted them before."

"Lucky for you I'm making extra." She grabbed a huge knife from her rack and sliced the chives in that rapid-fire way he'd only seen from the chefs on TV.

"Thanks, but don't you need to be getting on your way to your conference?"

She turned again and leaned her hip against the counter, looking at him curiously. "I'm not going until this afternoon. The ceremony, however, is in two hours so you should probably start the coffee if we're going to get there on time."

He took a cautious step forward into the kitchen. "You're coming to the ceremony?"

She offered a smile that seemed somehow sad. "I was always going to be there."

It seemed so dumb, in retrospect, to doubt her. She was kind and considerate and always put others first. But he also knew how much this conference meant to her. "But aren't you going to miss the conference?"

"My talk's not until tomorrow morning. It's not the end of the world if I miss a few sessions." She shrugged, but he could tell from her tight smile that it did bother her. "It's more important for me to be here for you and Julia."

You and Julia. It was the reminder that no matter what happened last night, nothing had really changed. She still didn't see a future where they were anything but friends. Barely a step above neighbors.

He opened her cabinet and grabbed two plates to distract himself from the frustration coursing through his body at that moment. He reminded himself that this was a good thing. He wasn't ready for the kind of talk they needed to have right now. Not until after the ceremony.

He set the table and made coffee while she finished cooking, as easy and comfortable as if they'd been doing this for fifty years. She slid the eggs onto their plates, adding a couple slices of toast. The smell alone was enough to make his stomach weep with joy. He took his first bite and moaned.

She grinned while carefully unfolding a napkin onto her lap. "The secret is to melt a pad of butter into the eggs. It gives them a creamy texture."

"If I'd known your eggs were this good, I'd have been over for breakfast from the moment you moved in."

A crimson flush swept over her cheeks. "How's your hand?"

"Not as bad as my ego. Julia's going to kill me when she notices."

"Are you nervous about the ceremony?"

He scooped up another rich bite and took his time swallowing. "Is it wrong if I say I'm not?"

She shook her head. "Why would it be?"

"I'm not nervous. I'm…" He flexed his fists, causing a searing jolt of pain in his injured hand, as he took his time searching for the right word. He hadn't allowed himself to admit what he was feeling until now. But Nora's brown eyes seemed to penetrate his thoughts, pulling the truth out of him. "I'm angry. Nothing about this ceremony has anything to do with me. I don't know what kind of flowers Mom liked, or what color she would prefer, or how she would feel about being immortalized in a stupid bench. I'm not doing anything but following Julia's orders, and I hate it. I hate that after ten years, I still have no idea how I'm supposed to think or feel or act. I'm just angry all the time."

She sipped her coffee, then added another spoonful of sugar. She tapped the spoon against the edge of the mug before setting it on the saucer. Eli hadn't known anyone who actually used saucers before her. "Do you want advice or do you want me to just listen?"

He ran his hand through his hair, regretting his answer before he even gave it. "Advice."

She reached her hand across the table and set it on his. He flinched, not ready for this kind of tenderness from her with so much still left unsaid, but he couldn't bring himself to pull away either. "There's no right or wrong way to feel. I didn't know your mom, but I know the children she raised, and I know she would be incredibly proud of who you are."

Every muscle in his body tensed, from his neck right through to his wrists and feet.

"Both of you," Nora added before he could argue. "I mean that. Even if I didn't know her, I would bet everything that your mom wanted to see you grow up to be a man who cares so deeply. A man who is fiercely loyal to his friends and successful in his field. No parent ever sees eye-to-eye with their kids on what path they're supposed to take to be happy in life, but I guarantee you she would be proud of who you are and what you've accomplished. And there's no rule that says this ceremony has to be your way of remembering her. You can do your own thing to remember her by."

"Like what?"

She smiled and tightened the grip on his hand. "Like forgiving yourself, for starters. It'll be a lot easier to come up with something meaningful if you're not focused on punishing yourself."

He'd never known someone who could cut through the swirling mess in his head like a hot knife and understand exactly what he'd been failing to figure out for months. He needed to do something that came from him. Something different from Julia's plans. His own thing. But what?

"You don't have to figure it all out right now. Forgiveness takes time."

He wasn't sure if she was talking about forgiving himself or her, but it was a visceral reminder that last night hadn't solved their problems. "Maybe too much time."

"I believe in you."

"Do you?" He hadn't meant to be sound so accusing. He didn't want to hurt her. He didn't want revenge. But he needed to know.

She withdrew her hand and fidgeted with her mug. "What I said at the fundraiser—what you overheard… It isn't what you think."

"You said I would destroy you. Pretty hard to misinterpret that."

"We. Not you. We." She tugged at the ends of her ponytail. "I never told you about my parents. They separated at the same time Gavin and I divorced. Thirty-five years together thrown down the drain."

"What happened?"

"They never belonged together. They're both academics, but they couldn't be more different. Mom's always been this free spirit with big dreams of travelling and adventure. Dad…well, his idea of adventure is using real cream instead of coffee creamer. He was married to his job more than his wife. They tried to make it work, but I guess they just couldn't keep sacrificing their dreams for each other anymore. And now they're both so miserable, they can barely function, much less enjoy their freedom."

"Just because your parents split up doesn't mean everyone else is doomed to fail."

"Maybe not, but after Gavin and I divorced, I lost everything. I'd given up my dream job in Toronto to follow him to Boston because I thought love was worth sacrificing for. But in the end, I lost everything. I had no friends. No house. No job. Nothing. I can't do that again. I can't start my life over anymore. I can't face that kind of regret again."

He clenched his hands into fists on the table, letting the pain fuel his anger once more. He hated the man who had taken away her ability to trust. "I wouldn't hurt you like that."

She shook her head. "I know. But I'm still me. The person who throws too much of herself into relationships. And the thing is, the way I feel about you is so much stronger than I ever felt about Gavin. Stronger than anything I've felt in my life."

She looked at him with eyes so wide and pleading, it felt like they were trying to communicate a secret message in those shimmering flecks of gold. She was falling for him, too, and it didn't just scare her. It terrified her. And he finally understood why.

He ran his hand through his hair and stood up. "I should go."

She didn't answer, so he collected the empty dishes and set them inside her dishwasher. She followed him silently to the door, watching as he slipped his shoes on and stepped outside into the gray drizzle.

"Eli," she called when he reached the bottom step.

He turned to look at her, drops of rain hitting his eyelashes.

She pressed her lips together nervously. "The thing is, I thought I was afraid of what could happen if things between us didn't work out, but after these weeks apart, I realize that I'm just as afraid of what will happen if we don't even try."

He bounded back up the steps and took her face between his hands. He placed a whisper of a kiss on her lips—the kind that finished without ending and held all the promises he couldn't articulate in words. He dropped his forehead to hers when it was over.

"We're gonna talk later. Okay?"

"Okay."

1 6

The rain didn't let up at all by the time the small crowd had gathered at the Holy Grale's back courtyard. If anything, it had grown stronger. Raindrops came down from the gray clouds in an urgent rhythm, splattering everything and making the air feel even chillier than it was. This kind of weather was inevitable in early November in the Pacific Northwest, but Eli still felt bad knowing Julia had been hoping for a sunny miracle.

Instead of herding everyone inside the brewpub, Julia enlisted Eli and Jake to quickly erect a white tent she'd had the foresight to keep on hand in case of rain. The floral archway wasn't holding up as well, but the white flowers—whatever kind they were—brought a nice bright contrast to the gray skies. He had to admit his sister had done a fantastic job to bring this event together.

Somehow it seemed fitting that he was stuck holding an umbrella over Julia while rain drenched his hair and clothes. He was soaking wet. The damn rain had even gotten into his underwear. But he refused to complain or draw attention to himself. It was Julia's turn to speak.

His sister held her notes in shaking hands and stepped up to the dais with Eli beside her, keeping her dry. "Thank you all for coming.

We're here today to celebrate a woman who was kind and smart and loving. Ruth Hardin wasn't just the best mom on the planet, she was also an amazing dancer—at least when it came to the chicken dance. She was also an incredible storyteller. When I was little, I used to beg her to make up bedtime stories for me. I was scared of the dark and she invented a different story every night about Julia the Superhero Princess vanquishing her enemies and darkness throughout the land, while always wearing the prettiest dresses. That was the thing about Mom. Even though we didn't have a lot of money growing up, she always found a way to give us what we needed, whether it was a jacket from the consignment shop that she bedazzled to look new, or a story about a superhero princess to take away my fear of the dark.

"One of my favorite stories about Mom is the time she decided to take us on a road trip when I was seven and Eli was nine. After we crossed the border, Mom realized she'd forgotten her wallet at home. In spite of our protests..." She paused to look at Eli. He encouraged her with a nod. "Mom turned the car around, but unfortunately she also forgot to gas up and we ended up stuck on the side of the road.

Julia laughed and the audience followed suit. She'd always been good at speaking in public and Eli was starting to regret agreeing to give his speech second—his yet-unfinished speech. He'd known it was dumb to wing it, but it wasn't like the hours spent trying to prepare something ahead of time had done him any good.

"Instead of panicking," Julia continued, "Mom dragged us to the side of the road and told us to pick out the most beautiful stones we could find. She made us hold the stones tight in our fists and make a wish. Not five minutes after we did, a car stopped. It turned out to be one of my old teachers, who was more than willing to help us out. From that day on, I realized that something as silly as wishing on a stone was powerful enough to make dreams come true. So if you will join me, please take your stone in your hand."

Eli's mouth pulled into a tight line. Unlike Julia, he hadn't actually believed his mom when she told him all he had to do was wish on a random piece of rock and all their troubles would be solved. Instead, he'd sulked and pretended to play along.

There had been a glass bowl full of tiny, smooth stones in every color waiting for the guests at the foyer of the brewpub when they arrived with a note written in Julia's perfect calligraphy instructing everyone to take one. He obliged this time, slipping a generic gray stone into his jacket pocket. He curled his fingers around the stone while Julia asked everyone to make a wish in their mom's honor, but it made the cut on his palm throb. The pain helped ground him and keep the guilt and regret from spilling over onto his face.

The audience dutifully complied and clapped when the speech ended. Julia looked at him with thin tracks of tears on her cheeks. "You're all wet," she said, surprise widening her hazel eyes.

"There wasn't enough room under the umbrella," he said gruffly.

She shook her head with a sad smile. "You're up."

He handed her the umbrella and stepped onto the dais. With all eyes focused on him instead of his sister, his adrenaline jumped, tightening his throat and making his bones feel like as weak as toothpicks. He didn't have a speech. He didn't know what to say.

Say something. Anything.

The nervous energy turned to panic, blurring his vision and making it hard to breathe. He gripped the water-slicked edges of the podium, but it didn't help. He closed his eyes to inhale slowly, and when he opened them once more he saw her. Nora. Blond hair bright against the gray sky, and steely confidence in her eyes when they locked on his.

You've got this, she mouthed silently to him.

He nodded, not looking anywhere but at her. "I thought I was going to stand up here today and tell you that Mom would have been proud of everything that we've accomplished, but I can't. I don't know how she would feel because she isn't here. And there's nothing more unfair in the world. For all I know, she'd hate that we turned a church into a brewpub, and would be scolding me that I should have become a doctor or a lawyer or something."

He stopped for a moment and almost laughed when he realized that was probably true. She would've told him a brewpub was a terrible investment. The audience seemed to tense, waiting for him to continue, but the only reaction he cared about was Nora's. She smiled, and he knew it was okay to keep going.

"Mom didn't always agree with the choices I made, but I always knew she loved Julia and me. Loved us enough to tell us when we were making dumb mistakes. Loved us enough to fight for our futures, no matter how hard it was for her to do that. She deserved the chance to tell me I was an idiot for moving to Shadow Creek and dragging my impressionable little sister with me."

The crowd laughed. Even the people in the audience who didn't know Julia well were aware she was anything but impressionable.

His shoulders relaxed and his voice felt stronger. Less shaky. "She deserved the chance to see that I have these amazing friends here, and that sometimes I can make good decisions. And I want to tell you all these amazing stories about her, but I can't because it still hurts too much. There isn't a day that goes by that I don't think about her or feel so damn angry that she hasn't gotten to see what we've created, or gotten the chance to put herself first for once and live her life the way that she deserved after Julia and I grew up.

"The only thing I can ask you all is to remember that nothing lasts forever. You can't waste time because you're scared. You have to hold on to the people you love now because you never know what will happen tomorrow." His voice had grown raw, words tumbling out of him in a rushed jumble. His chest was rising and falling like he'd just run a hundred-meter sprint. He ducked his head to gather himself, but when he looked up at Nora again, there were tears in her eyes, and it broke him.

His throat filled with all the emotions he'd tried to bury beneath his cement-covered heart, eyes stinging with the threat of tears. He didn't even realize Jake had left his seat until his best friend was standing next to him. Jake set his hand on Eli's shoulder and leaned toward the microphone. "Thank you everyone for coming. We're going to be serving a special bourbon-barrel aged stout inside the bar in honor of Ruth's favorite drink."

Jake pulled Eli into a hug, and when he finally released him, the crowd had shuffled inside. "You good?"

Eli met his friend's hard, concerned look. "Yeah. I'm good."

Jake's expression loosened into a smile. "Good, because it would be a shame if you didn't get the first taste of that stout." He clapped Eli on the back and urged him inside.

His legs were still shaky, but it was from catharsis, not nerves. He'd carried that unspoken anger inside of him for so long, it felt like a weight had lifted when he'd finally let it out.

Julia was waiting for him with a pint glass when they passed under the white tent and through the back entrance to the pub. She handed him the stout and wrapped her arms around his waist, burying her head in his chest. "You were amazing!"

He exhaled with relief. "So were you. Everything is perfect."

She looked so young in this moment, and he realized she'd been as desperate for his approval as he was of hers. "Thank you. Now let's get going—raise a toast, because everyone is excited to taste this beer."

She kept one arm around his waist and called on everyone to raise their glasses. Eli held up the pint and looked around the room at his friends, coworkers, and customers who had come to support him and Julia, feeling the kind of gratitude that was hard to put into words. He looked for Nora, needing to see her in order to rein in the emotions threatening to spill out once more.

But he couldn't see her.

"She just left," Julia whispered to him when the toast was over. "She had to leave for her conference."

His chest tightened with disappointment. Of course she would be leaving as soon as possible.

"You could probably catch her," Julia added.

He started to say something, but he didn't know what, so instead his mouth just hung open in a foolish expression.

Julia rolled her eyes and gave him a little shove. "Go. I don't know what's going on with the two of you, but I could tell by the way you were looking at each other that you need to talk. And you know Mom would have smacked you upside the head if you let a woman like her get away without a fight. I've got it from here."

That was the permission he needed. He dashed out to the parking lot just in time to see Nora's little gray Civic backing out of its spot. He didn't even know why he was chasing after her or what he wanted to say, but he needed to say something. She was leaving for three days and that suddenly seemed like forever.

Her red backup lights turned off. She drove toward the parking lot exit, leaving him behind on the wet asphalt with cold rain pelting down on him. He was too late.

He ran his hand through his hair and watched her drive off.

And then she stopped.

Nora glanced at her review mirror before pulling onto the road, then slammed on her brakes so hard the seatbelt snapped back against her sternum, knocking the wind out of her lungs. "Eli?"

He jogged to her car and rapped against the passenger side window. She scrambled to unlock the door. As soon as the little beep sounded, he climbed in. Rain had flattened his hair against his forehead, making him look so young. Like the rain and emotions from the afternoon's ceremony had washed away the protective shell he'd been wearing for the last few weeks.

"Hey."

"What are you doing?"

"We needed to talk."

She sighed. "I'm heading straight to Portland for the conference, and you're soaking wet." She reached over and cranked the heat, grateful she'd opted for leather seats when she'd bought this car.

He leaned forward and warmed his hands in the blast of heat from the center vent. "That's a four-hour drive, right? More than enough time to say what we need to say."

"You're coming with?"

He nodded. "You said the reason you've been pushing me away isn't just about me and my habit of destroying everything I touch."

She winced at the harshness of the words. God, how badly had she hurt him by saying that?

"You're scared," he added more gently. "Scared that we don't fit into each other's worlds and that it will end badly. But the thing is, you do fit into mine—so perfectly, it's terrifying. So let me show you that I can fit into yours, too. Give me this weekend to prove it."

Her fingers tightened around the steering wheel. "How?"

"We give it a chance, away from our lives in Shadow Creek. Just you and me. You dress up in a sexy suit in the morning and kick ass at your conference, and at night, you come back to the hotel to the handsome paramour waiting for you."

She laughed. "Paramour?"

"Sure. Your lover undercover. Your man who'll go down on the low down." He waggled his eyebrows, which made her laugh even harder.

"But you don't have any stuff," she said when she finally. "How are you going to brush your teeth?"

It was his turn to laugh. "After all we've been through, that's what you're worried about? I promise not to use your toothbrush. I'm sure there's a Rite Aid in Portland where I can buy a spare."

She exhaled, wondering if she was crazy for considering it. Last night had unsettled her so completely, she needed some time to sort it all out in her head. She'd been planning to use the conference as a chance to escape reality for a little while and really think about her life. What she truly wanted and needed to be happy. There was no way she could do that in an unbiased way with Eli there. He was like the sun, constantly pulling her toward him and brightening everything around him. But he could also burn her if he got too close.

He reached across the console and set his hand on her thigh. "I'm just asking for a chance, okay?"

"Okay."

He leaned back in his seat with a long exhalation of relief. "So, I bet you want to practice your talk on the drive up."

She held back a smile as she set the car into drive and pulled out of the parking lot, realizing that just maybe this man understood her so much better than she could ever realize.

17

Over the next four hours, Nora practiced her talk over and over again, finally nailing the timing on the nineteenth try. She knew it so well by that point, she could have recited it backwards without stumbling over a single word. She was finally feeling confident that she wasn't going to make a fool of herself.

She knew she was a talented chemist, but it was so much easier to step up to the podium with the clout of a top research institution behind her. Her research was so much smaller and more modest now —the kind of thing she probably wouldn't even have bothered giving a talk on until she had another few months' worth of results to back it up and make a bigger claim. She was going to have to work ten times as hard to earn the respect of her colleagues in the room.

It didn't surprise her that Eli could be so patient—he'd always been unendingly sweet with her—but it was a revelation to hear him ask complex follow-up questions about the science. She knew he was smart, but it had been years since he'd been a grad student, and his grasp of the concepts in her talk was almost as good as Doug's.

"If you didn't already have such a successful career, I'd be trying to convince you to do a PhD under me," she said right after taking the exit off the highway into Portland.

"Under you, huh? That's sounds so dirty, I'm almost tempted."

She laughed. "Okay, that was a little dirtier than I intended. I'm just impressed you remembered so much. We don't get a lot of grad students at Shadow Creek College, and the teaching schedule is so much higher that it makes it hard to actually get any real research done."

"And that's your passion, right?"

She nodded, keeping her eyes on the street signs while looking for the turnoff to the hotel.

"So why didn't you go to a school that's more research-focused?"

"I didn't have much choice. I quit my last job right before the New Year, and most universities finish hiring by that point. It was the only thing I could get. I don't hate it, though. It's just…different."

"Good different or bad different?"

"Both," she said honestly, slowing the car to a crawl as she turned into the hotel parking lot. "It's not as demanding, and I actually have free time for once in my life, but I spend more time in the classroom than the lab. I miss that part a lot."

He reached over and rested his palm at the base of her neck, massaging into the tense muscles.

She parked in the last available spot. Given how late she'd registered for the conference, she'd been lucky to get one of the last available rooms close to the convention center. The rain was still pouring down when they got out of the car. Eli hefted her suitcase out of the trunk and carried it toward the entrance.

"Just so you know," he whispered in her ear as they stepped into the lobby, "I meant it when I said I wouldn't borrow your toothbrush, but I can't make the same promise about your clothes. You're the most gorgeous woman I've ever met, but I think I could give you a run for your money in that little black dress of yours."

The struggle to keep the grin from her face was almost painful. "Only if you borrow my fake emerald drop earrings to go with it."

"Fake emeralds?" He scoffed. "I am a man of class. Nothing but real diamonds for me."

She laughed. "Getting a little full of yourself, Eli?"

"Nora?"

She craned her neck at the sound of the familiar voice calling her name, breaking into a smile when she saw who it was. "Dr. Lo?"

She crossed the few feet of space between her and her former supervisor. Dr. Lo greeted with her with a warm hug. "How many times have I told you to call me Robin? We're colleagues now."

"It's so good to see you," Nora said as they let go.

"You, too. I didn't realize you would be here." Robin looked like she hadn't aged a day in the three years since they'd seen each other. Her black hair was still barely touched by gray and styled in a chic but sensible bob, and there was no sign of wrinkles in her classic black suit.

"I'm giving a talk on nanoparticle polymer coatings for plasma-assisted solar absorption."

Robin smiled. "It's great to hear you're managing to keep up with your research."

Nora's own smile slipped. "A little. I'm sorry I haven't had the chance to respond to your email yet."

"The job offer is still on the table. We should have dinner to talk about it a little more. Are you free tomorrow night?"

Nora felt Eli's presence beside her without having to turn around. He rested his hand against the small of her back. She had no idea what he'd heard. "Our room's ready."

"Right," she said, as Robin raised her already sharply arched eyebrow. "Eli, this is Robin Lo, my PhD supervisor. Robin, this is Eli, my..."

She hesitated. What was he? Her friend? Her boyfriend? Yesterday, he wasn't even speaking to her.

"Friend," Eli offered.

"Boyfriend," Nora corrected, hoping to God he didn't object. The last thing she wanted was for him to think she was embarrassed by him, even if he did look like he'd been dragged in from a tornado, clothing rumpled and hair having dried into a mess.

He slid his arm around her waist and pulled her into him, holding out his other hand to Robin. "It's a pleasure to meet you."

"It's nice to meet you, too," Robin said, giving Nora a sly smile while keeping a firm grip on Eli's hand. "I hope you'll be able to join us for dinner as well."

Nora's stomach clenched. She really didn't want to talk about her professional future with Eli around—not when he messed up her ability to think straight just by being near—but there was no way to politely decline a dinner with the woman she owed so much to.

"I wouldn't miss it," Eli answered.

Robin gave them a quick nod, then headed to the lobby exit, heels clacking against the stone floor in her wake.

"That is one intimidating woman," Eli whispered when she was out of sight, shaking his hand like it had just been crushed by her grip. "I think I'm in love."

"I'd hit you," she whispered back, "but I think I've always had a little crush on her, too. There's speculation that she's going to win the Nobel Prize soon."

He picked up her suitcase and started walking toward the elevator. "I bet you'll get there first."

Nora laughed. "Not working at Shadow Creek College."

She hadn't realized how derisive she sounded until she saw the look of pity on his face. "You really miss your old life, don't you?"

The elevator opened and they stepped inside. "A little. But there are things I don't miss, too." The sinking feeling in her stomach dropped another league deeper. Had he heard what Robin said? She'd have to confront that fact sooner than later, but for now, she just wanted to close out the world and be with him.

He pressed the button for the fourteenth floor. The doors closed, and they were the only ones inside. She hated being trapped in tight spaces with complete strangers' arms and hips rubbing against her. Whenever possible, she took the stairs, but fourteen flights was a little too high for her not-so-athletic legs.

"So," he said in a low voice, flicking her hair behind her ear to expose her neck. He leaned forward and pressed a soft kiss to the sensitive spot behind her ear. "You never told me you had a boyfriend."

Her knees started to buckle as he trailed his mouth along her neck, but her stomach was tense with nerves. "You're more than a friend, Eli."

"Don't you think jumping to that label is a little forward?" His lips moved to her jaw. "After all, we've never actually made love as boyfriend and girlfriend."

Every molecule in her body heated up like she was a beaker held over a flame. She turned to him and pressed her hand against his heart. "I guess we'll have to remedy that. Good thing there's room for two in the king bed."

She rose up on her toes to kiss him, but the elevator dinged. She jumped back as the doors opened and a man dressed in running shorts and a T-shirt dripping with sweat stepped inside, dividing her and Eli like a fence. A smelly, wet, disgusting fence. His earphones were blasting so loud, she could hear every beat of the bad nineties rock music he was listening to.

Nora glanced at Eli. He pinched his nose and made a face. It was everything she could do not to laugh.

The elevator dinged a few seconds later, and the man stepped out, giving her the chance to breathe freely again.

She practically leapt toward Eli. "Where were we again?"

"Rushing to the hotel room so you can freshen up and catch the last of the sessions at the convention center while I figure out where to buy a toothbrush. And some new underwear. At least, that's what we were supposed to be talking about."

She pouted, and he responded by kissing the tip of her nose.

"Don't worry. There will be plenty of time to for me to show you exactly what the word boyfriend means to me later tonight."

The blare of the alarm clock was so loud the next morning that Nora woke with a start.

"Turn that damn thing off and go back to sleep," Eli grumbled. He curled his arm around her waist and pulled her toward him.

"I can't. I have to get ready for my talk."

He lifted his head to look at the time flashing in florescent blue lights. "It's six-fifteen. Your talk's not for another three hours."

"I know, but—"

He reached across her and slammed on the snooze button. "There. We've got ten minutes until it goes off again. More than enough time for what I've got planned for you."

He climbed on top of her and kissed his way down her sternum. Her tummy. He spread her knees wide and settled between them, pressing his lips to her hipbone.

The backup alarm on her phone went off with an obnoxious melody.

He groaned.

"Front desk should be calling any second now, too." As if on cue, a ring sounded from the phone on the nightstand.

Eli rolled off her with a sigh and got out of bed to answer the call. He grunted something at the front desk person and hung up.

"If we hurry, we might have time to grab a real breakfast in the restaurant."

He narrowed his eyes into a glare. "Not a chance, Princess. Only continental breakfast for you."

She raised her eyebrows. "And what about you? What are you going to eat?"

He grabbed her by the ankles and dragged her legs off the bed, spreading them wide once more until she was bared to him. "You."

Nora was gone by the time Eli had come out of the shower. After he'd brought her to a rapid, screaming orgasm with his tongue, he'd insisted she practice her talk once more rather than letting her return the favor. He knew her nerves were the reason she'd gotten up at such an ungodly early hour.

She'd killed it, unsurprisingly. Well, maybe a little surprisingly considering he'd been sitting naked on the bed watching her practice with the world's biggest hard-on.

It wasn't just her intelligence he found so sexy. It was the meticulous determination she brought to everything she did that blew his mind. Even if she was panicking on the inside, on the outside she was powerful and completely in control. He admired the hell out of her for that. His feelings for her were so primal and raw, there was no way he could keep denying them. And when she'd called him her boyfriend last night, it set off something powerful inside him. He'd waited so long for her to admit she felt the same way, but now he wondered if it was too late.

He'd overheard her supervisor mention something about a job offer. He'd finally made Nora his, and now she was going to leave him. How much time had he wasted being angry at her instead of understanding her fear and frustration?

Too much. But he wasn't going to waste any more.

He quickly dressed in yesterday's clothes and searched for the conference program online. Twenty minutes later, he stepped into the convention center, armed with a bran muffin and an extra-large coffee from the continental breakfast. No one stopped him as he headed to the conference room. With his jeans and sport blazer, he blended in with the crowd of attendees, and he'd been a mischievous enough kid to know how to sneak into places using nothing but confidence and bluster.

She was just setting up her PowerPoint when he snuck into the room. He slipped into the back row and slunk low in his chair. He wasn't arrogant enough to think she needed his moral support the way he'd desperately needed hers yesterday at the remembrance ceremony. She was a professional in her element. He just wanted to be there to witness her kick ass.

"Thank you for that wonderful introduction," Nora said in that same confident, direct voice she'd rehearsed a million times over the last twenty-four hours. Polymer chemistry hadn't been his favorite subject, and he couldn't honestly say that listening to Nora's talk changed his opinion any, but he was riveted by her. Hell, he'd sit through a million more of these talks if it meant being with her.

By the time she'd reached her acknowledgement slide, it had occurred to Eli that this was the life his mom had wanted for him. She'd been so damn excited when got accepted into his Master's program that she threw a party. She'd been convinced he would one day become a professor and that she'd be able to call at least one of her kids "Doctor." Instead, he'd panicked just a few short months into grad school and told his Mom he was thinking of dropping out. The classes were so much harder than he'd been expecting. He'd had to study his ass off every night even though he'd coasted through undergrad.

He'd probably never completely forgive himself for his mom's death, but he was finally ready to accept that he deserved to be proud of what he had accomplished. Watching Nora deliver a talk that was, frankly, dry as dust helped him realize he would never have cut it in this world. Instead, he'd built a good life for himself. He had a good job. A home. Friends. Nora. At least hoped she'd be part of his life in the long-term. His mom would have liked her.

He stayed to listen to the talk after Nora's before sneaking out again. She'd gotten a few questions from the audience, but it wasn't anything she couldn't handle. There was always at least one long-winded douchebag who insisted on repeating the one tangentially related fact he'd heard about the topic and asked "Have you considered that?" as if he weren't talking to an expert on the subject. Nora handled it with grace and her wicked intelligence. He doubted it was the first time she'd dealt with that kind of obnoxious prick, but it was sexy as hell watching her put him in his place.

Eli spent the rest of the day listening to talks related to the chemistry of brewing. It was a pretty big conference and there were more than enough sessions to keep him busy and out of Nora's hair. He promised her he would prove he could fit into her world, and that meant not distracting her from the networking and learning she'd come to do. But by the end of the day, he was aching to see her again.

He made his way back to the hotel room and tucked his plastic keycard into the slot. Nora was already there, running a big fluffy powder brush down her nose. He'd never been the type to care whether a woman wore makeup or not—but there was something weirdly adorable about watching her in this moment. Something intimate.

She turned when the heavy door shut behind him and smiled brightly enough to burn away the clouds for hundreds of miles. "Hey!"

"How'd your talk go?"

The corners of her lips twisted down, pulling her face into a sad frown. "It was terrible."

"What?"

She sighed. "I stumbled over every word, completely botched my methods slide, and there were exactly three people in the audience. One was sleeping, one was on this phone the entire time, and the last one was the moderator."

"That's not true—"

"Aha!" She walked over and jabbed her index finger into his chest. "You were there!"

He circled his hands around her waist and dropped his forehead to hers. "You thought I'd miss it?"

"You hate conferences."

"Yeah, but I don't hate you. In fact, I don't hate you so much, I'd sit through a thousand conferences if it meant more chances to test out the bounce factor on these hotel beds."

He could tell she was trying not to smile, but the corners of her mouth lifted, dueling with the serious expression tightening in her cheeks. "I don't hate you, either. Enough to put up with your awful taste in music, especially if you do that thing with your tongue that you did this morning."

He pulled her body closer until her hips were flush against his. "Well, good thing I don't hate you so much that I want to wake up every morning with you."

She tipped her head upward, brushing her lips against his chin. "And I don't hate you at all. To be honest, you're the best thing that's happened to me since moving to Shadow Creek."

His hands stilled against her body. He didn't know how much to read into her casually delivered comment. He wanted to believe it was a declaration of the feelings she'd been so hesitant to express. He wanted to carry her to the bed and show her just how grateful he was for her, too, but he kissed her sweetly on the forehead instead. "And I don't hate you enough to be on time for dinner. We should probably get going."

She sucked in a breath. "There's something I should warn you about. Robin's probably going to use this dinner to try to convince me to apply for a job with a start-up company she just founded."

He didn't move, but his stomach felt like he'd taken a direct hit from a battering ram.

"I'm not interested," she added quickly. "I just wanted you to be prepared."

His stomach unclenched enough to breathe again, but that nervous feeling still lingered.

She finished refreshing her makeup while he looked up directions to the restaurant where they were meeting Robin. It was cold, but the rain had faded to a drizzle so they decided to walk. She held his hand the entire way. It was probably silly, but he'd waited so long for her to finally be comfortable with this kind of display of affection. He couldn't go back to stolen touches shrouded in denial.

Robin was already waiting for them in the darkly lit Italian place. They barely had time to finish greeting each other before she and Nora launched into a conversation about their research, which continued right through until their meals were delivered a short time later. The excitement and passion seemed to explode out of Nora like fireworks—sparkling and dazzling as each new idea took shape. He'd noticed Nora had run through her routine of checking her silverware for spots and agonizing over the menu, but she didn't seem insecure about it like she did on their first date. She was comfortable in her skin around Robin.

For the first time, he realized that maybe Nora's insecurities weren't really about herself as much as it was about being in a place where people didn't understand her. But she had people in Shadow

Creek who knew her now, he reminded himself. People who love her.

Fuck, *he* loved her.

He leaned back in his seat and took a sip of his water. The ice cubes rattled in the glass from the slight tremble in his hand. He loved Nora and he had no idea how she would react if he told her.

Robin leaned forward, swirling her glass of burgundy-colored wine against the table. "Have you considered using a TEM?"

Nora tilted her head downward and began fidgeting with the cloth napkin on her lap. "We don't have access to a TEM at Shadow Creek College."

"We do at P-Tech."

"I really appreciate the opportunity, Robin, but I'm not ready to give up academia quite yet."

Eli's heart stumbled against his ribs. She'd warned him this conversation was coming, but he wasn't really prepared for it. Still, it wasn't his place to say anything, so he forked a mouthful of rigatoni Bolognese into his mouth.

"You're not ready to give up the freedom of a having a research program under your control," Robin said. "But I bet you'd be happy to give up the teaching. The grading. Hours spent in department meetings where nothing is ever accomplished."

Nora shrugged. "Sure, but it's part of the job. If I worked in private sector, I'd lose all control over my research."

"P-Tech isn't just about producing solar devices. It's about innovation. The position would involve developing your own research agenda. As long as it's in the field of solar cell technology, you would have all the freedom in the world. And access to all the equipment in the lab you could ever want. We need someone with your abilities and vision."

Nora straightened in her seat. "That's sounds amazing, but—"

Robin cut her off with a wave of the hand. "Just think about it, okay? But not for too long. We're starting interviews for the position next week and there's only so many strings I can pull with the board to get you in."

"Okay, I'll think about it," Nora said at the same time she reached beneath the table and squeezed Eli's knee.

He knew she was trying to reassure him she'd only said that to appease Robin, but it didn't help. Because it wasn't him she needed to reassure. It was herself.

18

"*I* think I'm going to have to stage an intervention about your taste in music soon," Nora said as soon as Eli settled on a radio station.

"If loving Diana Ross is wrong, I don't want to be right." He kicked up the volume a few notches, which Nora readjusted immediately. They'd been listening to NPR for most of the drive back to Shadow Creek and he didn't think he could handle one more informative public interest piece delivered in a slow, soporific voice. "This is one of my mom's favorite songs."

"And you've never been even a little curious about any of the new music that's been created in the last three decades?"

He laughed. "Your taste in music shouldn't be influenced by what's popular. It should be based on how it makes you feel."

"That's sweet. And a little insufferable. But mostly sweet. We didn't listen to music a lot in my house because my dad didn't like background noise, but I think that's because my mom only listened to Andean flute music and Nepalese folk songs."

"You never hung out at CD stores or went to concerts?" He couldn't imagine growing up in a quiet home. One of his mom's favorite things was to turn on their old, clunky stereo on Saturday mornings and dance around the kitchen while she made breakfast for Julia and him. She'd been a strict parent, but she'd always made sure they had fun in their lives.

She glanced over at him with a wry smile. "I may or may not have gone through an unfortunate boy-band craze in my tween years, but I'm not telling you any more about that."

The image of a nerdy, pre-teen Nora sleeping in an oversized Backstreet Boys concert T-shirt and plastering her walls with cut-out pictures from *Tiger Beat* was almost enough to distract him from thoughts of his mom. But there was a thread of an idea that had been niggling at him since the remembrance ceremony.

"What do you think about a scholarship fund?"

"What do you mean?"

His heart beat fast as he tried to come up with the words to explain what he meant. Ones that wouldn't make it sound silly or pathetic. "I was thinking I could set up a scholarship at my old college in my mom's name. It could be for kids from single-parent families who need the financial help. I've got a little bit of money I could put toward it."

She was silent as she overtook a big semi-trailer on the highway. A huge spray of water hit the windshield and her fingers tightened on the wheel. "I think it's a wonderful idea," she finally said.

"Yeah?"

She nodded. "One thing to consider is that you'll need to donate more than a little bit of money if you want the scholarship to be an annual thing instead of a one-off. Most scholarships need a major endowment so that they can use the interest to fund the award year after year."

His excitement deflated, leaving him feeling like a foolish child too stupid to understand the realities of adult life. He had a decent amount of savings, but nowhere near enough for what he was thinking. "Yeah, I guess it was a dumb idea."

"No," she said forcefully. "It's not dumb at all. It's a fantastic idea. You could fundraise the difference. You've already got some experience with that under your belt, and I could help you."

He smiled. "Wouldn't that be frowned upon? Helping a rival college?"

She laughed. "You matter more to me that any sense of loyalty I might have to Shadow Creek College."

"Because you're not sure you're staying there?" He almost didn't want to know the answer. She'd told him she wasn't taking Robin's offer seriously, but she'd been unable to look him in the eye when she'd said it. He hadn't wanted to make the drive back awkward by bringing it up earlier, but he couldn't sit here now making plans for the future when he didn't know if she would be around. He couldn't let himself feel the way he did about her if she was going to leave him without a single glance backward.

"It's hard to not at least consider a job offer like that. I have friends back home. My dad."

"So you're thinking of taking it?"

"No. I mean, I don't think so. But it's a big decision. It's not the kind of thing I can say no to without mourning over it. I miss my life back in Toronto, and passing this job up makes me feel like I'm losing that part of my life all over again."

"But you have a good life here, too. Julia and Clem and everyone else adore you." *I adore you, dammit.*

She sighed. "The way you feel about Jake? That's how I feel about Alice and Jessie. And my dad's really struggling right now. I'm worried about him."

Eli's phone buzzed with a text, saving him from saying something he would regret. "It's from Jake. He says there's another emergency at the Holy Grale. Do you mind dropping me off there instead of going home?"

"Yeah, of course," she said, pressing down on the gas even though she'd driven exactly the speed limit for the last four hours.

They were already close to town and it didn't take long before they'd pulled into the Grale's parking lot. He'd expected her to just drop him off, but she parked the car and got out.

"You don't have to stay," he said.

"You'll need a ride home. Besides, I could use a drink after driving for that long."

The after-work happy hour crowds were already filling up the place, but he spotted Jake near the bar. Clem and Julia were there, too, talking excitedly about something. Whatever it was, he hoped it wasn't going to swallow up the last of their operating budget or require another all-nighter.

"Hey, you're here," Jake said. "Come on back with me."

Eli turned to look at Nora, but Clem and Julia had already latched on to her arms and were dragging her toward the mezzanine. He followed Jake to the brewery room, his anxiety multiplying with each step.

With the din of the bar muffled by the heavy wood doors, Eli listened to the purr of his machines. Nothing sounded off. "What's going on?"

Jake didn't answer. He poured two pint glasses from an unmarked keg and handed one to Eli. "Taste this."

Fuck. Nothing made him angrier than an off-batch. He sipped the amber liquid, letting the flavors coat his mouth and tongue, searching for the defect. There wasn't one.

"This is my Matrimoni-ale." It was an exclusive brew he'd developed that they reserved for wedding receptions hosted in their courtyard.

Jake grinned so wide, he looked like he was five years old. "I know."

Eli stared at his best friend for a moment before finally cluing in. "Shit. You did it?"

"Yep. I finally proposed and Clem said yes."

"That's awesome! Congratulations!" He gave Jake a one-armed hug, careful to not spill his beer all over him. "I'm so happy for you."

This time, he really meant it. Jake had been engaged once before to a woman who made him miserable, but his relationship with Clem was different. They were meant for each other, even if it had taken the pair forever to figure that out.

Eli took another long sip of beer, letting himself sink into the flavor and enjoy the perfect blend of hops and malt he'd created. "You really had me going there. I thought I was coming back to a disaster, not an engagement."

Jake laughed. "Not a total lie. Tom called in sick, so you're on your own tonight. And you better hurry up, because we're almost out of Lord's Work Lager."

"I'll get on that soon," Eli said. "But first I have a better idea of how we can celebrate. I've got something I've been saving for just this occasion."

Jake held his pint glass up and clanked it against Eli's. "Whatever it is, I'm in."

Nora had worried about what kind of problem was waiting for Eli downstairs, but Clem and Julia seemed way too excited for it to be anything truly bad. They led her up to the library room, far from the noise of the main floor, and shut the door behind them.

"What is going on?" Nora finally asked.

Clem's cheeks turned bright red while Julia didn't even try to hide the gleeful expression on her face. "Jake proposed," Julia crowed, grabbing Clem's left hand and holding it up. A deep blue sapphire sparkled on her ring finger.

"Congratulations!" Nora hugged Clem. "That's so exciting."

"And kind of overwhelming," Clem said. She looked shell-shocked with her hair curling like a dark cloud around her face.

"It's a good thing you have the best event planner in town as your friend," Julia said. "You just need to trust me."

Nora couldn't help but laugh. When it came to organizational skills, Julia was the complete opposite of Eli. But the way they cared deeply for their friends and threw their hearts and souls into everything they did was completely alike. "You're in good hands. All you need to do right now is bask in the moment. And give me all the details of how he proposed."

Clem grinned. "God, I'm so lucky to have you two."

"Details!" Julia said. "And don't leave anything out."

Nora's phone buzzed. She reached inside her purse and ended the call without picking up. Whatever it was about could wait.

The phone buzzed again instantly. "Sorry," she murmured, pulling out her phone to see who was calling her so insistently. It wasn't just a half-dozen calls she'd missed. There were text messages, too. All from Jessie.

The one blazing on the front of her screen was so bizarre, she had to read it twice before the words even made sense.

Answer the phone! Your parents are in the hospital.

"Everything okay?" Clem asked softly.

"I...I don't know." The phone buzzed again and she answered the call immediately. "Jessie?"

"Oh thank god! You need to answer your phone when I call!"

"What's going on?"

"I just started my shift an hour ago and I saw your parents. They were in a car accident."

Nora's heart beat so fast, if felt like it was about to burst out of her chest. Jessie was a nurse in one of the emergency departments back home. "Both of them?"

"Both. Together."

"That can't be possible. Mom's in Italy."

"I don't know how," Jessie said. "But they're here. I saw them with my own eyes. They're alive, but I don't know much else. I've only got a few minutes and I'm using it to book you a ticket home."

"Oh my god." Nora covered her mouth with her hand. Her legs were shaking. Clem and Julia rushed to her side.

"There's only one flight out of Shadow Creek today that will get you here, and it leaves in forty minutes. I've just booked it and sent the details to your email. Don't thank me, just get to the airport."

Nausea rose in Nora's chest as she ended the call. Her limbs felt cold and hollow.

"What's the matter?" Julia asked.

Nora had to swallow back the panic in her throat before she could answer. "My parents are in the hospital. I need to go."

"You can't drive," Clem said. "You're shaking."

"I have to catch my flight. It leaves in forty minutes."

"I'll take you," Julia said, hooking her arm around Nora's and leading her toward the exit.

"I'll let Eli know," Clem offered.

Oh God. Eli. She didn't even have time to find him before she left. "Thank you."

"Don't worry," Julia said, dragging Nora down the steps. "It's going to be okay. I promise."

All Nora could do was put one foot in front of the other and hope to God Julia was right.

The back door to the Holy Grale banged open before Eli could light the waterproof match he'd saved for this very occasion. Clem burst through and stepped out onto their back patio, which, aside from him and Jake, was completely empty. The grounds were beautiful, but no one willingly came out here when it was raining this hard.

"This is where you are? I've been looking all over for you." She brushed her thick hair back from her face, revealing wide eyes. "Are you smoking cigars?"

Eli laughed. "If you're worried I'm corrupting your fiancé, well, you should be. But not with cigars. Something even better that won't ruin his breath for your post-announcement make-out." He held up the unlit firecracker and grinned.

Clem, who could usually find the humor in his and Jake's antics, didn't crack a smile.

Jake cupped her cheek with one hand, looking her in the eye with the kind of intensity that seemed to lock out everyone around them. "What's the matter?"

She was upset, Eli realized. Panicked even. She turned to Eli. "Nora's parents were hurt. She's flying to Toronto right now."

"What? I don't understand. Her parents aren't together. They're not even in the same country." His own words sounded distant in his head, like he was watching the conversation happen from afar. Memories of the night he'd gotten the same kind of call about his own mom ten years ago hit him like a thousand knife blades.

"I don't know," Clem answered. "But her friend Jessie called her twenty minutes ago from the hospital. Nora's already on her way to the airport. We tried to find you, but—"

He cut her off with an angry curse. None of this made sense. "I need to go after her."

Clem shook her head. "You won't get to the airport in time to make the flight."

Eli raked his hand through his hair. He couldn't let her deal with this alone. Not after she'd been there for him. Not when he didn't know if she would come back. Everything she loved was in Toronto, and if her parents were hurt...

Shit. He hadn't told her he loved her yet.

"Maybe not Shadow Creek Airport," Jake said. "But I bet there's still some flights from Seattle that would work."

Clem nodded and grabbed Eli by the arm. "My car's out front."

"You would do that for me?" Seattle was almost two hours away, and rush hour traffic would be picking up right around now.

Clem smiled. "Of course, but I'm doing it for Nora, too. Now let's go."

---

19

*I*t was almost ten in the morning by the time Nora finally stepped off the plane. Between the long drive back from Portland and the three-connection flight to Toronto, her legs felt like they'd been fossilized. Every part of her was stiff and sore.

She pulled out her phone, which was a silly thing to do since the battery had died before she even made it to the airport in Shadow Creek, but it was a normal, instinctive thing to do and she desperately needed normal right now. She'd managed to get an email off to her department chair before her phone died, explaining her absence and ensuring she had coverage for her classes. At least all the stress of meticulously preparing her labs and lectures months in advance would make it easy for a replacement to step in at the last minute.

She hadn't gotten the chance to call Eli, though. Thinking of him felt like a warm blanket had been wrapped around her shoulders, warding off the winter chill. God, she hoped he would understand why she took off without telling him first.

With no luggage to collect, she went straight to the taxi line and asked for a ride to the hospital. She stared at her phone the entire way. Somehow, holding it made her feel a little less alone, like a call from Eli or her friends or parents could pop on the screen at any minute.

Except, it couldn't. She didn't have her charger, and for all she knew her parents wouldn't ever be able to call her again.

Please be okay. No matter how much her parents frustrated her, she would give anything to know they would have another chance to nitpick about her clothes or her life or her job.

The familiar sights of the city she grew up in were a comfort, at least. She'd wanted to come back here for so long, but apparently she'd forgotten how bad the traffic could be in big cities. It was amazing how she could forget something like that in such a short time.

When she finally pulled up to the hospital, the agonizing slowness of her trip gave way to the frantic bustle of a busy emergency room. Loud voices, strange beeps, and distant cries of pain swirled around her as she looked for someone who could tell her where her parents were.

"Nora!"

She turned to see Jessie, dressed in pale blue scrubs. "Oh, thank God you're here."

Jessie pulled her into a hug. "I've seen them. They're stable, but your mom's been moved to a specialized ward for some additional tests. I'll take you there now."

Nora stomach seized. "Why?"

"She banged her head pretty hard, but it's going to be okay," Jessie said calmly. "It's a good thing the doctors are taking extra precautions."

Nora tried her best to believe her as they walked through the chaotic hallways. Within a few minutes, they'd arrived at her mom's room.

Jessie gave her one last hug. "I have to get back to the ER, but I'll find you when my shift's over. I'll let Alice know you've arrived, okay? She was here with them last night but had to go in to work this morning."

Nora nodded. She squeezed a dollop of sanitizer from the wall-mounted dispenser onto her hands and entered the room. It was a small space that smelled like antiseptic, with big windows, linoleum floors, and a simple monitoring unit next to the bed. And in the middle of it all were her parents. Her mom lay awake on the bed, batting a hand at her father, who was standing next to her with a sling on one arm and fussing with the settings on the adjustable bed.

Even though she was looking right at them, it was hard to believe her parents were here together. She hadn't seen them in the same room in over a year, and now they were bickering like they were still an old married couple. "Mom? Dad?"

"Nora?" Her mom's eyes lit up, but she sounded weak. "What are you doing here?"

"Jessie called me." She walked to the bed and gingerly hugged her mom.

"I always liked that girl," her dad said, now messing with the blankets at her mom's waist. "She's a good influence on you."

In any other circumstance, Nora would have laughed. Instead, she hugged him, too. He'd never been one for physical affection, offering a distant pat on the shoulder whenever she'd accomplished something important or skinned her knee, but this time he hugged her back, holding her long enough to make her feel every bit of the emotion he usually kept locked up behind his gruff exterior. "Tell me what happened."

"Some fool didn't know how to take a proper left turn," her dad grumbled.

"Yes, and that fool was your father."

"Hush, my little goldfish. You were distracting me."

Nora's head spun. That was the pet name her dad used to call her mom—a teasing reference to her short attention span and golden hair. She was suddenly flooded with memories of her mom cooking terrible, over-salted pancakes on the weekends, cajoling her dad to dance with her in the kitchen whenever one of her favorite songs came on the radio. The way her dad would protest until the sway of her mom's hips broke down his defenses.

Catherine giggled. She was lying in a hospital bed with a cast on her leg, cuts and scrapes over her body, and she was giggling.

"I still don't understand. What are you even doing together?"

Her parents looked to each other. Their smiles were giddy. Guilty, almost. Like teenagers caught making out beneath the bleachers. "It's kind of a long story," her mom supplied, reaching for her dad's hands.

Nora shuddered, realizing exactly how her mom had distracted her dad in the car. It was an image no woman should have to have about her parents. And it still didn't make sense. "You were supposed to be in Italy."

"I was. And it was terrible. Just like the yoga retreat, and my trip to Argentina. And New Orleans. And all the other places I dreamed of visiting when I finally retired." She patted her husband's hand. "And finally I realized there was nothing wrong with those places. It was me. I didn't want to do all those things alone. I was sitting on the edge of the Fonte Gaia in Siena, soaking in the beautiful architecture and watching two pigeons fight over an overly large scrap of bread someone had left on the sampietrini, and then I remembered what you asked me the day I left Shadow Creek."

Nora frowned. "I don't remember."

"You asked why we never tried to compromise. Sitting there, with the sun on my face, I realized I didn't have a good answer." She looked to Nora's father once again and took his hand. The smile that passed between them was so warm, the fear and worry that had wrapped like ice around Nora's heart finally thawed.

"So you're...back together?"

"We're not putting labels on it right now," he dad said, so thoroughly out of character that Nora had to laugh again. "Now help me with these damn tubes. They're all tangled up."

"They're just fine. Leave them alone and give Nora some money to get me a coffee."

"You're not allowed coffee yet."

"Fine, then." Her mom threw her arms up, setting off a frantic beeping sound from her monitor. "I'll have a latte."

Her parents seemed to forget she was even there, completely enthralled in their bickering, and Nora couldn't remember having been happier in her entire life.

Eli would have recognized the two women standing at the arrival section of the airport just from the photos lining Nora's house, but the big cardboard sign reading *Humperdinck* made it clear that Jessie and Alice were waiting for him. Somehow, the two of them had managed to track him down over his social media accounts to let him know what was happening.

It was more than he'd heard from Nora. He tried not to worry, knowing she'd left her phone charger dangling from the adaptor plugged into her car's dashboard, but he hated that she was dealing with all this without him. Hated thinking he was going to lose her.

She'd told him she wasn't taking the job Robin had offered, and at the time he'd believed her. But everything changed the moment she got on that plane. Her parents were facing a long recovery. She had to be at least considering it, and he couldn't blame her if she was.

"So, you're the neighbor who's turned Nora's life completely upside down," said Jessie, who he recognized by her short stature and curly brown hair.

"To be fair, she's turned mine completely upside down, too." His response earned him the barest hint of a smile, but they were loyal friends holding back any signs of approval until he'd earned it.

"I can see that," said Alice, strawberry-blond and tall in a way that gave her a natural elegance. "Don't think that flying across the continent is enough to absolve you from all the crap you put her through."

"Wouldn't dream of it. Thank you for letting me know what was going on and picking me up. If you hadn't, I'd probably be wandering around the streets of Toronto shouting Nora's name." He glanced at the giant windows stretching the length of the wall, noticing the heavy snow blanketing the ground. "And I didn't exactly dress for the weather."

He took a step forward, but the two women crossed their arms at the exact same time, subtly leaning into each other and blocking his path. He rubbed the back of his neck. This was going to be a little harder than he'd anticipated.

Alice drummed her fingers against her biceps.

Okay, maybe a lot harder. He turned on his best innocent puppy dog look. "I'm not here to talk her into coming home, I swear. And I really am sorry for being an ass."

Jessie harrumphed. "Then why are you here?"

"Because..." He inhaled, steeling his courage. "Because I love her."

"Okay," Alice said with a nod. "Let's go."

It had been years since Nora had been so tired. Even her bones felt fragile from the exhaustion, like they could crumble to dust at the slightest touch. Her parents had been discharged only a few hours ago, with strict instructions for bed rest. Her dad's left arm was broken and her mom had a concussion and fractured tibia. They were doped up on painkillers, covered in bandages, and arguing about everything from what route the cab driver should take home from the hospital to whether they should order sushi or Thai for dinner. It had been so long since they'd been a family like this.

It was so odd how almost nothing had changed. The furniture was exactly the same as when she'd last seen it almost a year ago, if a little more dusty. The bright throw pillows, garish paintings, and other little random splashes of color in the otherwise stuffy space hadn't been touched. But there was something different—a sadness hovering over the room like a fog.

In truth, it wasn't just her parents' separation that had created distance between them all. They'd barely had any real time together since she'd eloped with Gavin and moved to Boston. She'd been so consumed by work, she hadn't made enough time for them. In the three years she'd been living on the East Coast of the United States, she'd only managed a total of four visits home. Her family had broken down in that time. Every part of them. Their hearts, their relationships, and now, it seemed, their bodies. At least their bones would heal.

Once she'd settled her mom on the sagging, floral-patterned couch with a cup of Earl Grey, and her dad on his favorite cognac-colored leather recliner next to her, Nora made an executive decision and called in a sushi delivery order from her dad's landline. She organized the prescriptions she'd picked up at the pharmacy on the way back from the hospital into labeled pillboxes to make sure they wouldn't get mixed up, and cleaned the kitchen, which looked like it hadn't been properly wiped down in months.

She wandered into her dad's office next. Considering how bad the rest of the house had gotten, she was afraid of what she'd find. Unfortunately, her fears weren't unfounded. Coffee mugs lined the desk and there were books and stacks of paper everywhere. She returned the books to the bookshelves, but knew better than to touch any of the papers without her dad's explicit permission.

She was about to pick up a plate that had some kind of unidentifiable, mold-covered food on it, but stopped when she saw the photo perched on the desk behind her. It was one of her with her parents standing in front of the Ontario Science Centre. She must have been about seven or eight years old, if the terrible nineties fashion was anything to go by. Her parents had gotten her an annual pass, even though neither of them was remotely interested in the hard sciences. It was one of her happiest memories.

The weight of it all hit her at once, like she was caught in a hailstorm of emotions. She'd spent the better part of the last year being angry with her parents for their selfishness, and now she'd almost lost them entirely. They could have died in that crash. She could barely even remember why she'd been angry in the first place.

She'd tried so hard to convince herself that her parents didn't need her, but she was wrong. They couldn't function without her. Heck, they could barely keep themselves alive without her. Frustration seared into her skin. For months, the only thing she wanted was an excuse to come back home. Only now, home didn't feel like home anymore. She didn't want to leave her students, or her house, or Eli.

God, Eli. She could barely think straight when it came to him. He made her feel happy and safe and loved.

But none of that changed the fact her parents needed her.

The doorbell rang.

"Larry, go answer that," Catherine instructed her dad from the living room.

"No!" Nora jumped to her feet and wiped her cheeks dry. "I'll get it."

She was starving and the last thing she needed was her dad spending the next twenty minutes arguing with the delivery guy about the tip, or accidentally dropping the food. Aside from the complimentary coffee and cookies on her flight, she hadn't eaten anything in almost twenty-four hours. Her stomach rumbled in anticipation of actual food.

She opened the front door and gasped, unable to manage any other sound. She was struck silent by the absolutely impossible sight in front of her. Jessie and Alice were here at her parents' doorstep. With Eli.

"We come bearing get well gifts for your folks," Alice said cheerily, holding a bouquet of gerbera daisies.

"And a little something for you," Jessie added, pointing to Eli.

Nora didn't move. Her brain couldn't compute what her eyes and ears were telling it. "I...I don't understand."

Elis's expression twisted into something like trepidation. He was wearing the same clothes he'd had on for the last few days, looking almost as rough as she felt. Flecks of shiny white snow dusted his dark hair and shoulders. "I tried to call, but you didn't answer."

"So you flew here?"

The smallest hint of a smile crept onto his lips. "I didn't know when you'd be back and there was something I really needed to tell you."

Emotion welled in her throat, blocking everything she wanted to say. She threw her arms around his neck and sank into him. He held her tightly, pulling her into him and pressing a hand against the back of her head. It felt like falling into heaven—soft yet secure in all the right ways.

Alice cleared her throat. Hard as it was, Nora let Eli go in order to hug her friend. Jessie didn't even wait for Nora to finish. She burrowed into the hug like a cat.

"I still don't understand," Nora said when she finally let go of her friends. "How are you all here together?"

Jessie rolled her eyes. "I tracked him down on Facebook to let him know what was happening, but he was already on his way over."

"Did you really think we wouldn't take care of you?" Alice added.

Nora looked at Eli once more. "How did you get here? There weren't any flights."

Eli smiled. "Not out of Shadow Creek. Clem gave me a ride to SeaTac."

Nora's stomach flip-flopped. Seattle's airport was almost two hours away. He'd come all the way here. For her.

And she hadn't even let him inside yet. She moved out of the way to let them in. Eli shivered as he stepped inside, rubbing his hands against his arms. His jacket was too light for the wet, heavy snow and unrelenting cold of a Canadian winter.

"Is that the food? Don't tip unless they remembered to give you extra soy sauce this time!"

Nora forced a smile. "I guess it's time for you to meet my dad."

Alice and Jessie barged ahead into the living room. They'd spent so much time here growing up that it was practically a second home for them. They were used to her dad's gruffness and her mom's flightiness—so much so that they often referred to Nora's parents as endearingly kooky.

Eli laced his fingers through hers and started to walk down the hall. She stopped him with a slight tug of the wrist. "What was so important for you to tell me that you had to fly across the continent?"

He turned toward her with a grin and brushed a strand of hair behind her ear. "It's the kind of thing that needs to be said after I meet your father."

"I never told you that my dad is kind of—"

"Nora!" her dad yelled from the living room. "Where's the damn food? Your mother needs her miso soup!"

Nora sighed. "Kind of abrasive. Are you sure you want to go

through with this? It's not too late to run away."

His expression grew serious. He cupped her cheek with his hand. "I know how hard it is to get a call telling you that your parents were in a car crash. I'm here for you, even if it means having to explain to your dad I'm planning on spending the night in his only daughter's childhood bedroom." He kissed her softly, barely grazing his lips across hers, but there was a power behind that gentleness. The kind that could dismantle her fears with its delicate restraint in a way force and aggression never could. "Besides, I give good parent. Dads love me."

When they walked into the living room, her parents were exactly where she'd left them, only Alice and Jessie were sitting with them— Alice on the sofa next to Nora's mom, and Jessie on the arm of her dad's chair.

Her dad looked up from the pair of slippers Jessie had given him and locked his gaze on Eli. "If you don't have our miso soup, you better at least have an explanation for why you're holding my daughter's hand."

"Relax, Larry, that's her neighbor. He's a nice boy," her mom said.

"The turd-nugget who's been giving you grief?"

Eli smiled politely. "We've settled our misunderstandings as adults."

"Have you settled your face yet or are you always going to look like you're passing one out the wrong end?"

"Still think this is a good idea?" Nora whispered to Eli.

He swallowed, but kept his expression pleasant. "It's very nice to meet you, Dr. Pitts. Nora's spoken highly of you."

"Did that praise include mention of my machete collection?"

"Dad," Nora sighed. "You don't have a machete collection."

"No, but I'm suddenly inspired to acquire one."

Everyone else in the room laughed, but Eli just squeezed her hand tighter and whispered, "Any pointers for how to win him over?"

Nora shook her head. "You're doing great. Turd-nugget is actually a compliment. If he really didn't like you, you'd already be in tears and clutching the remaining tatters of your self-esteem."

20

"So..." Eli drawled as he followed Nora past the doorway, lugging his quickly packed bag over his shoulder. "This is the infamous childhood bedroom of Nora Pitts."

The room was filled with bookshelves, and posters of boy bands from the nineties.

"Infamous? Only if you're referring to the time Jessie stole her mom's bottle of limoncello when we were thirteen and got us all drunk during a sleepover."

"I'm both curious and a little creeped out thinking about you as a pre-teen cuddling your stuffed koala while chugging Italian liqueur."

"Let me spoil the surprise by admitting I threw up all over the floor and tried to cover it up by dumping my mom's perfume to cover the smell, even though I hate the smell of patchouli. She's bought me that perfume for every birthday since."

"I had no idea you had such a wild streak." He set the bag down on little bench in front of the mirrored vanity and looked at the brightly colored walls that were so different from the austere white décor of her home in Shadow Creek. "Or a thing for pink."

Nora groaned. "My parent's birthday present when I turned ten. I didn't have the heart to tell them I hated it."

He pulled her into his arms. She sagged against him, finally dropping the defense she'd been holding up for so long. "I brought you something that I think you're going to appreciate."

"You already brought yourself," she mumbled into his chest.

"Something even better. Hang on." He let her go to rummage in his bag. "This."

He held up a long white phone charger and her eyes went wide.

"Oh my god, thank you!" She pulled her phone from her purse and plugged in. "My battery died before I even made it to the airport and neither of my folks have cell phones. I've never felt more naked."

She kissed him, and it took every ounce of his self-restraint not to turn it into something more. Even in their exhaustion, passion smoldered between them, heating his blood with need. But he knew that wasn't what she needed right now.

Her phone beeped, signaling it finally had enough of a charge to turn on. She turned it on and scrolled through her messages. Her eyebrows knitted together right before she let out a little gasp.

"Yeah," he said sheepishly, running his hand along the back of his neck. "I might have sent you a few dozen texts."

"No, it's not that. It's…" She turned the phone toward him, revealing a photograph of a laboratory that was so high-tech and pristine, it looked like it was from a movie set. The kind of lab any scientist would kill for.

He swallowed the lump of nerves in his throat. "Robin isn't taking no for an answer?"

"No. In fact, she's upped the salary offer to…well, to a lot."

"And you're considering it?"

She sat on the edge of the mattress and dropped her head into her hands. "No. I don't know." Her words trailed off into a yawn.

"You need to get some sleep."

She looked down at the twin mattress set on a white-painted, wrought-iron frame, letting out a soft sigh. "I don't know how much sleep we'll get on this."

"As much as I hate that I won't be able to defile you in your childhood twin bed, I know you won't sleep well if I'm cuddled up next to you. I'll sleep on the floor."

She started to protest, but he shook his head. There was no arguing with the bags under her eyes and pallor of her skin.

She yawned, then said, "We should at least talk about—"

He spun her toward the bed and gave her a gentle nudge. "Sleep now. We can talk tomorrow."

Maybe by then his stomach would be able to handle the conversation they needed to have.

Over the last thirty hours, Eli had cooked so many meals and stuffed them inside so many freezer-safe containers, it felt like his fingers were going to fall off. Vegetable lasagna, turkey chili, lemon garlic chicken. He wasn't much of a cook and couldn't vouch for how good any of it would be, even with Nora's instructions. Then again, judging by the bits of food that Nora's dad had in his fridge, anything Eli cooked would be an improvement.

His basic renovation skills had been truly helpful, though. He'd installed a hand-held shower attachment and safety bar in their main-floor bathroom. He'd also moved the mattress down to the living room and taken care of anything that could be considered a trip hazard.

By the end of his second day there, they'd gotten Nora's parents as settled as they could in their home, though Eli hadn't made much headway in winning her dad over. He didn't blame Larry. Despite the man's obstinacy, he had a special bond with Nora. He'd watched his only daughter get hurt in the past.

But it wasn't Larry who Eli needed to win over. It was Nora. He still hadn't found the chance to tell her what he'd come here to say. She'd worked herself so ragged taking care of her parents there hadn't been a right time. Unfortunately, time wasn't something they had a lot of right now. It had been five days since he'd been at the Holy Grale. It was the longest he'd ever been away, and even though he wasn't eager to leave Nora, he needed to get back. Besides, she had things covered here. Other than serving as a human pincushion for her dad's sharp barbs, he wasn't much use here.

"Hey," he said gently, sliding a bowl of chicken noodle soup in front of her on the kitchen counter. "You need to eat something." It had been hours since she'd had any food, and darkness had already invaded the night sky.

She looked up from her phone with a sweet smile. "Thanks."

Her hair was pulled into a messy bun and exhaustion still painted the planes of her face with shades of gray. He never thought he'd use the word "unkempt" to describe her, but being around her parents seemed to wear her down like coarse-grit sandpaper. Seeing her family dynamic made him understand her so much more than before. She might be Catherine and Larry's daughter, but she was the care-taker in the family. The responsible one. There was a lot of love in her family, but that didn't make up for that kind of weight being put on her shoulders.

Her eyes flitted back to her phone in between spoonfuls. He didn't need to ask why. She was still thinking about the job offer.

"There's a flight back to Shadow Creek tomorrow morning," he said as she scraped the last bits of tiny yellow noodles onto her spoon. "I'm thinking of taking it. But only if you're okay with that."

She nodded. "You need to get back to the brewery. I know that. It's amazing that you came at all, and it wouldn't be fair to ask you to stay any longer."

"I'd stay forever if you needed me, but I don't think you do. You've got everything under control. I can't say the same about my assistant, Tom. He's good, but he still needs help getting the formulas right."

"I want to be selfish right now, but I can't. You have a life in Shadow Creek that you need to get back to."

He sat down on the stool next to hers and brushed a loose, wispy strand of hair behind her ear. "So do you."

The mix of emotions that battled on her face made him almost regret pushing her, but he couldn't leave without reminding her that she had another home to come back to. He could feel her being sucked back into her life here like water slipping through his fingers. He didn't want to lose her.

"In the last two days, I just found out my parents got back together and nearly died. What if they never fully recover? What if I leave and they fall apart all over again?"

"What if they're just fine? What if they're stronger than you think they are? It's one thing to take care of them right now, but you can't do that for the rest of your life. You've worked too hard not to remember that your dreams matter, too. *You* matter."

She stood up, brought her bowl and spoon to the dishwasher, then took his hand. She led him upstairs. Her parents had fallen asleep in the living room again—her mom on the sofa with her broken leg propped up on the armrest, and her dad on the leather recliner that was imprinted with the shape of his body from sitting there for so many years.

The house was old, and the heavy scent of wood from the thick-planked staircase added an ominous flavor to her silence as she led him to her bedroom. Without a word, she pulled her shirt over her head, folded it carefully, and set in on the chair. Her pants came next, then her bra and underwear. She stood in front of him like a flawless blank canvas waiting to be colored by his touch. She was so beautiful, it took his breath away.

She was perfect, but there was something fragile about her, like she was made of blown glass. He took a moment to memorize every detail of her body. The curve of her collarbone. The tiny birthmark on her hip. The way her thighs swelled with delicious softness.

He put his hands at her waist. "I never told you what I came here to say."

"I already know."

His heart thumped in his chest. She knew, but from the way she reached for the button on his jeans, it was clear she wasn't prepared to talk about it. Not with words. He retrieved the condom from his wallet in the back pocket of his jeans while she unzipped his fly.

He kicked off the rest of his clothes and lowered her to the bed beneath him. The old, metal frame creaked in protest from their weight. He teased her heat with his fingers until the soft, mewling sounds of her readiness tumbled from her lips. She arched her chest toward his, pressing her tightly beaded nipples against his skin. He slid into her and cupped her checks, holding her while he kissed her with a hunger he'd never experienced before.

He thrust into her, hard and slow. They'd had sex before, but this was different. This wasn't about losing himself in pleasure or the sweetness of her body. It was about filling her with his desire and his love, until she breathed it in like oxygen. "I need to say it, Nora. Tell me you're ready to hear it."

Her breath hitched—the only sound other than the chorus of their bodies gliding and bumping against each other. Doubt battered his heart, an uncomfortable sensation almost irreconcilable with the pleasure building inside him. He needed her to understand. He needed her to say yes.

She dug her fingers into his shoulders, lifting her knees up and locking her ankles around his waist. "Okay."

She wasn't ready to hear him say it. Nora had never lied to Eli before, but her basic instincts had taken control of her head and her heart. She was addicted to him. And she was terrified that as soon as he said the those words, her happiness would pop like a fragile bubble.

His slow thrusts brought her closer to the edge. Their movements were constrained by the tiny bed, leaving no room for anything but the press of their bodies.

"I love you."

Her orgasm overwhelmed her. The only thing grounding her to the world was the feel of his lips on hers. His tight grip on her hips, holding her like he would never let her go.

He settled on top of her when it was over, using one arm to hold most of his weight, then brushed her hair off her face. "I love you, Nora. I need you to know that."

She squeezed her eyes shut. She didn't have the words for what she felt. It was more than love. It was life-shattering, earth-shaking, blinding love. The kind where she could lose herself completely to him. The kind that could crush her identity and independence into dust.

The kind that was too strong to deny any longer. She opened her eyes, meeting his gaze as steadily as she could. "I love—"

A crash sounded from the main floor. A shriek—her mother's —followed.

Nora and Eli scrambled out of the bed at the same moment. They threw on whatever clothes they could find and ran downstairs.

"What's the matter?" Nora called out before she'd even made it to the living room. She flipped on the light and looked around.

The lamp that normally sat on the side table lay on the dark hardwood floor. Her mom clutched her broken leg and yelled at her dad to stop, while a blanket half-covered her head. Her dad was hunched over her mom, struggling with the blanket in a way that only seemed to entangle them both further.

"Hang on, Dad," Nora said when she realized the fringes of the blanket were somehow caught in his watch. "I'll fix this."

"No, no, I have it under control," her dad protested, pulling against the fabric, which made her mom moan with pain.

Her dad's stubbornness made it take twice as long to disentangle the mess and get everyone settled back down.

"I was just trying to get Catherine a blanket," her dad grumbled.

"I'm fine," her mom protested with a huff.

"You're not fine," Nora snapped. "You were almost killed two days ago. The doctors said it could be months before you're walking properly again."

"It's not ideal, but I've always felt like I was a fast healer. I'm sure I'll be walking sooner than that."

"Who's going to take you to your doctors' appointments? Who's going to cook for you? Who's going to make sure you don't fall down and make things ten times worse?"

"I'll do it. I'm her husband. Who else is going to do it?"

"No, Dad. I'll take care of it. I'm here now and I'll take care of everything." She didn't mean to sound so angry, but she'd only just figured out how to put her life back together. Now she was going to have to throw it all away in order to fix her parents' lives.

Her parents finally went silent, like pouting children after a scolding. Nora's chest rose and fell quickly. Then she remembered Eli was there, standing in the corner of the room. She met his eyes and felt the weight of everything slam into her like a freight train. She didn't need to explain. The resigned look on his face made it clear he already knew.

She wasn't coming back to Shadow Creek.

21

*N*ora barely slept that night, too exhausted to settle into a proper slumber and too scared that this might be the last night she spent in Eli's arms. The morning after was even more awkward as she watched him gather the few items he'd brought with him, offering her reassuring smiles that everything would be okay when it wouldn't be. Her eyes were swollen with unshed tears and fatigue, and her skin felt raw, like the slightest touch would make her bleed.

Her parents were still asleep when she crept downstairs to brew him a mug of coffee before his cab arrived. Thank God, because she couldn't face them right now. She'd finally found a place for herself in Shadow Creek and started to feel like she belonged. Not just because of Eli, though she'd never thought she could feel so happy because of a man. She'd made real friends there—ones who didn't hesitate to drop everything and help her out when she needed it. She liked her home. The community. Hell, she was actually coming around to liking her job, even if it wasn't exactly the career path she'd thought she would have at this point in her life. And now she had to give up all of it because her parents had decided to rekindle their marriage by getting frisky in the most dangerous way imaginable.

It was almost ironic, really, that she hadn't been able to see how much she actually wanted to stay in Shadow Creek until the choice was taken away from her.

The old, creaking wood stairs warned her that Eli was on his way down. She poured the coffee into a mug and slid the bagel she'd toasted and covered with cream cheese into a re-sealable plastic bag, tucking a carefully folded paper towel in with it. She wanted to send him off with a better breakfast, but it was the best she could do under the circumstances.

"That for me?"

God, he was a beautiful man. She'd always known he was good-looking, but it still astounded her that his heart was just as beautiful, full of selflessness and unfiltered kindness. "Yeah, I hope it's okay."

"It's perfect, thank you." He cupped the back of her neck, a touch that was as strong as it was tender.

She exhaled shakily. The air between them was heavy with all the things they hadn't said to each other last night.

A horn beeped from outside, signaling his taxi had arrived. He dropped his forehead to hers. "I meant what I said last night. I love you. If we need to be long distance, then that's what we'll be. I can come visit a lot, and eventually I'll have Tom trained to take over the day-to-day operations at the Holy Grale."

She curled her fingers into the hem of his T-shirt. "I can't ask you to do that."

"You don't have to. I'm not letting this thing between us slip away without a fight. You're the only person who's ever made me feel like I have an anchor to this world. You make me feel like I can accomplish anything when most of my life I've felt like a loser. Plus, we still haven't acted out my sexy scientist fantasy where you show up at my door wearing nothing but a lab coat and safety goggles."

She laughed because it was the only thing she could do to keep from crying. He crept quietly out the front door, leaving her with promises to call soon and a soft kiss on the lips. She watched his cab drive off from the living room window, fighting the urge to chase after him. Even if she did, she had no idea if she would beg him to say or tell him not to ruin his life for hers.

Instead, she walked back to the kitchen to make herself a pot of tea. The ritual of scooping the fragrant leaves into the infuser was familiar and calming, something she desperately needed at this moment.

"You're making a mistake."

Nora jumped. Her dad was standing at the doorway to the kitchen. She hadn't heard him wake up. "I'm not sure I'm prepared to take advice from you about relationships right now, Dad."

"I can't blame you for that. I haven't done a great job setting an example, have I?"

Nora poured the water from the steaming kettle instead of answering.

"But you should know more than anyone that there's value in the experiments that fail."

"Is that what you're trying to do with Mom?"

"It's what I need to do. I haven't done a very good job taking care of your mom. That's why our marriage fell apart in the first place. We've relied on you too much to keep our family together, and that wasn't fair. It's time your mom and I figured out how to take care of each other for once."

"You picked a hell of a time to start."

The smallest hint of a grin tugged at his thin lips. "So I did."

Nora sighed. "This isn't just about trying a new restaurant when Mom feels like Ethiopian food, or taking dance lessons with her. She needs serious care. It will be months until her cast comes off, and she'll probably need another surgery in the future. She'll need her stiches removed. Heck, you'll need your stiches removed and—"

Her dad placed his hand over hers. "And we'll figure it out. The hospital gave me a pamphlet for a homecare service. They'll send a nurse every day to help us with the medical stuff, and the bathing, and anything else. I've already called them. The nurse comes this afternoon. I also told my department chair that I'm retiring as soon as my leave is done."

Nora's jaw dropped so fast, she almost lost her grip on her mug. Her dad had never done anything so responsible before. She'd always been the one to organize them. Make the decisions and necessary phone calls. Her heart pounded. Maybe he was right. Maybe she didn't have to be the one doing it all anymore.

"Your mom and I agree. As long as you're here, we won't be able to prioritize our marriage the way we need to. And you won't be able to prioritize your life the way you deserve. You need to go."

"Even if it means chasing after the knuckle-brained goober?"

Her dad's expression darkened. "Yes, even if it means going after him. But if he ever breaks your heart, I have a colleague in the archaeology department with a collection of poison-tipped darts that he's been itching to try out, and I bet that turd-nugget's ego is a big enough target that I could take him down in one blow."

Eli had arrived at Shadow Creek airport in the late afternoon and spent the rest of the day working his ass off in the brewery to catch up for all the time he's spent away this week. There was a hell of a lot to do. The orders for the malt and hops were overdue and the floors hadn't been swept in days, and most importantly, they were running dangerously low on Lord's Work Lager—the Holy Grale's most popular brew.

His fingers were blistered and aching by the time the last patron stumbled out of the pub in the early hours of the morning, but at least he hadn't had to say much to anyone. Other than a quick explanation to Jake and Julia about what happened to Nora's parents, he didn't open his mouth for the rest of the night. Sometimes he thought it was a little ironic that Jake, who was as grumpy as a thirty-two-year-old man could get, was in charge of the bar while Eli was stuck in the back with the whirring machines, but today he appreciated the hell out of their arrangement. There was only one person he wanted to talk to, and she was 2,500 miles away.

He pulled into his driveway and tried not to look at Nora's house, though he'd never had very good impulse control, especially when it came to her. Mrs. Kocilowicz would be able to find a new tenant easily, but Eli couldn't imagine anyone but Nora there. Then again, what choice did he have? She wasn't coming back, and he couldn't blame her. If his mom had survived her car accident, he would have done anything for her. And even if he'd meant everything he told Nora about making a go at a long-distance relationship, he knew there were no guarantees it would work out.

He went straight to the shower when he got home. His bathroom looked damn good with the new tiles and fixtures, if he did say so himself, but it was small comfort right now. He tilted his head under the hot spray and tried to let the stress of the last few days wash off him.

An odd, loud sound rumbled through the room, shaking the walls around him. He wiped the water out of his eyes and looked around. "What the hell?"

It happened again. He turned off the shower and heard the faint beat of a Diana Ross song in the distance.

Another strident growl ripped through the air, attacking his eardrums like the claws of a feral raccoon. It was a sound he knew all too well. "No freaking way."

He threw on his boxers and ran outside to his backyard, barely believing what he saw. "Nora?"

She was in the middle of his yard, tugging awkwardly at the cord of his weed whacker in a way that put her at risk of losing more than a few fingers. An old-school stereo blaring music sat on the ground beside her. He ran down to the grass and gently pulled her hands away from the machine. She glanced up and pulled off her oversized ear protectors.

"You're going to kill yourself," he scolded, too frightened to process any other emotion right now.

"I had to get your attention somehow." She smiled, and that's when it finally sank in. She was here in his yard, blaring disco songs at him, and defiling his most cherished lawn implement.

"You've definitely got it now."

A few of their neighbors' back porch lights flicked on, but Eli didn't care about anything except the next few words out of Nora's mouth.

"I love you, Eli, and I'd never forgive myself if I just let you walk away without telling you. I love the way you make me laugh and the way you make me feel safe. I love the way you accept me for who I am —uptight, picky, and—"

"Perfect."

Tears pooled in the corners of her eyes. She cupped his face. "I love your kindness and your determination and your heart. The way you make every room brighten when you walk in. I love everything about you, even your crappy taste in music."

"Could you love his crappy music in the morning? Some of us were trying to sleep!" Budd shouted from his porch. Eli hit the off button on the stereo and Budd gave him a thumbs-up. "Now tell her you love her, too!"

Eli looked at Nora and grinned. "She already knows." He pulled her into his arms and kissed her. Applause exploded around them.

"What about your parents? The job?" he asked when he could finally bear to pull his lips from hers.

"My parents need to learn to rely on each other for a little while. And I don't want that job. Or my old life back. I want you."

"I want you, too, Nora, but only on one condition."

Her expression turned curious. "What's that?"

"You let me redo our first date."

She laughed. "Nah, I wouldn't change a thing."

EPILOGUE

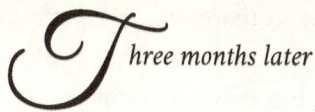hree months later

"The Ruth Hardin Memorial Scholarship Fund," Eli said as Nora examined the glossy brochure the university's development office had given them. "I still think we should have gone with Ruth Hardin's Get Good Grades Or I Swear To God I'll Kick Your Ass And Take Away Your Money Scholarship Fund. More authentic, you know?"

Nora laughed and unwrapped the plastic cover from the plate of freshly baked pistachio and lime sugar cookies she'd brought over. She'd spent a few weeks perfecting this recipe and finally gotten it right, and there was no better occasion to bring them out. Between the scholarship and the article based on her conference presentation topic she'd just gotten published in one of the top academic journals in her field, they had a lot to celebrate. "I know they're pretty eager to take your money, but I'm not sure they're that eager."

"Not just my money." He reached his hand across the counter and snatched the plate, pulling it toward him like a toddler clutching their favorite stuffed animal. "I really appreciate all your help."

It was true she'd matched his contribution, something she hadn't told him she was planning to do until today. Her parents, who were doing well after the accident and still happy together for now, had chipped in, too. But it was also the generosity of the Holy Grale's patrons who donated their change toward the scholarship and came out to their last-minute trivia and karaoke fundraiser nights. They'd managed to raise enough money in the short time to pay a full year's tuition for one student who came from a single-parent family, or was a single parent themselves, each year. In the end, though, Eli was the one who deserved all the congratulations. She'd never seen him more passionate and driven and *organized* about anything.

He grabbed another cookie from the middle of the plate and shoved it into his mouth. "Dear God, woman, these cookies are good."

Inwardly, she preened at the compliment, but outwardly, she rearranged the coiled pattern of the cookies so there wasn't a gaping hole in the middle of the plate. The jerk just picked up another cookie from the other side of the plate, derailing her carefully constructed arrangement even further.

But at least he was her jerk. Her lovable, amazing, perfect jerk who made food taste better and colors brighter and everything else in her life a million times better, even if he couldn't respect basic symmetry. It had taken her longer than she'd liked to realize to see how well they fit together, like discordant colors that came together in a perfect work of art.

"I think these are the best cookies I've ever had," he said reverently between bites. An odd, low rumble sounded from his direction.

She drew her eyebrows together. "Did you just...purr?"

He looked up, confusion on his face.

She heard another purr, but this time it sounded like it was even closer to her. Something soft and furry brushed against her ankle. She yelped and looked down.

A gray cat curled itself around her legs, meowing and purring. She bent down and picked the little guy up. He was a little fatter than the last time she saw him, but she immediately recognized him as the cat from the SPCA fundraiser all those months ago.

Eli frowned. "How did you get out of the bedroom?"

She looked up at Eli with astonishment while stroking her hand down the cat's silky back. "You got a cat? You hate cats."

"No," he grumbled. "We got a cat. I was going to surprise you tonight, but the little fucker is some kind of feline mastermind and escaped from my closed bedroom door."

The cat turned toward him and hissed. Eli scowled in return.

She scratched behind the animal's ear, soothing him. "I can't have a cat. It's not allowed in my rental agreement."

"I called Ms. Kocilowicz and asked if she'd make an exception. Apparently she still finds me very charming."

A kaleidoscope of emotions swelled inside her chest. "Why?"

He walked over to her and cupped her cheek. "Because you're worth it, and I wanted to give you another reason to always stay here with me."

She leaned into his touch. "You already are my reason. But this little guy is the sweetest gift ever. What should we name him?"

He grinned. "I don't know. Kinda looks like a Humperdinck to me."

She laughed. "Humperdinck is the perfect name."

The end.

EXCERPT FROM REAL KIND OF LOVE (BOOKS & BREWS SERIES, BOOK 1)

Don't miss REAL KIND OF LOVE, *book 1 in the Books & Brews Series:*

"For a woman who's never touched hard liquor, you're staring awfully hard at that bottle of whisky."

"Huh?" Clementine Cox tore her attention away from the rows of bottles behind the bar when she realized Jake Donovan was talking. To her. Even though the Holy Grale brewpub—named for its ale so delicious, it would make anyone drop to their knees in worship—was empty at this time of day, she still glanced over her shoulder before answering. "Oh, um, maybe I'm just in the mood for something different."

He shook his head and gave her the sexy half smile that seemed to compel every one of his female patrons to giggle flirtatiously and triple their tips. Everyone but Clem. Not that she didn't appreciate those dark brown eyes, broad shoulders, and jaw so sharp you could carve ice with it. The man oozed charm. She just wasn't the type to fall for it.

Fantasize about him on those dark, lonely nights in her bedroom? Heck, yeah. But she knew the difference between real and fake. Gorgeous, confident men like Jake did not sit around thinking about how to get a bookworm with frizzy hair in their beds. She liked herself just fine, but there was no denying she had nothing in common with him.

"You've been coming to my pub for over three years, sitting in that exact same stool every time, and never once ordered anything but a lager or coffee."

"People change," she said with a shrug. Especially after hiding in the bathroom for the better part of the night like a coward while two guys smashed through her dining room window and tore through all her belongings.

She'd spent all morning dealing with the police and her insurance company, which left her exhausted and well past her quota for human interaction for the next month. The broken glass, scattered clothes and mud-covered floors were bad enough, but the bastards had destroyed her bookshelf and entire collection of paperbacks with it. The shredded covers and torn pages were too intolerable to deal with right now, which is why she found herself back at the Holy Grale trying to escape reality for another few hours.

No one ever talked to her here. Until today.

Jake grabbed the bottle of 10-year-old Laphroaig off the shelf and poured two fingers into a small tumbler.

She picked up the glass he set in front of her, gave it a sniff, and winced as the alcohol fumes burned a trail through her nasal passages straight to her retinas.

He laughed and snatched the glass back. "Didn't think so. Why don't you tell me what you really want?"

She sighed and centered her white coffee mug in the exact middle of her coaster, a task made even more difficult because of the optical illusion created by the Holy Grale's slightly oblong logo. "You got anything that will put me into a state of euphoria so I can forget the last twenty-four hours and actually enjoy dinner with my family tonight and still drive without getting arrested?"

"Yep." Eli, the co-owner of the Holy Grale, set down the pint glass he'd been washing, threw the towel over his shoulder, and came to stand next to Jake. "It's called sex. Wild, monkey, make-you-scream-so-loud-the-neighbors-complain-then-ask-to-join-in sex."

Heat rushed to Clem's cheeks and she nearly choked on the sip of coffee she'd just taken.

Eli set his hand on Jake's shoulder. "Unfortunately, Mr. 'Health Code Violations Are A Very Big Deal' over here won't let me put than on the monthly specials list. And don't bother trying to get it with this guy. He's a little rusty. I, however, am a well-practiced expert. Just say the word."

The hard glare Jake sent Eli's way was uncharacteristic, but effective at silencing him. Thank god, because picturing wild, monkey sex with Jake Donovan right at this moment was not a good idea if she wanted to keep coming to this place. That kind of fantasy was strictly for when she was alone, under the covers, and could claim plausible deniability.

Clem was a creature of habit, and three years ago her inner muse had decided to dig her roots into this spot. Something about the rich smelling wood, the whirring machines of the adjoining brewery, and the haunting architecture left over from the building's first incarnation as a church had sucked her in. There wasn't another place like it in the entire state. No one bugged her while she treated this two-foot section of the mahogany bar like her own personal office. And the fact that it was right down the street from her little bungalow was a huge added bonus she couldn't replicate just anywhere.

"Uh, thanks. I'll stick to coffee this afternoon," she said right before accidentally knocking her cup and spilling the contents all over the bar. "Shit! Sorry!"

Thankfully, she had the presence of mind to move her tablet and notebook before they were destroyed by the river of caffeine winding toward them. Her BLT and fries didn't survive unscathed but she didn't have much of an appetite today, anyway. She carefully placed her belongings on her stool and grabbed a handful of napkins from the stack Jake was using to sop up the brown liquid.

He set his hand on top of hers, sending an unexpected jolt of heat zinging through her body. *Thanks a lot, Eli.* "Not your job. I fired you three years ago, remember?"

"And yet you still offer me the employee discount on every meal." She slipped her hand out from beneath his and let him get back to dealing with the mess.

"Really? I'll have to fix that," he said with another grin, wiping away the last bits of coffee. "One of these days."

"Thank you." Her words came out in a mumble, not because she didn't mean them, but because she did. Too much. The unwelcome rush of jumbled emotions swept through her body like a tidal wave, crashing in her stomach and tightening her throat.

She tried to hide her unease from her expression, but Jake's deep brown eyes zeroed in on her. He leaned forward and set his arms on the bar, forcing her to meet his gaze. "Hey, what's really going on?"

Shit. This is why he was so good at his job. He could gauge moods like he was hardwired with an emotional barometer, and know exactly what to say at the right time. It was a talent she admired but didn't possess. Her atrocious people skills and dislike of small talk, combined with a bad case of resting bitch face, pretty much forced him to fire her after two days as a waitress. But Jake had somehow managed to still make her feel welcome here when she kept coming back like an obsessed stalker. And for the last three years, he'd let her quietly sit on the same stool at his bar, head buried in a manuscript, taking piles of notes and occasionally mouthing out the words and accents to herself like a weirdo, not caring if she scared away other customers. Knowing exactly what she was going to order before she even opened her mouth.

Just like he knew at this moment there was more going on with her.

She forced a smile to her lips and resigned herself to opening up about what happened. She hadn't told anyone but the cops. Maybe it would be good to get it off her chest, and if anyone could listen to her without making her feel like a freak, it was him. "I'm just tired. My house was broken into last night. No big deal."

ABOUT THE AUTHOR

Sara Rider writes contemporary romance full of heart, heat, and happily ever after. She lives in British Columbia with her husband and daughters. She spends far too much time in public libraries and never leaves the home without her e-reader stuffed in her purse.

ALSO BY SARA RIDER

The Books & Brews Series
REAL KIND OF LOVE

The Perfect Play Series
FOR THE WIN
KEEPING SCORE
GOING FOR THE GOAL

"No big deal?" Jake came around the side of the bar to stand next to her with Eli following right behind. "Did they hurt you?"

She shook her head, though her heart pounded in her chest. The intruders hadn't done anything to her physically, but the break-in had left her in a cold sweat all night. "The cops got there pretty quick and arrested the guys who did it."

"Jesus, Clem." He pulled her into a hug, wrapping his muscular arms around her back. She stiffened from the unexpected physical contact. Not only had they exchanged more words in a single instance than they had in all the time they'd known each other—including when he'd sacked her, they'd moved on to touching. Full-body touching.

As the seconds awkwardly ticked by, the warmth of his body and the deliciously spicy scent of his skin chipped away at her discomfort. She let her exhaustion wash over her while he held her close until the pace of her breathing fell in sync with his, like he was recharging her soul. He rubbed small circles onto her back, and she melted into him. She was hugging Jake Donovan, and it felt *good*. Really, really good. God, how long had it been since she'd touched a man like this?

Too long. She was the epitome of boring. No risk. No romance. No adventure—except for the many hours she spent lost in a good book. After everything she'd been through, maybe she deserved to be just a little bit reckless.

She set her hands on his lower back and traced the muscles along his spine. He inhaled sharply and buried his fingers in her hair, holding her tight against his hard chest. A strange tingling erupted deep in her belly, snowballing in potency as it descended toward the apex of her thighs.

"Aw man, let me in on that action." Eli threw his arms around both of them and squeezed them together in the world's most awkward group hug. "It's okay, let it all out. Uncle Eli is here to collect your tears."

"Can't breathe," she managed to say while sandwiched between the two men. They disentangled and she retreated back to her stool. Her eyes flashed toward Jake like metal to a magnet. His irises looked like they'd deepened three shades, staring at her with an intensity that made her wonder if the spark she'd felt when they touched wasn't just in her head.

"You got anyone you can stay with tonight?"

Maybe it was the gruff tone in his deep voice, or her overactive imagination, but that question felt more loaded than a simple inquiry from a concerned friend should. "I'll be fine."

"You want us to come over and play bedtime bodyguard?" Eli asked with a wink.

Jake gave him a small shove. "What about your family?"

She laughed, grateful once again to Eli for breaking the tension. "I'd rather spend another night with my robbers."

"They can't be that bad," Eli said with a frown.

"You've never met them. If they find out about this, they'll be camped outside my house for the next five years wearing matching berets and T-shirts that say 'Cox Avengers,' or something equally embarrassing."

Eli sputtered. She wished she'd been joking, or at least exaggerating. She loved them, but it was hard being the black cloud in a family of rainbows.

"Better than not having any family," Jake said cryptically. He returned to his spot behind the bar and refilled her coffee mug, this time adding a splash of Bailey's.

"I know." She shifted uncomfortably, realizing she'd just hit the point in the conversation where everything turned awkward because she'd said or done the wrong thing. Like usual. She downed half her coffee in one gulp, grateful to have something to occupy her hands as she recalibrated to the changing atmosphere in the room.

Julia, Eli's sister, came through the backroom door a moment later, eyes fixed on a clipboard in her hands. "Hey, Eli, we need to talk."

"Not now. Clem's about to give us all the juicy details about her crazy family."

"Yes, now." She pointed to the back office before giving Clem a small smile. "Sorry. Business emergency."

www.ingramcontent.com/pod-product-compliance
Lightning Source LLC
Chambersburg PA
CBHW031726170626
46808CB00005B/1903

"No problem." Except that for the fact she would be alone in the big bar with Jake without Eli's humor as a buffer.

She quickly finished her drink while Jake went back to work, preparing for the happy hour crowds that would be trickling in soon. She didn't usually take anything in her coffee, but the small shot of creamy, sweet alcohol warmed her throat just enough to make her feel a little more human.

Hopefully it would be enough to get her through another Cox family Sunday-night dinner extravaganza with enough energy left over to clean the mess waiting for her at home. She checked her watch and realized there wasn't any time left to procrastinate. If she delayed any longer, the onslaught of phone calls and texts asking where she was, if she was okay, what hospital room she was in, and whose kidney she needed, would begin.

She opened her wallet to grab a twenty-dollar bill, but Jake shook his head. "It's on the house today."

"You really don't have to do that."

He leaned over the bar and took her hands in his. "I know. But I'm doing it any way. Same way you don't need to ask for help right now, but you could."

She cleared her throat. "You know you're never going to get rid of me if you keep this up."

"Not something I'm worried about. I *am* worried about you not taking care of yourself or asking for what you need."

A shiver ran down her spine. "I'm fine. Really."

"At least let me walk you home, Clem."

Her heart thumped in her chest. She might be shy, but she recognized that burning look in a man's eye when she saw it. After the ordeal she'd been through over the last twenty-four hours, there'd been a restlessness building inside her chest. A need to do something reckless and remind herself she was the one in control of her life, not the assholes who'd trashed her place. Doing something reckless with Jake was starting to seem like exactly the kind of thing she needed. "Okay. Sure, that would be—"

"Well, you sure moved on fast, Jake."

Clem jumped out of Jake's grasp and turned around to see a tall, gorgeous brunette walking toward them. The woman took hold of Clem's hand and shook it with the force of snake devouring a small rodent. "Hi. I'm Kelly Vanderburgh. Jake's fiancée."

Fiancée? She winced, realizing she'd completely mistaken his earlier kindness for something totally different. Like a fool. This was why she didn't open up with people. "Nice to meet you. I was just leaving. Thanks for lunch, Jake." She wrenched her hand free from Kelly's and gathered up her things.

"Clementine—" Whatever Jake was about to say next was cut off by Julia and Eli bursting back into the room.

"Oh crap," Julia said, adding to Clem's confusion.

"We should get a move on, Jakey. Wedding's only a week away."

Wedding? Clem wasn't good with people, but she'd never before misread a situation so badly in her life. She headed to the door without a single glance backward, hoping she was fast enough to outrun her mortification.